MW01169380

Lucinda's Solution

Lucinda's Solution

NANCY ROMAN

Lucinda's Solution

Copyright © 2017 Nancy Roman. All rights reserved.

Cover and Formatting: Blue Valley Author Services

No part of this book may be reproduced, scanned, or distributed in any printed or electronic form without permission. Please do not participate in or encourage piracy of copyrighted materials in violation of the author's rights. Thank you for respecting the hard work of this author.

This is a work of fiction. Names, characters, places, and incidents either are the product of the author's imagination or are used fictitiously, and any resemblance to locales, events, business establishments, or actual persons—living or dead—is entirely coincidental.

DEDICATION

For my grandparents, great-grandparents and all their siblings. Their stories of immigration and epidemics and determination and poverty and war - and love - inspired me. And inspired this book.

CHAPTER 1

1913

I WAS TWELVE WHEN MY SISTER Catherine got married. I did not know how I would live without her.

Yes, I still had Malcolm and Amelia. But to be perfectly honest, I never much cared for them. Malcolm was what my mother called 'high-spirited' but my father called a 'vociferous savage.' For once I thought my father may have been correct. There did not seem to exist in the entire house a chair he could not knock over or a plate he could not break. Or a spot on his body that did not have a bruise, slowly turning green. I found it rather miraculous that he had any teeth left in his head. My mother said Malcolm would outgrow it. I had my doubts.

Amelia was the opposite. The opposite of hellion in this case was not angel. It was mouse. Where Malcolm ran headlong through any obstacle, and his fearlessness was startling – he jumped from the veranda roof into the hydrangea at three – Amelia was a cowering baby. Afraid of dogs and horses and insects, afraid of the dark and of thunderstorms. Weepy, my mother called her. Tiresome, I thought.

"She's sensitive," explained my father. Oh, Father was infatuated. Amelia had blond curls and dimples, and liked – or appeared to like – to pray.

Amelia wasn't the beauty of the family, however. That was Catherine. Catherine had a creamy complexion that flushed easily in the most attractive way. Her eyes were bright blue, her lashes lush, and her dark hair was thick and gleaming.

My father found her vain and shallow. But she was not. It was confidence, not vanity that brought that color to her cheek. I won't deny that Catherine loved attention, especially the attention of men. But she loved men because she loved to laugh and men loved to hear that laugh. All men; boys too. Even Malcolm strove to make Catherine smile, turning somersaults and picking daisies. He would even sit in her lap for more than one minute.

The only man not susceptible was my father - Catherine's joy was an embarrassment for him. Piety was the only admirable attribute.

And Catherine was not pious. If Springfield had hosted a society for heretics, Catherine would have provided the biscuits.

Not that she didn't attend Holy Mass on Sunday. On the contrary. She looked forward to it.

"How nice it is to see all the families dressed up, the children all shined and gleaming. To exchange hellos with all your neighbors."

My father disapproved. "Sunday services are solemn occasions. Not social ones," he lectured.

"Nonsense, Daddy," she answered - which only incensed him further, as he liked to be called Father, for a reason that was obvious to all - "Church is very social. Jesus told us to love one another, and that is exactly what I am doing."

And Church was where Catherine noticed Roger Blaisdell's cousin Martin, who was visiting from Connecticut.

Connecticut! She had her pick of all the men in Springfield. And she chose the one from Connecticut.

I did not know how I would live without her.

I did not know how soon I would have to.

CHAPTER 2

MY PATERNAL GRANDFATHER OWNED THE lumber yard on the south end of Springfield. But he didn't make much money at it until he started delivering coal. He would say, "Coal is cheap but it sells expensive." The demand for coal was so great he needed to add a second wagon for deliveries. My father was sixteen and wanted to study for the priesthood. But my grandfather refused. So Father quit school and hauled coal.

My father would have preferred the priesthood, and he would have been a priest whose parish flourished. His business acumen would certainly have garnered him a cathedral. At Benedict Lumber, he soon added a third coal wagon. And a furnace repair service. And since there was not as great a need for coal in the summer, and the three wagons sat idle, and idleness was a sin - therefore, ice delivery.

The ice house was my favorite part of the Benedict empire. Malcolm would chip off shards with the pocket-knife that he was not supposed to have. Catherine would steal a bit of honey from the larder. We would feast among the cool dark igloos. Even Amelia would not tattle, so refreshing was the secret treat.

So for a girl of eighteen who still enjoyed childish escapades, it astonished me that Catherine would decide to marry after knowing Martin Blaisdell less than two months.

He was as charming as she was, though in a much quieter way. He watched rather than led. The first time he appeared at our dinner table - which he accomplished by bringing Mother white roses - Martin was deferential with my father, who grew as puffed and flushed as the ham he was carving. And yet I detected from Mr. Blaisdell an undercurrent of mockery.

That was the moment I fell in love with Martin Blaisdell myself. He had brown hair that tended to curl, but not so much as to be feminine, rather just enough to soften his forehead and partially cover the tops of his large ears. He had blue eyes, and so bettered the chances that Catherine's children would be so endowed. I have blue eyes myself. He dressed in expensive, but not new, clothes. Quality but not Vanity, as my mother would say.

My mother liked Martin Blaisdell too. But she was reluctant to agree to Catherine's marriage. She herself had married young and against her wishes, as her parents had too many daughters, and were glad to get rid of the first three posthaste. In my role as familial observer, I could see that she only sometimes loved my father. She respected his business ability and appreciated that he was a good provider. Her other married-off sisters were not as fortunate. Certainly they were not poor - their father had seen to that when brokering the deal. But Aunt Helen's husband was stingy with his wealth, and required Helen to beg for each nickel. Aunt Margaret's husband had a preference for liquor and loose women. Father was not lecherous or mean. Just opinionated, humorless, and unrelentingly pious. Not so bad really.

Martin Blaisdell was not humorless. And Catherine loved to laugh. Together, they were in a constant state of mirth. Either heads down suppressing inappropriate giggles or heads thrown back in full and loud hilarity.

Mother, being naturally light-hearted herself, enjoyed their happiness. Still, she worried about Catherine taking on such responsibility as marriage at only eighteen.

"Marriage is a serious undertaking," declared Father. "You cannot snigger your way through the life-long commitment - not to mention the holy sacrament."

"Oh Father," Catherine argued, "Marriage may be serious, but Love is joyful."

And she would not be dissuaded.

I had no objection to Catherine marrying. I loved the idea of more babies in the family, especially if she and Martin could produce one who was jolly, and perhaps a balance between Malcolm's temerity and Amelia's timidity. And I certainly thought that Martin was a handsome and charming man. I thought so to a fault.

My grievance was the distance between Springfield, Massachusetts and New Haven, Connecticut. Two hours by train. Cheaper by trolley, but you had to transfer in Hartford and again in Meriden. Probably half the day, although Martin seemed to manage to do this often enough.

I would imagine the least expensive way to travel would be by automobile, but first you would have to submit to the expense of buying one, which was an unnecessary extravagance, according to my father. My mother wholeheartedly agreed, but she often wholeheartedly agreed out of simple loyalty. I ventured she would love to drive up to church in her own automobile.

Catherine assured me that Martin would purchase an automobile in just a few years, and then they would make the trip to Springfield every week. But in the meantime, they promised that they would visit one Sunday a month.

One Sunday a month! As if I could bear thirty days with my mother the only congenial person in my household.

So as Catherine was determined to marry, I became determined to keep her in Massachusetts. It was logical and practical for Martin to move north rather than Catherine move south. Why should he not work for my father at Benedict Lumber and Fuel?

Which is exactly what I said the next time Martin took his place at our dinner table.

"Father," I said, "You need an intelligent assistant in order to expand your business. You can add tools and hardware to your offering, and Martin has that very experience."

Seated beside me, Catherine reached under the tablecloth and gently squeezed my knee, which was our secret signal that we were on the right track in manipulating our father. I was delighted to think that perhaps her hopes were in the same direction, although she had spoken just the previous day of the opportunities that New Haven offered.

"Nonsense," replied Father. "Springfield has more hardware stores than we need. And Martin has an excellent position in New Haven."

"But even if you don't want to be in the hardware business, you should still consider the future. Now that you are fifty, you need to ensure that Benedict Lumber will be in good hands should anything..."

"Fifty is not old," my mother interjected, as she was well aware that my father worried incessantly that he was about to speak to God through more direct means than prayer.

"But you have so much knowledge," I carried on. "You need to impart everything you have learned to someone dependable and hard-working - and who will be part of the family."

"Martin will be family, of course," Father replied. "But Malcolm will inherit the business."

"Malcolm is seven years old. It will be ten years before you can even start to train him." And ten years before he can add, I thought.

"Oh, we have plenty of time."

I looked at Malcolm, who was smashing peas with the back of his fork. My father had better start Malcolm immediately.

"Besides," my father added, "it is a wife's duty to follow her husband. Wheresoever thou goest, there goest I."

I suppressed a laugh. "Ruth said that to her mother-in-law, not her husband."

"Which makes the point even more so. It is the husband's family that takes precedent, not the wife's."

Martin finally spoke.

"Lucinda, it is very sweet that you would like Catherine and me to live in Springfield, but your father is correct - I have a very good job in New Haven, with a very good future for me. I'm a supervisor at the plant, and I will soon be a manager."

"And Martin really loves working there," Catherine said.

And everyone at the table except my father, and perhaps Malcolm, was well aware that Martin would not love working for my father. Father was a decent man, and a fair boss, in his own way, which was that he made every decision and closely supervised all work. His employees were decently paid and kept safe. But none would say he enjoyed it.

I did not give up, however.

I entered my father's study - after knocking and waiting for permission to enter of course - the following evening. Father was at his desk with his newspaper to one side and the Bible to the other. Directly in front of him were a comb and a small hand mirror. This made me curious, but also hopeful. My father was a vain man, and perhaps I could appeal to his pride.

"I'm worried," I said to Father. "I'm worried that your knowledge is so vast it will take years for you to impart all your wisdom. And Malcolm will not be ready for quite some time. What will happen to the business and to

Mother if you do not start right away, and then something happens that denies anyone the opportunity to understand the complexity of Benedict Lumber and Fuel?"

"I have been reflecting on that myself," said Father. "Our dinner conversation has left me disconcerted. I must confront the possibility that I could expire before Malcolm comes of age."

I was astounded. But not nearly as astounded as I was to hear what came next.

"So, Lucinda, I have made a decision. I should start forthwith transferring my knowledge to someone who can then teach Malcolm when the time is right."

"An excellent idea!" I said.

"I think it is. That is why I think that you should start coming into the office every day after school, and full time this summer."

"ME? Holy Cow, Daddy, I'm twelve years old."

"Language, Lucinda!"

In my utter consternation, I forgot to use my father-approved vocabulary.

"I actually thought you were eleven. Twelve is even better."

"But Father..."

"Listen to me, Lucinda. I am well aware that a lumber yard - indeed, any business, but especially the rough world of strong-backed men - may not be an appropriate place for a young lady. But I am also unfortunately aware that you are the most astute of all my progeny. And although you are only eleven...no, twelve... I will be honest with you. I do not see much prospect for you with regard to marriage. You are no beauty and you are too outspoken to charm a young man into marriage."

"You already think I will be an old maid?"

"We need to be realistic, Lucinda. I do not see a husband in your future. So we need to secure a satisfactory life for you as a spinster. Comfortable even. You can learn the business and be an invaluable asset to your brother. Which will ensure that you will always have a home with your brother and a decent income - since it will be through your efforts that our business thrives."

I excused myself, saying to my father that it was much to consider, but I was surprised that I could respond so calmly when my head was on fire, but the rest of my body so cold.

"We'll plan your schedule at breakfast," he said as I stumbled away. I did not forget, however, to close his door quietly, as required.

I went out to the second-floor veranda. It was just a small balcony at the top of the front staircase, meant in earlier years, my father had said, for men to have a cigar before bedtime. No one ever used this space now except me. In fact, it was kept locked, due to Malcolm's propensity towards human aviation. I had found a spare key about two months earlier, and kept it behind the urn on the landing.

This turn of events was quite overwhelming.

My father wanted me to learn the business. My father thought I was too ugly and cross to ever secure a husband. My father's business was full of roughnecks. My father expected me to go to work at twelve years old. My father expected that I would run the company for his dolt of a son, in return for a roof over my head. My father thought I lacked charm.

My father thought I was the smartest of his children.

The most astute of all his progeny.

And that is how in my attempt to manipulate my father, he instead manipulated me.

CHAPTER 3

A T BREAKFAST THE NEXT MORNING, my mother was disconcerted to hear of my father's plan.

"Lucinda is still a little girl," she said. "She does not belong in a lumber yard."

"She is shrewd and practical," answered Father. "I need to disseminate the practice of conducting a successful business. For all our sakes."

"She cannot work among all those coarse men," argued my mother. "And she will be trampled by the wagons that constantly come and go. No one will even see such a tiny thing."

Which I was not. I was the third tallest girl in my class. Only the Olmstead twins were taller and they were older than I by ten months.

"I will be careful of her innocence and feminine weakness. She will work in the office. She will be my assistant."

And he winked at me. My father. My father winked at me.

Amelia at that point prepared herself to cry. It looked to be genuine, so distraught was she at my father's unprecedented display of affection towards me. It almost made the thought of spending the next forty years working for my father seem appealing. I had passed the night in abject regret of having brought the idea to my father in the first place. I'd meant for him to worry about his death in order to require Martin's services, not mine. And in the long dark sleepless night, I saw how my father's technique of destroying me by calling me homely and unpleasant had made me more vulnerable to the flattery that accompanied the disparagement.

Catherine chimed in. "Your assistant! How grand!"

My father sipped his coffee and looked magnanimous. "Yes, Lucinda will be an invaluable assistant."

"And what is the rate of pay for such an invaluable assistant?" Catherine asked.

Oh, my father may have outmaneuvered me, but Catherine was the final winner of the game.

Father looked stricken. Of course, he had not intended to pay me. But now he was obliged to do so or admit that I would not be of help.

"I've given that considerable thought," he said, although I could certainly see the calculations he was quickly running in his head. "Most of my workers are paid fifty cents an hour. But as an apprentice, and a female apprentice at that,

I think it would be more than fair to start at twelve cents an hour." Father nodded, agreeing with himself. "More than fair."

I couldn't really disagree. I had no idea what folks earned. I was rich when I had a nickel. I looked at my mother and Catherine. They didn't look shocked one way or the other.

"How much do I have to work? I still want to go to school."

"Of course you will stay in school. We have years to teach you the business. But no shirking either. You will have great responsibilities. You leave school at 3:30, correct?" He did not wait for me to answer. "It should take no longer than twenty minutes to walk from school to the lumberyard. So I will expect you at 3:50 every day. You can come home with me at 6:30. Except Friday. You may have Friday afternoon off. And then on Saturdays, we can go to work together at 6:00, but you can go home at noon."

I could not do the math in my head the way Father could, but I recognized that this would be over one dollar a week. My mother instantly realized the same thing.

"A child cannot have that kind of money!" She looked at my unhappy face. "Even a responsible girl like Lucinda," she added.

"I'll save it!" I said, proving to her that I was indeed a responsible girl. "I'll save it and go to college."

Now it was Father's turn to reveal a horrified face. "Now, now, Lucinda. Very few women go to college. It isn't appropriate."

"But some do!" I said. "Helen Keller went to college, and she's blind and deaf. Harriet Beecher Stowe went to college - at her sister Catharine's school. And I have a sister Catherine, even though it's spelled a little different. It was meant to be!"

"Differently," said Father.

"What would you study in school?" asked Catherine.

I knew what I wanted to study, though it wouldn't suit Father any. But it was a long way off anyway. I didn't even want Father's job, but now I had to have it. It was just a matter of pride and defiance, and according to Father, I had an abundance of both. So I gave an answer that would not meet resistance from either of my parents.

"I would train to be a teacher," I said. "That is a suitable position for an unmarried lady."

"Unmarried?" said my mother. "Why ever do you think that?"

I handed the butter to Amelia. "I just have to be realistic," I said. "I'm no beauty."

"Nonsense!" said Catherine. "Why Martin said this weekend that you are quite striking. Individuality should be prized."

"Like having your eyes a bit too close together?" I asked.

"Your eyes are not too close together," my mother said. "They are just the perfect distance for you."

"They are practically touching," I said. "They would probably actually touch if it wasn't for the beak I have in the middle of my face."

16

"You have an elegant nose," said Catherine. "And intelligence in your eyes and brows. And perfect lips that someday some boy will greatly admire."

"No one would want to kiss you," said Amelia.

"I would kiss you," said Malcolm. I almost did kiss him at that moment, if it weren't for the jam spread evenly across his cheeks.

"Enough nonsense," declared Mother. "You will all marry and give me pretty grandchildren. And perhaps you will go to college one day, Lucinda. We will save for it with your generous salary from Father. You can keep ten cents each week from what you earn, and the rest goes into the bank. And you must have Mondays free as well as Fridays. I will not have you relinquishing your piano lessons."

And so it was settled. I had a job.

CHAPTER 4

I T WASN'T SO BAD.

I made the trek to the Lumber Yard right from school on Tuesdays, Wednesdays, and Thursdays.

The first day Sister Michael ran after me for heading in a direction not home. I explained that I would be working for my father three days a week. She told me I needed a note from my parents that would allow me to walk anyplace but home. I never even realized the sisters watched us, but then again, I wasn't surprised either. Those nuns watched how we placed our boots in the cloakroom. They knew what aisle our family chose for Sunday Mass. They knew if we made the slightest pencil mark in the books that had been used in the school for the past century. (Truly. I had a history book that mentioned the recent end to the "War Of

The Rebellion" and it was as pristine as it had been under President Grant.)

I explained to Sister Michael that my father had only allowed me twenty minutes to walk more than a mile-and-a-half and I could not even stop to discuss a permission slip. Sister Michael knew my father. She gave me a little push in the right direction and said, "Hurry." I heard her holler as I trotted away.

"Bring your permission note tomorrow!"

My father showed me around the place that first day. He was proud of all his bins and stacks and nails. He was nearly as proud of me when he introduced me to his employees. I did not quite get the same glow of loving ownership that the roofing shingles received, but I would say I did get considerably more than the tarpaper.

Everyone was very polite. Some of the men doffed their caps, but most just touched their fingers to their caps and kept on working. There was no way they would take an extra second to be polite when it meant they would have to stop working in front of my father. He seemed appreciative that they could say *"How do you do?"* and continue to throw the sorted wood into the right cubbyhole.

Jack O'Hara was the man who worked the customers. Jolly Jack, he was called by everyone. Father told me later that one always needed someone with the common touch to ensure that the customers come back.

"I don't deceive myself," he confided. "I don't have it. But you can always hire it. However," and he lowered his voice further, "you need to watch those personable types very carefully. A soft heart sometimes gets in the way of making a fair profit. But I have a prize with Jolly Jack. As honest as he is friendly. So I pay him well. And I have his three sons working too. I'm hoping that one will be like Jack, and keep the public happy and his hand out of the till. You must watch all three and tell me which one might replace Jolly Jack. You have to prepare, you know. The Irish, with their high color and their penchant for drink - they often die young."

I nodded seriously. Jolly Jack did have rosy cheeks and a big belly. He was about Father's age. He could die at any moment.

I also learned that although my father was well-known for paying fair wages, he was judicious as to how his employees were paid. The fellows with the strong backs were paid the least. "You can always get another set of muscles," Father said. Of course, the combination of brains and brawn put workers into a different category. The men who could think and make decisions were rewarded. But those were kept to a minimum. It was dangerous to have the men out in the yard second-guessing you. "A few smart ones who can see how to stack the lumber efficiently, and keep the men from killing themselves. That's all you need. And those rabble-rousers who would stir up discontent - well, I steer them over to Patterson's," he added with a chuckle.

Then there were those who could handle a team and could be counted on to make accurate deliveries. And the ones who had good reading and arithmetic skills, who could plan schedules or add up orders in their heads. Their wages were good, and they sometimes received a little extra in their pay packet.

"The rules of the Yard are simple: come to work every day on time, work hard, and don't steal. Don't drink either - not on the job, anyway. And you'd be surprised how many folks want a nip in the morning. I'm lax on the coarse language though. I'd like to fire every person who took the Lord's name in vain, but then I'd be here alone." He laughed again. This amazed me. Two laughs in one conversation. I had not heard so much in one week. "I might even have to fire *you*," he said, "from what Amelia tells me about your salty tongue!" At this I laughed too, but my father did not laugh this time.

"On this I am serious, Lucinda. Your mother and I will be gravely disappointed if you pick up bad habits here. There is much to learn, but not all of it is good."

CHAPTER 5

J OLLY JACK'S THREE SONS APPEARED to me to be from separate mothers. The oldest, Samuel, was gaunt and stern. He worked the delivery schedules and calculated wages. He'd put the cash in little envelopes, and demanded that the empty packets be returned within three days for re-use. Father loved him for his frugalness. But the other workers detested him.

The middle son was Richard. He was strong and tanned from the sun. He took much pride in displaying his arm muscles. He removed his shirt as soon as the temperature rose above freezing. He was well aware of his handsomeness, and flirted with me, although he knew I was the boss's daughter and only twelve. Or perhaps because I was the boss's daughter and only twelve. What a coup it would be to become son-in-law to Benedict Lumber.

I had heard (and asked Catherine to explain, but she would not) that Richard had children but no wife. Without a clear idea what this exactly meant, I was given to understand that this was not a good thing, and that perhaps Richard was not bound for heaven.

The youngest of Jolly Jack's boys was Peter. He was sixteen. He had Irish-red hair and more freckles than stars in the sky. He wore thick glasses - "My mum thought I was as blind as a bat, but Dad said no way... he never leaves a crumb on his plate." Peter drove one of the delivery wagons. It appeared the horses competed for his love, which he doled out as if they were his own offspring.

"This is my Zeke," he said as he introduced me to a big black horse with a prominent sway to his back and yellow hooves. "Isn't he a prince? And this bay, this is Carthage, who is older than all the wood in the forest, but still strong and fit." And I regarded the old tailless and almost toothless wreck.

"Don't tell your papa, but I let them stop every day at the meadow by the river. Just a few minutes. There's some fine clover there, and it puts them in good humor for the rest of the afternoon."

Peter also brought carrots for his team, and I had the impression that he did so because the carrots were beneficial to their eyesight - he usually ate a few himself. "Just taking care," he said. He also indicated, just in case I thought he was cheating my father by taking ten minutes to pamper the horses every day, that carrots were expensive.

"Maybe you could grow some yourself," I suggested.

"Oh, a garden! Wouldn't that be sweet? That's what I'm going to do when I am out on my own. Have a big garden with all sorts of fine vegetables. And fruit trees. I give apples to these fellows in the fall. I can get the bruised ones cheap."

"How long have you worked here?"

"Since I was fourteen. But I didn't get to drive the wagon until I was fifteen. Best year of my life."

"So far," I added.

Our conversations never went on longer than a few sentences. Peter was diligent about not shirking on the job (except for the meadow break, and I wondered what he did in those ten-minute respites he gave the animals). And of course I was careful that my father did not see me talking to any of the men for long. But he did ask me to size up the O'Hara boys, and so I considered this part of my responsibilities.

I managed during one short talk with Peter to ask him about his plans for the future.

"Well, just like you said… to have a garden."

"But what job do you see yourself doing?"

"This one for sure. Me and my horses."

"What about seeing to customers, like your father?"

"Ah nope. Can't read."

I was appalled. A man of sixteen who cannot read? But perhaps it was just his poor eyesight, and not any lack of learning. I didn't quite know how to ask this, however.

I hoped that Father did not ask which of Jolly Jack's sons he should groom for Jack's expected demise. One stingy and unpleasant, one burly and destined for hell, and one with a kind heart who couldn't read a bill of sale. Maybe I could encourage Jolly Jack to give up the drink.

As far as my own duties went, watching the O'Hara boys was just a small part. Father taught me inventory and ordering. I went to the bins and counted shingles, nails, and other supplies every day. From those numbers I made a chart, and determined over the course of two months, what the average usage was, and so calculated when we would need to order more and how much to order.

My father was delighted by this, as my charts and projections turned out to agree with his own ordering schedule. By delighted, I mean that he said, "You did not put us out of business this week, Lucinda."

He instructed me as to seasonality. If one ordered as much in the Fall as we had done in Spring, we would be spending our cash for product that would sit on the shelf. "You cannot eat shingles, Lucinda. So you must forecast properly." And he gave me huge old ledgers of the previous ten years, which I was to study and chart the ebb and flow of the lumber business. He was to test me on this by October. If I passed (or rather, as Father put it, did not fail too wretchedly), then I would start on the prestigious coal business.

"Aha," I said. "Without studying I would say that coal transactions go up when the lumber transactions go down!"

"You must not be so full of yourself, Lucinda," he said. But he pulled from his pocket a butterscotch candy, which I am sure had been originally intended for Amelia.

CHAPTER 6

I MANAGED TO KEEP UP WITH my schoolwork (Mama's first priority) and my piano lessons (Mama's second priority) as well as learning the lumber trade (Father's only priority). My own priority was to spend every other available minute with Catherine before I lost her to Connecticut.

It was to be a grand wedding. This surprised me as I had expected Father to be loathed to fund such extravagance.

But as arrangements advanced, Father grew more and more magnanimous. He indulged Catherine more than I had ever seen him do. He had shown such steadfast disapproval of Catherine's so-called flippancy over the last several years, but suddenly seemed to have a change of heart. He was determined that she should have the best dress in all of Massachusetts as well as a fine lace veil, and a trousseau that would rival those New York City society brides who embarked on a European Tour as honeymoon. It became my mother's role to be the rational decision maker. And in my Father's increasingly pleasant mood, he also took great pride in Mother's level-headedness.

I heard at the lumber yard that Mary Patterson, the daughter of Father's rival, Randolph Patterson, had eloped to New York City with an Italian. Whether this scandal affected my father's generosity I cannot say.

Catherine wanted everything and nothing. She took great pleasure in the attention and the extravagance. She danced around the house wearing her laundry-day clothes and her magnificent veil. But on the other hand, if my mother pronounced that there would be only two tiers to the wedding cake and not four, Catherine would say, "That sounds perfect."

For the truth was that Catherine only wanted Martin. All the accompaniments were a joy, but superfluous.

"We are going to have such a sweet life," she told me as we prepared for bed just a few days before the wedding. "You should see the quaint little apartment we have rented in New Haven. We're going to be just like in 'The Gift of The Magi' - except without me having to cut my hair, of course. Because we tell each other everything. Martin's so intelligent, and he even believes that I am intelligent too."

"Well, of course you are intelligent!" I said.

"Oh no, not like you. I know how to ridicule things I don't like. That's not intelligence. It's vanity."

"Did Martin tell you that?"

"Martin says I have sound reasons for my ridicule, but that I need to understand them before I criticize. That's what he does - he laughs at Life but he knows why."

"I think that is the very definition of a cynic."

"He's not a cynic. He is quite an optimist. I would say ... maybe a skeptic."

"Well that should suit you well," I said.

"Lucinda," said Catherine, looking at me with sincerity. "Don't work for Father if you don't want to." She paused. "I mean, when you are old enough to decide," she added.

"I rather like the charts and figuring out the future. But I know I don't like watching every move people make. I always thought I would like being bossy, but now I'm seeing that it's much pleasanter to let folks do as they please. Father likes to tell people they are wrong."

Catherine laughed. "True enough. But the world needs the bossy types too, and Daddy provides jobs for a lot of men, and so he supports a lot of families. And if he wasn't bossy and a bit of a tyrant, he may not be successful, and then those people couldn't provide for their families."

"Can you be nice and be successful?"

"Yes! But Father is not so bad, you know."

I was surprised Catherine was defending him so.

"I didn't think you liked Father very much," I said.

"Oh, I love him. I know he's not perfect, and he *is* a bit of a tyrant and he's tiresome and boring sometimes. But he took on a life that he didn't want and he's made the best of it."

"Isn't that what I should do then? Stay with Father and teach Malcolm so he doesn't botch it all up?"

She shook her head. "Not at all. Father accepted his responsibility and it has made him solemn and tiresome. I want you to be happy and light. Like I am. I am going to do what I love. Laugh with Martin every day in our little home and have lots of happy babies."

"What if I don't want babies?"

"Do you know what you do want?"

"I think I want to be a muckraker."

"A what?"

"I want to protest in the streets and write for a newspaper and get justice for people!"

"Oh," she laughed, "So you DO like to tell people when they're wrong!"

CHAPTER 7

W HAT CATHERINE DID NOT TELL me was how to know when I was old enough to stand up to my father.

But oh, the wedding was as splendid as that of Alice Roosevelt. I would argue that Catherine was certainly lovelier. Father had decided that we would not hire carriages or motorcars. He prayed for excellent September weather - I could say that he ordered God to provide a beautiful day, and God complied.

And we walked to St. Sebastian's church in procession. Father engaged a violinist to provide the beautiful solemn music as we strode the four blocks in our finery. The accompaniment ensured that all the neighbors (those not invited) had the opportunity to come outside or lean from their windows and applaud our prestigious group. I rather believe there would have been a marching band but for the fact that Father found tubas to be reprehensible.

Catherine had wanted me to be her maid of honor, but Mother thought I was too young to witness a marriage certificate. My cousin Bertha was given that role, and in compensation, a dress was designed for me in pale silvery blue satin with a lace sash to match my sister's veil. Still, I cried at the thought of not standing by my sister's side at the altar, and Mother added the loan of her second best strand of pearls.

A beautiful gown was not something I normally prized, but I will confess to taking some comfort in the surprising notion that I might not be as homely as my father had previously indicated. Indeed, he seemed rather taken with my appearance that morning, and suggested I walk at the head of the procession strewing flowers from a basket. Well, that was a silly notion, as we did not have more than a single bouquet of flowers for me to carry, and I wasn't about to prance down the streets like some childish idiot. But it was a nice idea nonetheless.

So Father and Catherine headed the procession, with me following alongside cousin Bertha (in pink), and my mother next in line with Amelia and Malcolm by the hand on each side.

Martin was waiting at the church with his cousin Roger and a small contingent of family. We Benedicts, on the other hand, had invited every drop of blood on both Father's and Mother's family tree, and in addition every acquaintance, customer, vendor, plus any politician who may someday do our business some service. And numerous clergy.

The service was literally heaven - with a boys' choir and high Mass and the monsignor in white and gold vestments looking like the Pope himself. I have a suspicion that my father might have written the Holy Father himself, who perhaps sent the robes as a nuptial gift.

Catherine was radiant. Martin was calm and could not stop smiling, even during the most solemn of the scriptures. The remainder of the congregation wept, such was the beauty and emotion evoked. Even Malcolm sobbed just a tad, although that may have been induced by the pungency of the tonic applied to his cowlick.

All but me. I did not cry at all. Not when all the guests had said their goodbyes. Not when Catherine and Martin had said their goodbyes. Not until I carefully hung my beautiful dress in the mahogany wardrobe and brushed my hair and put on my summer nightgown and turned out my light. Then lying in the dark bedroom on a moonless night - then I wept.

I did not know how I would live without Catherine. I did not know how soon I would have to.

CHAPTER 8

1918

BY THE SUMMER OF 1918, I was finished with school. For the time being at least. I was still endeavoring to convince my father that I should go to college. He was by principle opposed to women receiving an advanced education. Knowledge in excess of basic skills was not a fiscally sound investment, as a woman would not be able to pursue erudite endeavors once she became a mother. That Father had determined five years earlier that I would not marry was my best argument, and I was beginning to see some small signs that he may be relenting.

I had served Father well at Benedict Lumber in those years. The business had thrived, and the profits had grown. I had an aptitude for inventory management, and found it quite satisfying to order just enough product to meet demand, neither running out nor having merchandise sit unsold in the yard.

I was careful to maintain my Father's concept of femininity, and did not take up cursing or tobacco chewing, although I will admit that I did on Thursday evenings enjoy a beer with the O'Hara boys. My parents, I can only believe, were unaware of my participation in Payday Darts and Brew at Corcoran's Bar on High Street. Or more specifically, behind Corcoran's Bar - for much of those five years, Peter O'Hara and I were too young to enter the bar, so Richard, the middle boy, would bring our beers out to the yard behind the bar, where we would sit on the stoop and relish our bad behavior. Once Peter came of age, he would still sit with me outside. "It's hot and noisy," he said, "and besides, not a proper place for a lady."

The eldest O'Hara boy, Samuel, had gone off to the Great War, and it seemed that he was showing a capacity for leadership that may serve him well when he returned. I believed that strong, bull-like Richard would have been the better soldier, but he was discovered to have unhealthy lungs and was exempted. To my surprise, he seemed relieved to stay out of the war.

Peter was expecting to be called up soon. He was eager to join Sam and prove his worth in battle. I knew this would not happen. Despite calling upon my father to equip Peter with better spectacles (I argued that it would be safer in the yard if he could see the workmen running back and forth so near his wagon) - he was still nearly blind. But I let Peter keep his dream of soldiering. What good would it have done for me to point out what he surely knew but would rather deny?

The boys' father, Jolly Jack O'Hara, had defied the gods, and was still behind my father's counter in 1918. I knew this could not go on forever, as Jolly Jack grew more rotund and red-faced with each passing month. But I no longer had to worry about which of his sons would take over his role. Because in March, Malcolm had turned twelve, and came after school to work at Benedict Lumber, much as I had at the same age.

And wonder of wonders, Malcolm was splendid.

He was big and sturdy for twelve, and he could carry lumber with the men. And curse like a sailor.

And although mathematics was not his strong suit, he seemed to have a special talent for filling orders and writing bills of sale quickly and error-free. Knowing when to cut a deal, extend credit, or demand immediate cash payment seemed instinctive. He could laugh behind the counter like Jolly Jack with men four times his age. And he had only been on the job part-time for five months. Here was Jolly Jack's successor and the inheritor of Benedict Lumber all rolled into one strange packet.

I was a little jealous at times of the pride that Father showed in Malcolm. No customer or dealer came into the Yard without my Father braying in a new loud voice, "You must meet my son, Malcolm. A young man with the world at his command!"

So a little jealous perhaps. But on the whole, very relieved. I did not really want to spend my life in the lumberyard. I wanted to go to school.

I had not lost my desire to be a news reporter and a reformer. Indeed I had portraits of Upton Sinclair and Ida Tarbell on the wall above my bed. And to my great satisfaction - as well as my vanity - I had already made a small impact.

I had witnessed in Father's own business an injustice. Father had several colored men working in the yard. They performed the tasks that required the strongest of men. These colored gentlemen worked long hours, took no breaks, and were never late or absent. Yet they earned only half of what the white men made.

I brought this up to Father and he was mystified that I thought this to be unjust.

"These men would not work at all but for me," he declared. "Patterson would not hire them. He has no black men at all at his lumberyard."

"But they do the same work! Don't they have to eat the same food? Pay for the same roof over their head? Support their families?"

"No," he answered. "I have seen that they do not eat the same food or have the same types of rents. They live cheaper. So they need less money."

I thought about this for a week. I had Peter show me one Sunday afternoon where the colored people lived in Springfield.

The following week, I brought up the issue with my father again. I explained that I thought the colored men lived in lesser apartments because of the money, and not the other way around. "They do not live cheaper because they can. They live cheaper because they have no choice.

I think they would have nicer homes for their wives and children if they could afford it."

"But we cannot afford it."

But I had done my arithmetic.

"We have only six colored men. They make twenty-five cents an hour. If you gave each man thirty cents per hour, that is only one nickel more per man. Over the course of the week, it is still much less than you would have to pay if you had to replace one of those colored gentlemen with a white man. We could raise the price of a five-pound box of nails by a penny and cover the cost, and our nails would still be fairly priced as compared to the thievery that Mr. Patterson charges."

Father looked at me somewhat suspiciously, but I could tell he was interested.

"And just think of how those colored men would be grateful to see more money in their pay packets every week. Why they would work so extra hard for you! And they would still be making much less than the white men, so the white men would not have any reason to be angry."

"Can we really increase the price of nails and still be lower than Patterson?" he asked.

"Yes. I went there myself last week, and their prices of nails are 18% higher than ours."

"Just five cents. For just the six men, correct?"

"Yes - that's all." I added, "You will see it will be worth it." I dropped for a moment all my business manner. "Please, Daddy."

"All right. Go ahead then, Lucinda. You are quite the reformer."

I did it that very week. My original intention had been to make all the men equal -white and colored both, but after doing my research, I knew that was impossible. Negroes never made what white men made. To think that they might would be as crazy as thinking that women would earn the same as men. That idea would certainly make Father laugh. But for these men, working fifty-five hours each week, that $2.75 would at least let their wives put a better meal out for their children.

I decided that setting a reasonable small goal was the best way to reform the world. Success could certainly be measured in nickels.

I was delighted. And determined to go on to college to learn where I could find extra nickels.

CHAPTER 9

Initially, Catherine had kept her promise to visit us in Springfield one Sunday a month. She and Martin would take the train up from New Haven, arriving around eleven in the morning. With having to change trains in Hartford, I knew that they would have left Connecticut very early in the morning. I wondered (to myself only) whether this meant that they were skipping Sunday Mass.

The following year, however, Catherine's visits grew scarce. There was a delightful reason for this. Catherine was in the family way, and by June of 1915, I had acquired a nephew. Jonathan, named for my father, was a cherub of a boy with a round bald head and round cheeks and round blue eyes. He laughed as much as Catherine. But her condition made it uncomfortable to travel, and then after the baby was born, it was just increasingly difficult to carry the baby and all his accoutrements and at the same time keep him hushed and good-natured during the long ride.

And in October of 1916, Catherine and Martin added a daughter to their family. Charlotte was as tiny as Jonathan was round, and appeared to have Father's penchant for serious concentration.

So visits gradually dwindled to just a few times per year.

A few times, the family made the trek to New Haven instead. I rather liked it. The train was interesting, and New Haven was quite wonderful. Catherine and Martin had a tiny apartment not far from Yale University. Yale took my breath away. The beautiful dark buildings and young men striding with intelligent purpose into the future.

Catherine's home was tiny. The family lived up on the third floor of a lead-windowed brownstone. They had a large kitchen with a small sitting area and one bedroom. Some of the older buildings in the neighborhood had much more impressive architecture, but the advantage of this place was modern plumbing and even a W.C. "So much easier with the babies," bragged Catherine. The children slept in cribs which made walking through the bedroom all but impossible. Catherine told me that it was fine - she just climbed over the bed to get to the dresser.

"And I can see myself so much better in the mirror when I stand on the bed anyway. The bottom half of me, that is," she joked.

We didn't all fit around her kitchen table for dinner. But Malcolm took his meal on his lap in the sitting room.

I thought it was perfect and romantic. However, I did speculate that things would only get tighter as the children outgrew the cribs.

"The Carmichaels next door have three older children," Martin explained. "And they have a cot in the sitting room that the two boys share quite nicely. The girl gets the horsehair sofa, which is warm in the winter."

Warm in the winter meant stifling in the summer, and that is what we learned as the seasons changed in New Haven. Amelia took to fainting during the peak of the day in July. And shivering a bit too much to be authentic in December.

And so our own visits dwindled too.

Catherine wrote me weekly. The children were thriving. Martin had changed employment and was being groomed for promotion. It was just a matter of time before they would be able to move into a larger apartment. Not that there was anything wrong with their quaint little abode. And she wrote of music and art and museums and all the activities that surrounded the university.

"I wish you could go to school here," she wrote.

"No matter about our small space; I would build you a cubby under the kitchen table if that were possible. But there are no programs for women. Not at Yale or anyplace, as far as I can determine. But life in New Haven is grand. Perhaps when you finish school you can find a position here. That is, if you are determined to remain a spinster and a reformer. I can attest to the sweetness of married life, however, if you are so inclined. Martin is a fine man. He has a good soul. And he is handsome, as you may have noticed."

We all had letters from Catherine each week. We read them at the dinner table and they became part of our dessert tradition. Amelia and Malcolm read their letters in their entirety. Catherine wrote to Amelia about all the fine shops in New Haven and the old woman in a neighboring building who had the most marvelous collection of dolls. This although Amelia was growing far too mature to swoon over dolls. But Catherine's descriptions may have been at the request of Mother, who could see that Amelia was increasingly prone to swoon over boys.

To Malcolm, she wrote about baseball tournaments, as well as Egyptian artifacts and other museum discoveries. And automobiles. New Haven was a becoming a babel of motorcars, and Catherine described in great detail the mechanics as well as the hilarity that often ensued from the clash of unreliable vehicles and ornery horses.

I read almost every line of my letters aloud, only omitting the parts about my college aspirations, and of course, Catherine's effusive compliments on her husband's good looks, as that seemed to me to be Catherine's private thoughts that my father and mother need not hear.

My parents also skipped paragraphs; it was obvious that there existed much more writing on the page than was repeated at the dining room table. Mother read mostly about the precious babies, surely the most clever of children ever born. And Father read about Martin's career and his slow but steady progress.

I was quite sure that the parts that my mother skipped were those of loneliness for us, despite Catherine's happy marriage. And I suspected that Father omitted Catherine's exhortations on my part. She was as determined as I that I should further my schooling. And I believed she may have used a tactic that I had not considered: My father's pride.

To be the first Benedict with a degree. Think how my father could trumpet that to Randolph Patterson and the officers at the Knights of Columbus. And that he was broad-minded enough to encourage a daughter in such intellectual pursuits.

I believe that Catherine was relentless in her entreaties. As my Father skipped down through whole paragraphs, his eyes would involuntarily dart to me. And eventually she won.

In August of 1918, Father relented.

He announced at dinner that he had given great thought and copious prayer - my father used the term 'copious prayer' on a frequent basis - that I should perhaps go to college after all.

"I would like you to take another year at home to transition your duties at the yard to Malcolm, during which time you should apply to certain institutes of higher education where you may pursue either teaching or nursing, whichever you prefer."

Well, I was overjoyed. Not that I desired to be a teacher or a nurse - those pursuits were not in my plans. But the idea that I might in one year be in college. I was overcome.

Father continued, "I would prefer that you attend a Catholic university, but that doesn't seem viable if we would have you stay in New England. While I believe you may receive a fine education at the University of Massachusetts, you would be required to take classes alongside men. And that would be worrisome to me."

"But I work alongside very rough men every day at the lumberyard," I pointed out.

"Yes, but I am there to protect you," Father said.

"And me," Malcolm added. "I would never let any of those men harm you or talk rough around you. I would fight any fellow that would disrespect you. He wouldn't even have a jaw left when I was through!"

"Why, thank you, Malcolm," I said. "You are my knight in shining armor."

"Back to the subject at hand," said Father. "I have made a list of a few women's colleges that are acceptable to your mother and me. At the top of the list is Mount Holyoke. There you would get a superior education, and still be close to home."

"Mount Holyoke!" said Mother. "How marvelous that would be!"

I was near tears at this point. College. And Mount Holyoke at that. It was more than I could even imagine.

"This is an expensive proposition," continued Father. "So I will expect you to save even more of your wages than you do currently. You must show us that you are committed to this proposal."

"Oh Father, I will save every penny. I need nothing this next year but the paper and ink to apply. You have made me the happiest girl in the world!"

CHAPTER 10

IN SEPTEMBER OF 1918, NEW England was ravaged. It was influenza.

All through Massachusetts and Connecticut, families were wiped out. Unlike other epidemics, the disease spared many of the small children and the elderly, while strong and healthy young adults fell victim. Folks who were fine on Sunday were dead on Tuesday. The wagons collecting the dead were overwhelmed with bodies, and although it was sinful and disrespectful, bodies were stacked one atop the other.

Schools and businesses came to a halt, or operated amidst worry and sorrow.

Jolly Jack fell ill during the first weeks of the scourge but survived. Not as fortunate were two of the colored workers in the yard and several of our coal customers. Our neighbor to the south of us lost three daughters.

So we Benedicts were lucky. Or so we were told.

We lost only one.

At the beginning of November, when the worst of the epidemic seemed to have passed, Catherine died.

CHAPTER 11

W E RECEIVED A TELEGRAM. WE had a telephone, and Martin had access to the phone of his landlord. But he telegraphed. I believe that Martin could not bear to hear any of our voices. Or perhaps he could not bear to hear his own.

The telegram read:

I am so sorry, Dear Mr. and Mrs. Benedict. Catherine has died from the influenza. The children are well. Please come immediately. Martin.

Father hired a car to bring us to New Haven. Mother sent Amelia and Malcolm to Aunt Helen, but I was adamant that I would not be left behind. It took several hours to drive down, and the only words spoken were Mother's: "This is surely some terrible mistake."

But it was not. We arrived at Catherine's apartment to find Martin sitting on the stoop with his head in his hands. It took several minutes to determine that Catherine had already been taken to a mortuary somewhere in the city - Martin could not remember where - and the babies were with a neighbor, although Martin was not sure which one.

We begged and cajoled Martin to come with us back up to the apartment. He declared that he could not go in. "I must wait here," he replied, and continued to sit in the cold. My father finally convinced him to get up by sternly reprimanding him.

"Martin, you are putting your family in jeopardy with your self-pity. Get up, sir, and open your apartment and let your mother-in-law out of the cold. And then we shall find your children. And make proper arrangements for Catherine."

And Martin rose and apologized. We went up the stairs and into the apartment, where we found the landlord's wife feeding Jonathan and Charlotte.

My mother snatched up little Charlotte and began to weep. "Oh my Catherine," she cried.

Father said to Martin, "Come sit here on the sofa with me." And when Martin obeyed, Father wrapped his arms around Martin and said rather imperiously, "Now you go ahead and cry, young man."

I stood in the kitchen and watched. Watched my mother weep over Catherine's daughter and Martin weep in my father's arms.

Jonathan, then three, said, "Can I have more pudding, please?"

CHAPTER 12

MARTIN'S LANDLORD WAS ABLE TO supply us with the information as to the location of Catherine's body, and Mother and Father left with Martin to make arrangements to bring her body back to Springfield for burial. I thought Martin would object, but he seemed relieved that we would take her home.

I stayed with Jonathan and Charlotte. I didn't have a tremendous amount of experience taking care of children. When Amelia and Malcolm were infants and toddlers, my mother did not trust me at such a young age to handle them. So my care of them was no more than patting their cheeks, or perhaps feeding them little spoons of applesauce. When they were older, I was often in charge of seeing that they did not eat dirt or fall down the stairs, but other than that, I avoided them as far as was possible.

NANCY ROMAN

Jonathan and Charlotte were three and two, respectively. A small infant who could not move by itself would have been quite a bit easier than watching these two tumble and climb and occasionally swat at each other. Charlotte was still in diapers, but I had watched my mother do that duty often enough that I managed to pin her into her nappy without sticking her. Jonathan, on the other hand, needed to use the little potty chair that resided in a corner of the kitchen. I had not seen Malcolm's privates since I was six years old, and I suppose I must have suppressed the awful memory of the unpleasant look of boy parts, as I was a bit surprised at his little thing nestled in what appeared to be a soft dumpling. I managed to pretend that it was normal - and I suppose it was, after all.

Within two hours, Jonathan began to cry for his mother, and I was ill-equipped to console him, as each time he sobbed "Mama," I wept myself. Distraught, I drank a small thimble of some rye whiskey I had found in the back of a cabinet, and sat for a moment with Jonathan on my lap and held him close. I considered giving Jonathan a taste of the whiskey as well, but he finally fell asleep on his own.

I laid him in his crib, and took up Charlotte.

She babbled and giggled and tried to tell me something about her dress that I was not able to understand. I suppose if you listen to a baby's voice every day you understand what they are saying, or at least enough to get by. All I understood was "Auntie" and "No No." I sang her a song from my memory about an old gray goose, and she started to sing along a bit. Catherine must have remembered the same song. There is a line in that song - "Go tell Aunt

Rhody the old gray goose is dead." Why would you sing about death to a little child?

"Let's sing *Twinkle Twinkle Little Star* instead," I suggested, and Charlotte was happy to do so.

Both of the babies were napping when my parents and Martin returned. My mother looked in on both cribs.

"You were wonderful with the children," said Mother, although she had no real evidence to prove this was so.

It was decided that Martin and the babies would come back to Springfield with us and stay until after the funeral and burial. Martin sat as still and silent as a stone while my mother packed clothing for him and the children. I packed up a few of the children's toys. I chose those which seemed most worn, since those would be the ones that were most likely also the most loved.

The hired driver was fetched and he brought the car around.

"I think that is everything," said Mother.

"No," said Martin, speaking for the first time in many hours. "We need a dress for Catherine."

And he went to the bedroom and opened a pine wardrobe that had been painted to resemble cherry. He took out Catherine's wedding dress.

"This one," he said. "It is her most beautiful dress. Do you think it would be right to bury her in her wedding dress? Is there any rule about such a thing?"

"It will be perfect," said my Mother.

CHAPTER 13

C ATHERINE WAS BURIED ON A Monday. The day it was announced that the Great War had ended.

Martin and the children stayed in Springfield for a week. Martin mostly sat in the sitting room in his funeral suit. My mother took care of Jonathan and Charlotte, and tried to teach me how to manage two restless children, keeping them happy and safe, while letting them still be children.

It amazed me how resilient they were - or rather how short their memories were. They asked for their mother quite often, but were easily distracted by a toy or a cookie. It was a blessing, I imagine, although I found myself angry that Catherine might be so readily forgotten. It would have been easier for me, and perhaps for Martin too, had they cried relentlessly, as we all wanted to do.

But we kept up appearances. I played with Charlotte, dressing and undressing her dolls, and Malcolm pulled Jonathan in a small wagon.

We tried to postpone the decision that was inevitable.

Martin could not take care of the children and also provide an income. The children needed to be taken care of while Martin worked.

Mother suggested that Martin move to Springfield, and take up employment with my father. This had been my original goal five years ago, but my intention had been to keep Catherine close. Now we may have Martin and Catherine's children, but Catherine was lost to us. We needed to focus on the children. If Martin moved in with us, my mother would raise the children with my and Amelia's assistance.

But there was a complication to this plan. Martin's employer in New Haven lost six employees to influenza. They needed him. They finally offered him the promotion that Catherine had so hoped for. He wanted that position. He wanted to work there, not for my father.

And they needed him as soon as possible. Three days after the funeral Martin packed the children's things and hugged my mother and thanked my father and boarded the train back to Connecticut.

I went with him.

I was to care for the babies during the day. I learned as quickly as possible from Mother how to properly prepare food for toddlers, and how often to feed them. And when they should nap and when to awaken them, and how to handle tantrums and arguments.

I didn't think I could do it. I didn't think the children would be safe under my inexperienced care. I didn't think I could handle Martin's profound grief. I wanted my mother to go to New Haven with Martin and let me take care of Father and Amelia and Malcolm. I knew those three. I may not have much affection for them, but I could keep them alive. But that made no sense for me to stay. I was the one - finished with school and wrapping up my own duties with Father - who was free to go.

I took three dresses besides the one I wore, two nightgowns and an extra pair of shoes. I wore my winter coat. This could not last forever. Martin would make arrangements for a housekeeper and nanny. I would go home in perhaps a month, and continue my plans for my education.

Of course, there was no real room for me in the tiny apartment. I slept on the settee, and changed into my nightdress after everyone was in bed, and rose before sunrise to wash and dress again.

Not that it would have mattered. Martin stumbled through the mornings and evenings, and spent most of his day at the factory.

He spoke very little. He did make an effort with the children, playing on the floor with blocks and dolls, but he had lost that lighthearted merriment that I had witnessed before Catherine's death. On our infrequent visits last year, he would swing the children high over his head until they squealed with delight. I had not seen him repeat that one time in the weeks that followed. I prayed for the melancholy to fade.

The children often picked up on his sadness, and their response was not reciprocal sadness, but demands for attention. Usually, they would wait for their father to leave, and then present me with their most dreadful behaviors.

Jonathan would throw his toys and scream. I would stand helplessly out of the path of the heaviest missiles, and wait for his anger to dissipate. Then the tears would flow. Not just his. I would cry with him as he pounded his little fists against my chest.

Charlotte's reaction was more chilling. She would stiffen on the floor, and refuse to move, or even meet my eye. As small as she was, she was nearly impossible to pick up in this ossified state. I found that the easiest thing to do was to lay on the floor with her.

"We are playing Statues," I explained to Jonathan, and he would lie down with us. Eventually, Charlotte would sleep.

I loved best their nap-time. I would sit with my book and savor the quiet. Sometimes I filled the hour writing letters of application to college. Letters I could not mail. I cursed Catherine for leaving her children. For leaving me.

One Saturday, not long before Christmas, I took the children out to play in the recent snowfall. As I bundled them up against the cold with extra trousers, and scarves and mittens pinned to their coats, I begged Martin to come with us.

"Please, let's have an hour where we can laugh with the children. The fresh air will do us all good."

He agreed, and donned his coat and hat and dragged out a small sled that he had stored in the basement. He pulled the children with breathtaking speed along the snow-covered street, and they hollered and cried, "Faster, faster!" He lost his footing eventually and fell into the snow, where the children climbed over him and piled their snowy selves on his chest. We went in rosy-cheeked and drank warm milk and Martin read a story about Christmas.

It was our best day.

And later that night, after the children had been put down to sleep, Martin said, "I am both happy we had such fun this afternoon, and devastated that I could smile. Catherine should be here and I don't want to be happy ever again."

"I can't imagine that Catherine would want you to be sad for the rest of your life. She loved to hear you laugh more than she loved anything in the world. She would want to hear you laugh again."

"Well, she can't. She can't hear anything buried in the ground in Massachusetts. Please spare me the 'looking down from heaven' nonsense."

I was stunned.

I knew that Martin may have shared Catherine's heretical views, but this sounded more like atheism than agnosticism. But as doubtful as I was myself of the Catholic view of heaven and hell, I was not ready to relinquish my father's passed-along devotion. Not completely. Although I understood Martin's utter discouragement. God let this happen.

"I won't argue about Catherine's ability to watch you live your life," I said. "How about if we just put our attention to creating some joy for the children? Without having to worry whether this makes us feel better or worse. Because probably nothing will make us feel better. But the babies are too young for lifelong sadness."

Martin nodded. "I can agree to that. I love these babies. And it was good to see them smile today. I would not want them to grow up to be as miserable as I am."

"You are not miserable," I said. "Or if you are, pretend once in a while to not be."

"Granted," he said. "Would you like a small whiskey?"

And we drank more than one and we toasted Catherine and Father Christmas. And went to our separate rooms to undress in private and sleep that heavy drink-induced dreamless sleep.

CHAPTER 14

WE TRAVELED BACK TO SPRINGFIELD for Christmas. Father had always maintained that Christmas should be the most religious of holidays, with a sacred emphasis on prayer and very little on gifts. I remember just before Catherine's wedding receiving a hairbrush with an ebony handle and a very small box of chocolates.

But this Christmas was different. Mother seemed determined to make this holiday jolly and not morose. I never saw such a mass of presents. And a big tree, which we decorated with popcorn and cranberries and stars that Amelia cut out of yellow paper. Jonathan and Charlotte were mesmerized.

That did not mean there were not multiple church services to attend. Including a memorial mass for Catherine, during which Charlotte cried throughout, and Jonathan clambered over the seat and slammed the kneeler up and down relentlessly. Martin and I, trying to contain him, ended up laughing, which was just terrible. Finally, Mother picked up the naughty little boy and carried him out.

I think it was at that moment - when Martin and I laughed aloud in church - that my Father decided on the next necessary step.

The morning after Christmas - it was a Thursday - Father asked me after breakfast to come to his office where Mother and he needed to speak to me. I left Martin with Jonathan and handed Charlotte to Amelia.

I thought - hoped - that perhaps my father had engaged a domestic for Martin and I would be released from my duty in New Haven. I was sad at the thought that I would be away from the children, as I had been with them now for a month, and my attachment was growing. But I knew that the situation could not be maintained.

And indeed, that is how Father started.

"The situation with you in New Haven is unacceptable," he said. "It is not proper for you to live with a man not your husband."

"I agree," I said. "I think we should find a domestic to care for the children, and I will go on to college as planned."

Father shook his head. "No servant should raise our grandchildren. It is your duty as Catherine's sister to embrace these children as your own."

I had thought it worth the try. But I knew where my responsibilities lay. My own ambitions were selfish in the face of this tragedy. "I do love them. I'll care for them. I can do that for Catherine."

"But you cannot live in sin," he said.

I had already worked out a solution to this dilemma, which I had planned to share with Martin on our return to New Haven. But under the circumstances, I presented the plan to my parents now.

"Yes, I agree, it's difficult for us both. The apartment is very small, and I have no room of my own. But I have been thinking that with Martin's promotion, we could perhaps move to a bigger space. There are some nice two-family homes very near Martin's work. I think maybe we could rent an apartment with two bedrooms, and then later, when Martin receives further promotions with more money, we could actually buy one of those two-family houses, and I could live on one floor, and Martin could live on the other... and the children could come to me at breakfast and stay until their father returns from work. I can prepare dinner and then the children can return to Martin for the evening."

I continued, "Once the children are a bit older, and in school during the day, I think perhaps I might be able to find a teacher's preparatory course somewhere in the vicinity. There are many colleges in New Haven, and some are considering the admission of women."

Mother was nodding her head, and I could see that she thought that this might be a plan that could work for the near future.

But Father shook his head. He stood up and turned his back and addressed me while not facing me.

"That will not be satisfactory. You would still be residing in a house with a man who is neither your husband nor your brother. It is immoral."

"But he is my sister's husband, so he is my brother!" I exclaimed.

"It is a mortal sin!" he said.

"It is not a sin. I am caring for my dead sister's children. That is holy, not sinful."

"There is a solution to this dilemma," he said, still not facing me. "I think it would be best that you and Martin should marry, and raise the children as your own."

"No. Never!" I cried. "*That* is what would be immoral! I cannot take Catherine's husband as my own!"

I looked to my mother, and she lowered her eyes, but I saw that the tears were already there.

"Martin will just take the children and you will never see them again!" I cried.

And what Father said next was the most stunning of all.

"Martin has already agreed."

CHAPTER 15

I RAN IMMEDIATELY TO THE BEDROOM that Martin had shared with the children for the past week - Catherine's bedroom.

I flung open the door, and Martin was on the floor with Jonathan, playing with a wooden train that had been a Christmas gift. I ran out to the kitchen where I had seen Malcolm, grabbed my brother by the arm, and dragged him to the bedroom.

"Take Jonathan for a few minutes. Get him a piece of pie," I said, and Malcolm, confused but cooperative, picked up the little boy and carried him off.

"How could you?" I asked as soon as we were alone. "Why? Why did you tell Father that you would marry me?"

Martin sat down at the end of the bed. Catherine's bed. He shook his head.

"The children need a mother. They like you. You like them."

"Catherine has been dead for six weeks. Six weeks! And you are willing to remarry? Remarry her own sister?" I cried in frustration. "Did you ever love her at all?"

"Oh my God, Lucinda. I loved her with my whole heart. I think every day that I may not be able to draw another breath without her."

"Why then would you marry me?"

"What difference does it make? What difference does it make now? What difference can marrying possibly make to me now? All I have is the children and the children need you. They will have a mother. I will provide for them and you."

"What difference does it make? Maybe it makes no difference to you. What about me? It may make a difference to me... asking me to give up my life to raise your children!"

He looked at me for the first time. Truly looked. He stood. "Oh, Lucinda, I'm so sorry. I was not thinking about anyone but the children. I have no right... your father said I was endangering your soul."

"What will you do now?" I asked.

Martin shook his head again, as if trying to clear it after a long sleep.

"I don't know. I should move here, I know. Perhaps your father will take me on at the lumberyard. If not, I can find something. Or.... give the children to your mother, if she will have them."

He cried then.

"But I can't," he sobbed. "I cannot give my children away."

I took him by the hand and we sat back on the bed, side by side. A mortal sin, I'm sure my father would say. I would say I was offering comfort to my brother.

"Tell me, Martin, what exactly you do in your work that you cannot do here?"

"I am not a toolmaker any longer," he replied. "Except in the most general sense. I am an engineer. I design parts for airplanes. I help people fly. I helped the brave pilots who fought in the Great War. It was why I did not go overseas to fight. I was needed here."

"Mother of God and Holy Cow," I said, mixing my slang and certainly committing blasphemy.

Martin laughed, but without any humor. "You've got that right. But what difference does it make now? The children must come first. I will ask your father to give me a job in the yard. I will do anything."

We sat silently for quite a while. I took his hand.

I said. "Did you know that my father told me when I was twelve that no one would ever marry me? I believe he may have been wrong."

"He was."

CHAPTER 16

THE WEDDING WAS SCHEDULED IMMEDIATELY. Saturday. Father arranged it all. Monsignor Curran agreed that Martin and I could be married in the church in a private service.

On Friday, I went to Benedict Lumber for the first time in seven weeks. I said my goodbyes to Jolly Jack, who enveloped me in his arms.

"Truth be told, girl, you have been like a daughter to me these last years!" And he cried profuse tears, although to be fair, Jolly Jack cried profuse tears at least several times a week.

I went around to the back of the yard and waited for Peter to come back with the horses. The yard had been transitioning to delivery trucks for the last year - Father had been brought along to the 20th century with Malcolm's encouragement - but Peter still drove the old wagon with the now-ancient team.

I sat on a bale of hay and shivered, although it was a warm day for the end of December. Forty minutes later I watched him drive in. He didn't see me in the shadows, so I sat silently while Peter unhitched the horses. He put away the tack, and brushed Zeke and Carthage, cleaned their hooves and fed them two carrots each, all the while cooing to them about being the best creatures in existence.

"You two are the loveliest smartest animals in Springfield. You are the loveliest animals in Massachusetts. You are the loveliest in New England. The loveliest in the whole of the United States of America. In the world. In all the planets."

"What comes after the Universe?" I asked, jumping up.

Peter laughed. He wasn't the slightest bit surprised or embarrassed by his effusion.

"The Heavens!" he answered.

He led Zeke to his stall, and I took Carthage and led him to his.

"It's so good to see you, Lucinda," said Peter. "I didn't even know that I missed you until you are in front of me and then I think to myself, '*Now the world is straight!*'"

"I'm back, but it is only to say goodbye."

"Are you off to school then?" he asked. "Off to write about injustices and dirty dealings? To save the universe?"

"No. I am off to save a family."

"Catherine's, I expect," Peter said.

"Yes, Catherine's. Mine now, soon. It has been decided that I will raise her children. I'm to be married to Martin." I added, "Tomorrow."

Peter spun around to face me. "Jesus, Lucy!"

"Don't swear, Peter!"

"It's so fast. And you're so young... what are you now, fifteen?"

"Seventeen."

"Well, if I knew you were ancient I would have married you myself!"

"Very funny," I said.

He turned and gave old Zeke another carrot. "Seriously, Lucinda, I had a mind to marry you."

"You did? Oh, Peter, that's so nice to know." I sat down on an upturned bucket. "I would have made you miserable."

"That's likely," he said. "How can you be married so soon? What about the Banns and all?"

"Monsignor got a dispensation from the Bishop. Martin needs to return to Connecticut right away."

Peter sat down on the packed dirt of the barn floor facing me where I perched on my makeshift chair. He sat so near me that I could feel his breath against my leg. I thought for a moment he would put his head on my knee. I wouldn't have stopped him.

"I saw Catherine once," he said. "I was about ten. I think she must have been the age you were when you first came to the yard. She was so lovely it was a minute or more before I could get a breath."

"Yes. She was beautiful for sure."

"You look like her, you know."

"Ha," I said. "Only to someone with your poor eyesight."

"I see well enough."

I couldn't think of anything to end this conversation. "Her children are as pretty. And they are smart and happy too. They have my heart already."

"And Martin?" Peter asked. "Does he have your heart?"

I looked away. "He's a good man."

"I wish I had married you a year ago," he said.

"Oh Petey, you would have made a fine husband. And you will. You will find a girl as beautiful as Catherine, who will see your good heart."

"I will have a farm and seven children. All redheads. They will have so many freckles, the neighbors will call us the Spotted Farm."

"When you find the girl, I would ask your brothers for advice. Ask Samuel if your girl is smart enough. But ask Richard if she's beautiful enough."

"Oh, I may be blind as a bat, Lucinda, but I know for a fact that smart and beautiful are the same thing."

CHAPTER 17

THERE WAS NOT TIME TO acquire a nice dress for the wedding.

My mother had given me a beautiful dress for Christmas. But it was red, and Father was adamant that red would not be appropriate for the sanctity of a marriage ceremony. He said this without any trace of irony, as if marrying my sister's widower within two months of her death was perfectly proper and even sacred.

Mother had me try on her own wedding gown, which had been packed in tissue for the past twenty-seven years. It was quite pretty and it would have been a fine sentimentality, but it had yellowed. And it was two inches short. But it was a lovely gesture and I was tempted to wear it anyway.

But in the end, I wore my pale rose dress that Mother had made me for Charlotte's christening two years before. Then I was Charlotte's godmother. Now I was to be her mother. So it was fitting, I suppose.

There was no procession to the Church. No violinist. Not even a bouquet. At the last moment, Mother had realized this and wanted Malcolm to run out and buy flowers, but I told him that I was fine, and he should not ruin his good shoes running out in the slushy half-frozen rain.

Mother gave me her best pearls. "And you must keep them," she said. "It is my wedding gift to you."

A hired automobile drove us to the church.

I walked down the aisle on my father's arm, just like any other bride. To my surprise, an organ started up, and played a solemn *Abide With Me*.

Mother walked in the processional on Malcolm's arm. Amelia had Jonathan and Charlotte by the hand.

Martin waited at the altar with the Monsignor. Martin wore his best suit. It was the suit he also wore to bury our Catherine. But it didn't matter. He wasn't really there anyway.

As Monsignor Curran blessed our marriage, he told us, "This marriage is a product of tragedy. But you are blessed for loving the children more than yourselves. So although this marriage starts in tragedy, I believe the Lord will ensure that it grows into love."

Martin put a ring on my finger - to this day I do not know where he came by this ring, but I suspect my Father bought it. He kissed me lightly at the priest's encouragement, and managed to smile.

CHAPTER 18

WE HAD A LIGHT LUNCH at my parent's home that was no longer my home. Ham left over from Christmas dinner with cheese and apples. My mother had somehow produced a pretty cake, and the babies were joyful.

I packed a small trunk, as I didn't think there would be room in Martin's apartment for too many of my possessions. Catherine's clothes still hung in his wardrobe, and I could neither wear them nor throw them away. I would wait until Martin decided on his own to dispose of them.

Because of the trunk and the many Christmas presents the children received, we did not take the train back to New Haven, but instead, my father sent Malcolm out to fetch the car that had brought us to the church.

The icy rain had turned to snow, and the combination made for slippery, treacherous roads. The driver crawled through the streets, and we watched towns pass by us at a pace that seemed we could have improved upon by walking. I worried that my trunk, affixed to the back of the motorcar, might not be waterproof enough, and the few things I brought might be ruined.

"They'll be fine," Martin reassured me. "Everything will be fine."

But it was cold in the car and the children were tired and cranky. I felt near to tears, and knew I was not the only one. Martin took Charlotte in his lap and buttoned her up inside his coat, giving her a cozy hideaway and the warmth of his body. I took Jonathan in my own lap and let him wear my beaver hat. He could see his reflection in the glass, and made faces at himself, and so we all felt a bit better.

We arrived in New Haven well after midnight. We took the children up immediately, and Martin and the driver made two trips with the baggage. I worried about the poor man driving back so late in such poor weather, and offered to let him stay the night, though I had no idea where we would put him.

"I have a cousin just six blocks from here," he said. "And he owns a drinking establishment, so I will recover quite nicely from the trip." Martin gave him a generous tip to supplement what Father had paid him. "Have a few on us," he said, "And Happy Christmas."

I put Jonathan down in his crib in the clothes he was wearing, since he was fast asleep and deserved to stay so. I changed Charlotte out of her soiled diaper and dressed her in her heaviest flannel nightgown and warm booties. She insisted she was not sleepy and sat in her crib sucking her thumb. Soon, though, she let herself fall backward and I covered her sweet sleeping form.

Martin and I stood in the darkened bedroom for a few moments, watching them sleep and listening to their calm even breaths.

"What do we do now?" I asked finally.

He touched my fingertips. "Nothing. Not for right now. Go to sleep."

I went back to the sitting room, to my small sofa where I had been sleeping for six weeks. As with Jonathan, I did not bother to change out of my travel clothes, but simply pulled a blanket over me. And tried to sleep. My first night as a married woman.

CHAPTER 19

LIFE SEEMED SOMEWHAT ROSIER IN the morning. It has stopped snowing, and the sun was bright and melting the snow on the pavement. The children were excited about getting out to play as quickly as possible, as Amelia had given them little snow shovels, and they wanted to try them out before the snow had completely disappeared. I bundled them up and brought them out to the back of the house, where they could dig in the snow until their noses were red.

It was Sunday and I suppose we should have gone to Mass. Martin had not yet gotten out of bed. When we returned from our outdoor activity, with wet clothes and running noses to be seen to, he was sitting at the kitchen table with coffee and a book of Sherlock Holmes stories, which had a been a gift from my mother. To me, she had given *My Antonia*, the new novel from Willa Cather, and I hoped I would have a few moments each day to read it. I had my hour during the children's naps. And evenings, I suppose.

The children ran to their father snowy and squealing, and he scooped them up and deposited one on each knee.

"Now who would like a sip of coffee?" he asked.

"Me! Me!" they cried.

He tipped his cup to their lips and they pretended to have a big sip.

"I dig in the thnow!" said Charlotte.

"Come, we need to get you into dry warm clothes," I said, and they scooted off Martin's lap and ran to me.

"You can drink Papa's coffee too," said Jonathan. "You need to be strong so you don't die."

Martin went pale. We met each other's eyes and shook our heads. Neither of us had been aware that Jonathan knew his mother was dead. We had kept both children away from the funeral with cousin Bertha. We were also not sure he knew what it meant to be dead.

I took him in my arms and said, "Jonathan, I am big enough without coffee to snatch you up and tickle you like the big brown bear in your alphabet book!" And he giggled and wiggled out of my arms, and ran off to the bedroom to fetch the book. The moment passed.

"We have almost no food in the house," I said to Martin. "The shops I know are not open on a Sunday. Is there a place where I could buy some bread and potatoes, and perhaps a chicken for dinner?"

"I'll go," he said, grabbed his coat and ran from the house. He was gone for three hours.

"I'm sorry," he apologized when he finally returned, handing me a sack. "I stopped at a church and I found it comforting. I stayed quite a while. It was quiet and peaceful. And then the shop I had intended to go to wasn't open after all, and I could not even remember where there was another store in all of the city. It was as if the city got turned around on me, and I didn't recognize the streets. It must be the snow."

"Do you know, when I was reading Sherlock Holmes a year or two ago, I got so wrapped up in the story, that I walked out for school one morning and was surprised to find my street? My brain somehow expected London."

"Ha! I have snow *and* Sir Conan Doyle. What handy excuses. Anyhow," he continued, "I bought us a nice big chicken and some oranges as well as potatoes, bread, milk, and cheese."

"And coffee?"

"Oh no! Are we out? I used up the last of it, didn't I? I'll go out right this minute."

"Don't you dare leave. The children will be up from their naps any moment now. We'll have tea. There's plenty."

"Can we have some right now? With an orange? I'm cold and starving."

And like any married couple in the whole world, we sat with tea and oranges and talked about Sherlock Holmes and the news of the day, while the children napped.

CHAPTER 20

MARTIN RETURNED TO WORK THE next morning. I was burning with curiosity the entire day, wondering whether he had told the other men in the factory that he had gotten married over the Christmas holiday. How in heaven do you explain such a thing? I suppose it was fortunate that I did not have to - if you can suppose a benefit to being completely friendless.

We weren't the only people to do it - marry, that is. With the devastation wreaked by the epidemic, many young families were without fathers or mothers, and were quickly - too quickly - filling the loss with substitutes. Children had to be cared for; families had to be provided for. In addition, there was the War. Fathers lost to the War left families without means. Many young widows went back to live in their parents' home. But many sought to find a spouse posthaste. The Church acted as matchmaker in several cases that I read about - a war widow and a widower from the influenza were paired recently at St. Michael's parish, resulting in a family with a mother and father not yet twenty-five, with seven children.

I suppose I should have found it a blessing to have just two children at seventeen.

With a man who was good and kind and not a stranger.

If only I had the slightest idea what to do with the children. Or the house. Or the meals. But especially the children. My affection for Jonathan and Charlotte was growing with each day, and it's not as if it were my first day alone with them. I had been with them for the last six weeks. And I managed to keep them happy and safe, fed and clean.

But back at home - my former home, I mean - watching my mother's smooth and sweet competence with the children left me feeling that everything I had been doing was all wrong. I was awkward and short-tempered. I alternated crazily between neglect and over-protectiveness. Mother said the most reassuring words to me: that I possessed a natural gift and that she could see the children adored me already. And also that Martin, despite his grief, could see this too, and the knowledge that I was there for his children was easing his pain. But all those kind words seemed like shallow platitudes - a way of flattering me into submission, much as Father had flattered me into the job at the lumberyard.

As much as I had managed to keep the children from falling out the windows or down the stairs for more than six weeks, it was different now. I was not their kindly young aunt meeting their needs on an emergency basis. I was their mother.

It terrified me.

How could I be their mother? It was too big a responsibility. Jonathan stuttered sometimes. He laughed easily, but a few minutes later he would be in tears over a missing bunny or his blocks falling over. Charlotte was so serious. What two-year-old took so much to heart? She held a pencil with a strained grip, her little tongue sticking out with intensity. She asked me *"Why?"* at least twenty times a day, on subjects as diverse as peeling a carrot or having two ears. So smart. And yet she was still in diapers, with no indication that she wouldn't remain so throughout her existence.

Yet I was supposed to guide them through their young lives. See them through their illnesses both big and small. Walk them to school, and make sure their lessons were completed. Teach them to get along with other children, maybe learn a sport or a musical instrument. Bring them up in their religion. Show them the ways of the world and the choosing of careers and spouses.

The ways of the world? I was still waiting for someone to show them to me.

But I managed.

I managed in small increments. I continued just as I had the weeks before.

On Martin's first day back to work, I rose at five and made him breakfast. I sent him off with a lunch pail filled with bread and chicken, two pieces of fruit and a half dozen of my mother's Christmas cookies wrapped in a napkin. He kissed the children, still sleeping in their cribs. That morning he kissed me too - a small, light, barely-there touch of his lips to my forehead.

I had more than ten hours before he would return. I let the children sleep until seven, which gave me a bit more than an hour that I reserved for myself. I read the newspaper.

The children woke up hungry, but happy. I fed them porridge and milk while they were still dressed in their nightclothes. Then I bathed them together. My mother had warned me that in short order I would need to separate their little bodies, but they seemed oblivious at the moment, and it was much easier to wash them as well as watch them together. How in the world does a mother keep an eye on one child in the bath and another who knows where?

Martin had only a small, primitive icebox, so that meant I needed to shop nearly every day. The first month I had been in New Haven, the weather had still been temperate, which was lucky, since it had allowed me the opportunity to seek out the butcher and the greengrocer, and other shops. Martin's landlord had written directions to the very best and most frugal of the shops that were an easy walk.

Now that the weather was cold, I was grateful that I was already an expert at this part of daily life. I bundled up the children, and we walked to find tonight's dinner. Martin was generous with the money he would leave for the shopping, so I was free to buy whatever I fancied. He usually praised my cooking, while eating very little.

The walk home had often proved more difficult, and this day was no exception. With many blocks still to go,

Charlotte complained that she was cold and too tired to walk further, and I had a sack of groceries to also contend with.

"Let's go," begged Jonathan. "I'm cold too. Make her hurry up."

But Charlotte sat down on the snowy walk and would not move. I picked her up, and tried to balance the child and the provisions. I waddled a few steps and slipped a bit on the ice. I managed to keep upright and also keep from dropping Charlotte on her head, though she screamed in fright. A tin of baking powder and some precious butter fell from my sack.

Jonathan then started to cry. "My butter is on the road! I won't have butter for my bread!"

"Let's all get a breath," I said, and sat down on the curb. I held both crying children and thought about having a nice tantrum myself.

But I could not. I was the mother. I was the person who solved all problems.

"Here is what we will do, Jonathan," I said. "Pick up the tin and put it in my pocket." He smiled and did so. "Now pick up the butter and put it in your pocket. Did you ever have a pocket of butter before?"

He laughed. And I became a little more of a person who solved all problems.

"Now you see, the bag is not so full. But I think it is still very heavy. There is a slice of ham and some potatoes in there. Can you count the potatoes?"

"Six!" he said.

"Well, that is a lot. But you have one more pocket, and I think you might be able to fit a potato in there."

"It fits!" he shouted, as he stuffed a small potato in his pocket. "You have another pocket too... do you want to put a potato in your pocket?"

"That would be a wonderful idea," I said. So Jonathan put a potato in my pocket too.

"Now, Charlotte," I said, seeing that she had stopped crying, and had become very interested. "You have no pockets. But if I carry you, can you carry one big potato?"

She nodded.

"That's marvelous. So Jonathan, now that the sack is ever so much lighter, I am trusting you to carry it all the way home. Can you do that?"

"I could carry it even when it was heavy!" he said.

And we made it home.

I gave the children a lunch of steamed carrots and bits of the chicken from the previous night. The heavens smiled down upon me - it was time for their naps.

I washed some clothes in the sink and strung them out on the porch landing. I swept the floor and made biscuits, which I did not burn too badly and which were still warm when the babies awakened, so they had a nice treat. I set both children on the floor with the new Christmas train, while I prepared the rest of dinner.

Martin came in just before six. He hugged the children, exclaiming, "Oh my darling babies, I have missed you so much!"

"I had a pocketful of butter!" said Jonathan.

"You did?" asked Martin, eyeing me suspiciously.

"Long story," I said. "But the result is this: We need a pram."

And Martin said the most remarkable thing.

"We have one."

Of course. Why would they not? That evening, after the children were asleep Martin brought me down to the cellar, where he had a roped-off square of space. And in addition to the sled we had taken out weeks ago were a pram, and a wagon, and even a small hobby horse and ice skates.

"I suppose I should have shown you where everything was back in November," Martin said.

"It's fine," I said, "I feel like it might be Christmas again."

CHAPTER 21

WE HAD A FEW VERY ordinary days. Martin went off to work. I made meals and played with the children. Cleaning the tiny apartment was simple; laundry was much more difficult because the weather had turned frigid. Hanging the wet garments on the porch clothesline was a miserable task, and the clothes froze like empty scarecrows. I took to hanging a few things in the cellar on the ropes that marked Martin's storage space.

The cold weather was rough on the children too. I bundled them up for the shopping, but their little noses were red and their feet ached through their boots. I sought help from the landlord's pleasant wife, and left the children in her care while I ran to the market as quickly as I could. I began to wear an old coat of Catherine's under my own coat. It would have been a better fit to wear the coat over my own, but I couldn't bear the thought of being seen in her clothes. Each time I wore her coat I hid it quickly in the back of the wardrobe before I went downstairs to Mrs. Battle to fetch the children.

While the chill made me lethargic, the same could not be said of Charlotte and Jonathan. They had all the energy of toddlers and seemed to borrow more from someplace that they perhaps inherited from Malcolm.

I dragged the hobby horse from the cellar up to the third floor, and they loved rocking as if they were galloping through Texas. After just twenty minutes, though, we were paid a visit from Mrs. Giametti from directly downstairs. Her husband was home from the War, where he had been gassed. He suffered from severe incapacitating headaches, and the hobby horse banging on his ceiling was beyond his tolerance. I apologized immediately, realizing why the toy had been in the cellar in the first place, and lugged it back.

When I was replacing the hobby horse, I noticed a large box thrown into a corner that did not appear to be in anyone's marked space. Perhaps discarded from some large delivery. I checked the box and it was clean and in good condition. It wasn't heavy, but it was wider than the stairway. I pushed and prodded and finally deposited it in the middle of the kitchen.

I turned the opened end to the floor, and with a small knife cut a door and window into the side. Jonathan immediately recognized the potential, and it was all I could do to stop him from jumping up and down and causing further injury to poor Mr. Giametti.

"This is your house," I said. "I believe it may need some pets and furniture and dishes."

Jonathan ran to the bedroom for his bunny and Charlotte's teddy. Then he dragged in a pillow and the toy tea set.

"Come on in," he invited Charlotte.

She gave one of her rare smiles and crawled into the box.

The children were still in their playhouse when Martin came home. He nearly fell over the box opening the door, as I had moved it far away from the stove as I cooked.

"What do we have here?" he asked.

"A houth!" Charlotte answered.

"Well, then." And he knocked, making a clacking sound with his tongue.

"You can't come in," said Jonathan. "You are too big for our house!"

"Then I will huff and I'll puff and I'll blow your house down!" He shook the sides of the cardboard lightly and the children screamed in fake terror.

Maybe I wasn't so bad at this after all.

CHAPTER 22

S EVERAL DAYS LATER I RECEIVED a package from
my mother.

Along with some good heavy stockings for me
and the children were two large squares wrapped in scraps
of old bed sheets. My portraits of Upton Sinclair and Ida
Tarbell. A note attached to Miss Tarbell's photo read:

"You are still you."

I hugged the photo to my breast. I still wanted to be
me. But if I became Catherine instead, perhaps I would
have a better life.

"Why are you crying?" asked Jonathan, who had climbed
out of his crib to stand behind me. "Who is that lady? Is it
your Mama?"

"No, darling," I said. "Grandmother is my Mama." He
looked doubtful as to this confusing relationship. I sat him

on my lap. "This lady is Miss Ida Tarbell. She writes books and articles for newspapers."

"Does she write stories like my bear story?"

"She writes stories that make people's lives better."

"Like my angels book," he said.

"Yes. Just like that."

"What are you going to do with her picture? You can put it on the top of the wardrobe where Mama's picture is."

I kissed the top of his head. "No, that spot is for your Mama. I will hang this picture, and that one too, of Mr. Upton Sinclair, by the settee in the parlor. That way when I go to sleep at night I will be able to see their faces and think about how many people they helped. And that will make me feel very good."

Jonathan picked up the note from my mother. "What does this say?"

"It's from Grandmother," I answered. "It says, 'Jonathan and Charlotte are my favorite people in the world. Make sure they take their naps and don't climb out of their cribs.'"

"I'm too big for my crib," he said. "Write back to Grandmother and tell her that I climb out because I am not a baby, and I need a bed. Tell her I need a bed."

I need one too, I thought.

CHAPTER 23

THE NEXT DAY, AFTER I laid the children down for their naps, I took my clothes from my trunk and laid them on Martin's bed. I had been living out of that trunk for nearly two weeks, putting my dress and undergarments back at the end of every evening and my nightdress every morning.

I am still me, I thought. And I am here. I live here.

I opened Martin's wardrobe, where Catherine's lovely clothes still hung like ghosts waiting for her to return. I took each dress and folded it carefully and put it into my trunk, replacing the space in the wardrobe with one of my own dresses.

I placed her shoes in my trunk as well. Her nightdresses. Her fancy undergarments and her plain everyday ones.

I threw nothing away. It wasn't mine to discard. Perhaps after a time, I would ask Martin if I could put these lovely items in in the poor box at the church. For now, they were safe in my trunk.

I took the children out on my shopping errands. It was not so cold as it had been and they enjoyed the fresh air. Charlotte rode in the pram and Jonathan held obediently to the carriage's side. He prattled about Noah's Ark. We endeavored to name every animal we could think of. Lions, Bears, Giraffes, Elephants, Rabbits, Horses. "Cows!" said Charlotte. "Monkeys!" said Jonathan. "Kangaroos!" I said.

I had a small inspiration.

I counted the day's grocery money. I could buy a nice pork loin. It was difficult to find good vegetables in the winter, but there might be some decent sweet potatoes or a butternut squash. But not this day. I went into the market and bought eggs and an inexpensive slab of bacon. "We are going to have breakfast for dinner," I told the children.

"Hoorah!" said Jonathan.

I had one dollar and ten cents left. I put the eggs in the pram tucked out of the way of Charlotte's feet.

"Do you want a pocketful of bacon today?" I asked Jonathan, who happily took the wrapped slab from me. Too big for his pocket, he tucked it inside his jacket. "I've got a tummy full of bacon," he declared. "And when I eat it up I will have a tummy full of bacon again!"

We walked to the general store where I had strolled up and down the aisles a few days before, looking for a box of straight pins. This time I knew which aisle I wanted. In bins across the shelf were small carved wooden animals.

I picked up Charlotte to show her. Jonathan was already hopping from foot to foot.

"I think we need our own Noah's Ark," I said. "We have one dollar today and we need two of each animal, because Noah had two. They are five cents each so we can pick out ten different pairs of animals. The rest we can save and buy another day. So Jonny, you pick out five, and Charlotte, you can pick five."

Well, if that wasn't the best thing ever. Jonathan chose the exotic animals: monkeys, giraffes, elephants, hippopotamuses, kangaroos. Charlotte went with the sweet-faced familiar animals: cats, dogs, horses, cows, lambs. We filled a basket with their selections.

"Oh look!" I said, "I have ten cents left. So I get to choose an animal for the ark too!" I added two birds to the basket. "The ark has to have doves - so Noah will know when life is back to normal."

When we arrive at home, I took the cardboard box, and turned it upside down, so the open end was on the top.

"This is the ark," I explained. "And you, Jonathan, are Noah, and Charlotte, you are Mrs. Noah. And you need to gather all the animals, because I think it is starting to rain."

Martin was not upset that I spent the grocery money on the wooden menagerie. As a matter of fact, when our simple supper was ready, he instructed the children to line up the animals two by two on the kitchen table, as it was 'feeding time.' They giggled throughout the meal, pretending to feed bits of bacon to the figures.

And Martin was not even overtly upset when the inevitable happened. And by inevitable, I do not mean the milk spilled by a thirsty giraffe. It was the inevitable - even proper - outcome of this remodeled family.

Charlotte handed me the doves and said, "You feed birds, Mama."

We knew it would happen. It was supposed to happen. I was here in this apartment in New Haven as the legal wife to the husband and mother to the children. The children could hardly be expected to call me Auntie forever.

But that first *'Mama.'* Oh.

Even Jonathan was taken aback and immediately looked to his father. I think both the boy and I expected Martin to be angry, or at least correct Charlotte immediately.

To our surprise, Martin said, "Yes, Mama, feed your doves."

Jonathan audibly sighed in relief. He looked to me and smiled. Martin smiled also, but with a soft sadness.

"Papa," said Jonathan, "Mama" - he looked at me - "Mama said we will save our pennies to buy more, until we have every kind of animal."

"I'll save too," said Martin. "I would like a rhinoceros."

"You need TWO rhinotherutheth!" said Charlotte.

"Then I will have to save twice as hard," said Martin.

Late that night, from my nest in the parlor, I thought I heard Jonathan crying. I tiptoed to the bedroom, wanting to quiet the boy before he woke his exhausted father or his baby sister. I peeked into the room. It was not Jonathan crying.

Martin sat on the edge of the bed. In the dark, he stared at the open doors of the wardrobe. The wardrobe with the portrait of Catherine atop and my clothes inside.

I crept away.

CHAPTER 24

I
T WAS FINALLY SPRING. THE temperate weather was
so welcome, I nearly cried in relief every morning that
I could walk outside without shivering. How I had
missed my father's many fireplaces.

There was a lovely park nearby. With a decent place
for me to sit while the children skipped and ran and even
turned a crooked somersault. Even more delightful, there
would often be another young mother or two who would
join me. Several times a week, for perhaps a whole hour, I
could converse with a woman. It felt like years indeed since
I had spoken to someone even remotely like me.

These women talked mostly of housekeeping and
children and husbands. They were mainly good-natured
and amusing, but I had nothing worthwhile to contribute
on any of those subjects. Although I loved talking with

them, I wondered if they ever thought of anything else. I did not see any world significance in rubbing lemon oil onto a table. One day, enjoying the company of two nice young mothers, I asked what they thought of Mr. Lenin and the upheaval in Russia. And they knew of it, and had definite opinions. They believed it was disgraceful, but brought about by the horrible conditions of the poor in Russia. They hoped it would not lead to war. I was ashamed that I had considered myself superior. These women were not foolish nor empty-headed; they had never been asked.

There was one particular mother who was a suffragette. Constance Hadley was well-educated, cynical, and droll. Her daughter Sadie was four, and was prone to hollering and whooping like a red Indian. Constance would yell back, "Good for you, Sadie. Stay loud. Girls do not have to be quiet!" I believed her husband was a socialist - or worse, although I was not sure what could be worse. I found Constance both shocking and completely wonderful.

I confided in her my desire to be a journalist and fight for the rights of people, especially colored people.

"The colored people in this country have it very bad indeed," she said. "If I were you I would concentrate on demanding better education for the children."

"Why not better jobs for the fathers and health services for mothers?"

"Because I think our generation is already lost. Work on the future."

"Are you really from Connecticut?" I asked.

"Ha!" she laughed. "Boston!"

I loved Constance from that moment forward, but I privately disagreed. I thought children could get better educated if they lived in nicer neighborhoods. That could only happen if their fathers made better wages. I still wanted the extra nickel for my father's workers.

Constance also supplied me with some good practical advice. Charlotte was now two and a half, and still not out of diapers, and Constance early on discerned that the children were not my own, and so I had not been a factor in training Jonathan.

"Look," she said. "The major issue with babies is that we make them so comfortable. Charlotte doesn't care about wetting her nappy because she doesn't really feel it. Your diapers are too good. And you scoop her up and change her immediately so she never feels discomfort. Once a baby has reached an age where she has some control - which is *now* by the way - you need to let her feel awful when she soils herself. Just put her in regular undergarments and when she is soaked or soiled and hating it, you say, 'Well, there, now that you are in big girl clothes, you have to tell me when you need to go, BEFORE you need to.' One week at most, she will figure out when that is."

And Charlotte did. I kissed her and praised her. Charlotte, that is, not Constance, although the other would have been entirely appropriate as well.

Constance's biggest favor to me, aside from her intelligent discourse, which was like a banquet to a starving soul, was directions to the public library.

What an institution was the New Haven Public Library! A ten block walk from our home, it was an enormous, beautiful, classical repository of entertainment and information. It possessed an entire separate wing for children's books, and allowed the children to borrow two books each week. And in addition, it hosted a reading hour every Wednesday morning, with a beautiful old woman who held my children and a dozen more in rapt open-mouthed attention.

And for me? More books on more subjects than I ever dreamed existed. I borrowed the novels of the Brontes and Jane Austen, and the poetry of Emily Dickinson, and once in a while, to prove I was open-minded, I would read a book by a man. And there was Art and History and Geography. These last were also appreciated at home by Martin and the children. The little ones would sit with him at the table while I did the washing up, and he would point out exotic places with stories of India and China and Africa (mostly invented, I believe, but thoroughly enjoyable.)

As Spring progressed, I felt refreshed with the smallest thimble of optimism.

CHAPTER 25

WITH APRIL CAME EASTER, AND we packed up the children and traveled to Springfield to spend the holidays with my family.

My mother was overjoyed to see us. She hugged everyone and exclaimed how the children had grown and thrived under my care.

"Mama lets us carry the shopping," said Jonathan, and Mother wept in both joy and sorrow - with joy that the little boy called me his mother, and in sorrow that his true mother was gone from us. My father showed more restraint, but I could see that he was gratified and perhaps self-satisfied that he had done the right thing. He had pressured Martin and me into marriage, and just look, his magnanimous expression boasted, it has turned out splendidly.

Malcolm had appeared to grow very tall in just four months, and Amelia was the woman of fifteen that I had never been at that age. She was not required to work at the lumberyard, so I consoled myself that I had at least been grown up enough to drink with the O'Hara boys on Thursday evenings. She was astonishingly pretty though, and I feared that Peter O'Hara, if he had seen her, would be as lovestruck as he had been over Catherine. I hoped not. I wanted him to find a beautiful wife. But I did not want that wife to be Amelia.

We arrived on Saturday afternoon. My father and Malcolm took the small bags we carried with us upstairs. Mother explained our accommodations.

"Amelia has taken over your room, as it is sunnier and larger than her bedroom. We thought of turning her little space into a nursery for the children tonight, but considering they are not so familiar with the house, I thought it might be more comforting to them to keep you all together. So I had Malcolm carry Amelia's bed into Cath... into the guest bedroom...for the children. They are little enough to be both accommodated by the one bed, I think."

"That's fine," I said. And I made my way up the staircase to the west bedroom that had always been Catherine's. The room possessed a large feather bed, and now, tucked under the eaves, a small bed that still bore Amelia's pink quilt. I unpacked our Easter Sunday finery and hung them in the closet that had been empty since Catherine married Martin.

Dinner was loud and happy. Father kept attempting to instill some decorum but the babies were excited to see their grandparents and did not show any evidence that they had foregone their naps. Jonathan told of his adventures in the ark, which by this time had been replaced by a sturdier box, though it was in constant need of repair. And he prattled on about the library and the playground and Mrs. Battle and Mrs. Constance Hadley, and even Mrs. Giametti and Mr. Giametti's headaches. There was not a secret to be held in his little friendly head.

"Mama has pictures of book people in the parlor, so she can see them at night," he said. I'm not sure what my parents deduced from that comment. I was fortunate they did not pursue it and he progressed merrily to carrying potatoes in pockets.

After dinner, Father suggested we retire to the drawing room for Easter vigil prayers, but in short order, both of the little ones were asleep, Charlotte on my lap and Jonathan on Mother's.

"It's been a long day," said Martin, "with the Holiday to come, so we'd better excuse ourselves and get the children to bed. Thank you so much for a wonderful meal."

With that, we said goodnight with kisses all around. Martin took Jonathan from Mother, and we made our way to our bedroom. Catherine's bedroom.

We stood for a moment, each holding a sleeping child.

"Let the children sleep in the large bed with you," said Martin. "I'll sleep in the small bed, of course."

"Of course," I said.

We all attended Easter Sunday services together. The children were well-behaved considering how long the Mass went on. I had given each child one more wooden animal pair for the ark as an Easter gift - tigers for Jonathan and ostriches for Charlotte, and I let them play quietly behind me on the pew. I told them all animals needed to whisper in church, and they agreed that the animals would be obedient. And when I prayed during the service, I prayed that the children would reflect well on my mothering, and that they would not reveal how little we attended church in New Haven.

Later, I helped prepare the Easter dinner with Mother. She was surprised and pleased at how efficient I had become in the kitchen. Before taking on a family of my own, I had been little interested, and was less an asset than a nuisance.

"How accomplished you have become," said Mother. "And you look so well and fit. I would venture to say that your temperament has greatly improved. There is nothing like the love of family to bring you peace."

"I thought you had instructed me to stay true to myself," I teased. "If I become patient and sweet-tempered no one will know it's me."

"No chance of that," she said. "But you seem a happier version of you."

"Well I love the children and I am becoming a competent mother. And baking bread does suit me in some ways more than ordering nails for the lumberyard."

"And Martin?" she asked. "How is your husband?"

"He's good to me, and a loving father. He still mourns so terribly. He tries though to put on a good face for Jonny and Charlotte." I did not add that he had still not taken me for a wife. And perhaps never would.

CHAPTER 26

B Y THE SECOND WEEK OF May, the weather had turned to instant summer. The winter coats and boots were packed away in mothballs in our cellar space. I thought that I could use Jonathan's coat for Charlotte, but offered Charlotte's coat to one of the women I met at the park, for her infant daughter to use the following year. "Oh no," she said. "It is too pretty. You must keep that for your next child." I felt ashamed and exposed, and so readily agreed that I should have thought of that myself. So the tiny blue coat was wrapped in tissue and placed with the rest of the winter things in the box that had been the ark. The children had grown weary of that game anyway, although not of the wooden animals. The animals were, in turn, a farm, a circus, and best of all, a zoo.

We went to the library and borrowed every book on zoos that we could find. And when I wrote to Mother to tell them about the children's latest obsession, she found a wonderful big book in Springfield's best store and sent it along to them - an early birthday present for Jonathan.

Martin promised the children that as part of Jonny's birthday celebration the next month, we would all take the train to the Bronx Zoo. They spoke of almost nothing else from that moment.

Turning four turned out to be a problem for us as well as a joy for Jonathan. He could not be kept in his crib. And moreover, he did not fit. He took to crawling into bed with Martin. It was a solution that symbolized deeper issues for me than a little boy growing up.

I had now been married nearly five months. It seemed I had been permanently installed on the sofa.

I had no one to confide in. No one to ask whether this arrangement was a blessing that most women would have appreciated. I spoke in vague terms to Constance as we watched the children run in the park.

"Do you ever disagree with your husband?" I asked.

"Ha!" Constance replied. "You would be more correct to ask if we ever agree."

"How do you bring up sensitive issues that you disagree upon? Do you ever get your way?"

"Occasionally. What sometimes works for me is appealing to his pride."

"How do you do that?"

"Well, last fall I wanted a new stove very badly. I could not do the simplest things with the stove we had. So one evening I said, 'This stove is terrible. It is a shame that we are too poor for a new one.' Well, Thomas' pride couldn't bear the idea that I thought we were poor, and he went out and purchased a new stove."

This surprised me. First, that a Bolshevik like Constance cared about cooking, and even more surprising, that her husband, who was even a more committed Bolshevik than she, would not want to be thought poor. And then of course, surprised that this would work.

"If that had not worked, what else might you have tried?" I asked.

"Well, you could get him drunk."

104

CHAPTER 27

I THOUGHT ABOUT CONSTANCE'S ADVICE FOR several days, but each time I imagined the prospective conversation I backed down.

Then an opportunity presented itself.

I figured that it would not hurt to add a bit of drink to the mix. So after the children had been put down for the night - Jonathan in Martin's bed, and Charlotte in Jonny's crib that was slightly bigger than her own, I took out the half bottle of rye whiskey from the cupboard. I poured Martin a generous glass, and a thimbleful for myself, to add something to my thimbleful of courage.

"Martin," I said, "we are in dire need of additional beds."

"I know," he replied. "Jonathan has gotten so big. And he kicks," he laughed.

"This is a very nice apartment and convenient for your work. I like it here. Many of the other tenants have foregone the parlor and turned it into a bedroom. I think we should do that for Jonathan and Charlotte. Buy beds and put them in the parlor."

He took a large drink of whiskey. "I suppose," he said.

"And I need a bed as well. I cannot continue to sleep on the sofa. My health is deteriorating from such poor sleep, and I need to be fit to be the best mother for the children." I drew a breath, drank my sip of whiskey, and continued. "Mr. and Mrs. Giametti's apartment has two bedrooms. Mr. Giametti is still not well enough to seek work, so they have decided to let their second bedroom. They have put up a posting in the stairwell."

Martin looked at me through narrowed eyes.

"So I would like to tell the Giamettis that we will lease the bedroom. And each night once the children are settled for the night, you could go downstairs and sleep there. And I will stay here in this bedroom so I can be available for the children if they need me. And I know that you are exhausted in the evening from your long hours. I think we can make it work."

Martin put down his glass.

"Are you telling me that you are willing to let the neighbors see that husband and wife do not share a bed?"

"I see no other choice," I said. "I know it will be embarrassing. But there is no alternative. Unless..."

"Unless?"

"Husband and wife share a bed."

CHAPTER 28

S O WE BECAME HUSBAND AND wife. In sleeping arrangements anyway. We bought a small bed for Jonathan and placed it in the parlor. We moved the larger crib for Charlotte to the room as well, and hung heavier drapes to keep out the morning sun and the street noise. Jonathan was thrilled, although a bit fearful to be alone with his sister for the first time in his young life.

"Look what I have bought for you," I said, handing him a present that I had wrapped in colorful paper and tied with one of Charlotte's hair ribbons.

Jonathan's eyes opened wide - as did his little mouth, making a perfect O - and he tore through the wrapping. Inside was a small pewter bell.

"This is your special power. Like a king summoning his servant. When you ring this bell, I will jump up and run to you. '*Here I am - just for you!*' I will say."

"For real?" he asked.

"Yes," I said. "But this is a very big power. Mama gets very tired at night too. So you must be careful to use this power only when you need to."

"If I get scared, will it be okay to use the power?"

"Absolutely. That is exactly what the power is for. And you may ring the bell if your sister is scared too. Because she is very little, and she may be scared more than you, because you are almost four and very brave. But I will come when you ring your bell."

"I think this is a very good idea," Jonathan said gravely.

That evening I kissed the children goodnight and sat in the kitchen for a very long time. I justified this by telling myself that I wanted to be sure on this first night that if Jonathan tested his bell, I would be able to run to the room and prove to him that I would be there immediately.

Jonathan did ring his bell quite soon after I turned out the light. I jumped up and ran to the room.

"I thought I heard Charlotte cry," he said.

"It's a good thing you called me then," I reassured him. "I will tuck her in more securely, and that should comfort her."

"Could you tuck me in again too? I think I might have gotten up, even though I know I'm not supposed to," he said. And I wrapped him up even though the night was warm, and kissed his cheek.

But that was early in the evening, and they had now been asleep for hours. My nighttime chores were done, my book finished, the newspaper read, letters to my mother and Amelia in their envelopes. Still I lingered. I considered putting Jonny in Martin's bed, and sleeping in his new cot myself.

This is what I wanted, I told myself. I am a wife and it is time to be a wife. Time for Martin to be a husband to a living wife rather than a dead, though dear, one.

I left the kitchen light burning - to allay any fears from the children as well as to ensure that I did not stumble myself should I need to go to them. I tiptoed into the bedroom.

Martin was already asleep, on the side of the bed against the wall. At least he had left room for me. It encouraged me a bit.

He slept on his back with the blanket pulled to his chest. His shoulders and exposed arms looked like marble in the dim light filtering in from the kitchen. He wore his undershirt. I knew he slept in his underwear. Occasionally when I went into the bedroom late at night to tend to a crying child, he would have already risen to take the baby in his arms. "We're fine," he'd say, "Go back to bed." Except of course if Charlotte had soiled her diaper. That was women's work, by some sort of federal statute I believe, and he would hand the child carefully to me

It's possible that Martin's underwear had been a concession to my presence from the beginning. I don't know. How would I know what intimacy he shared with my sister? Or whether he would ever share it with me?

I undressed with my back to him, in case he should waken. Given the warm night, I chose my lightweight nightdress. It was plain but pretty. I loosened my hair. I laid down on the bed beside Martin, and I felt him stir.

"Goodnight, Lucinda," Martin whispered. And he turned on his side with his back to me.

I was so relieved. I was so heartbroken.

CHAPTER 29

ALTHOUGH I AWAKENED VERY EARLY, Martin was already up. I couldn't imagine how he had climbed over me in order to escape the bed, but he was gone. A magician.

I rose quickly and wrapped a dressing gown over my nightdress, ran a quick brush through my hair, and entered the kitchen. Martin was not there. In the parlor, which was now a bedroom, the children were still asleep.

I checked the icebox, I picked the coffee pot up from the stove and shook it lightly. Empty. He had not eaten, or taken a lunch, or made coffee. He was gone.

If he meant to leave me with the children over sleeping arrangements, I would need to decide what to do quickly. Pack up the children and get on a train for Springfield, I imagined. Maybe that would be for the best after all.

My mother would help me with the children. My father might employ me in the lumberyard. Perhaps it was not too late to ask Peter O'Hara if he still had a mind to marry me. Maybe he would, if Father could persuade the Bishop to have my marriage to Martin annulled. If I could bring myself to admit my failure.

I woke the children and bathed and fed them. They were excited about spending the night in their own room. Even Charlotte said, "my room," pointing to the parlor.

"Were you okay too, Jonny?" I asked. "Not afraid, I don't think."

"No I wasn't scared at all," he said. "It was quieter. Papa snores sometimes. I don't think I like the clock tick-tock. That sounds bad."

"I will move the clock out of the room tonight," I said.

"Mama, were you afraid in your new room?" Jonathan asked.

"No," I said. "I have your Papa to protect me."

The day was long. No other women appeared at the park. I shopped a bit, although there were no bargains to be had, and I spent too much on a mediocre piece of beef. I put the stringy unappetizing hunk to simmer on the stove, hoping it would be passable as a stew. I made cookies with the children and burned one batch so badly, we threw them out the window for the pigeons. That, at least, had the children laughing.

By six o'clock Martin was still not home. I fed the children my poor excuse for stew, and gave them lots of bread and butter to atone for the disastrous meal. I did the washing up, leaving Martin's unused dishes in their place at the head of the table.

Then I took the children onto the big feather bed, the bed where I had lain near but not touching their father, with the zoo book my mother had sent us. We read the story twice through, and then went page by page and gave all the animals names.

"Constance!" said Jonathan of the giraffe, "because she is so very tall!"

"Malcolm!" said Charlotte of the pig. "Because he can eat so much!"

"Mr. Giametti," I suggested of the bear. "Because you wouldn't want to wake him when he is sleeping."

We decided the flamingo was Amelia, the lion was Grandfather, and the lioness was Grandmother. Jonathan was happy to be the monkey, and jumped on the bed making silly faces until we all fell over in laughter.

That is when Martin walked into the bedroom.

"What is this? A party? Why was I not invited?"

"You can be the elephant, Papa!" exclaimed Jonathan, and Martin let out a big trumpet roar and threw himself upon the bed.

He landed on top of me.

He was quite drunk.

I scrambled out from under him.

"Oh my," I said to the children, "Look how tired Papa is! That's because it is way past bedtimes, and we must all get into bed quickly."

"Play zoo!" Charlotte insisted.

"We will play again tomorrow. Now it is time to sleep." I said.

I carried her to the parlor, with Jonathan reluctantly following. We said our prayers. I went through their small repertoire of *Our Father*, and *Hail Mary*, and *Now I Lay Me Down To Sleep*. I had changed the words of the last one to 'If I should cry before I wake, I pray the Lord my tears to take.' I wanted no more death in this house.

As reluctantly as the children went to bed, that is how reluctantly I made my way back to the bedroom. Martin was asleep, face down diagonally across the bed. He was snoring. I considered going back to the parlor and squeezing in with Jonny. But I changed to my nightdress and brushed my hair. I sat down on the edge of the bed and unlaced Martin from his shoes. I tried to ease him over to the far side of the bed with a gentle push on his shoulders. He was motionless. I pushed slightly harder, but he was unmovable. Finally, I gave up, and laid down in the small space left me, my back against his left shoulder. In his stupor, he turned on his side and put his arms around me. He enveloped me as if I were a bird in the nest of his body. I felt the warmth rise from his chest and his breath against my neck. Never in my life had I been so close to a man.

I did not think I would sleep, but the activity of the day and the stress of the evening finally overtook me.

Some time in the night I awoke to the weight of his body. I was rather surprised that my own frame could hold such weight so easily - that I was not crushed beneath him - that I still breathed.

His mouth found mine. His hands found my breasts. He penetrated me.

The night before my hurried wedding, Mother had described what she called *Marital Intimacy*. She had told me it would hurt, and quite a lot, but that over time the hurt would stop and it would become nice, even pleasurable. "Bear it until it reaches that place," she said. "It is worth it."

And so I did that night. I cried out only once. And then I bore the hurt. I drove my mind into the future, when the pleasure would overtake the pain. I let the tears flow noiselessly.

Martin thrust into me the final time. His body shuddered above me. "Oh, Catherine!" he cried. He tumbled off me, and turned his back.

I rose from the bed and went to the small lavatory that Catherine had been so proud of. I washed myself of the mix of Martin's fluid and my blood.

Martin still had his back to me when I returned to the bed. I held him in the same nest that he had held me earlier in the evening, one arm around his shoulder. I touched his hair and caressed him as he wept.

CHAPTER 30

Martin did not look at me throughout breakfast. He concentrated on his coffee and his eggs, while I sat with my hands in my lap.

He was out the door and halfway down the first flight of stairs, when I heard him stop. He came back up. Standing in the doorway, still not meeting my eye, he said, "I can't."

"You can't what? Be married to me?"

He shook his head. "Oh, no, Lucinda, Nothing so harsh. I just can't talk... about it... not now. I'm sorry. Give me time."

"I'll wait," I said. "Not forever, but I'll wait."

"I'm sorry," he said again, and left.

Another long day ahead. I concentrated on scrubbing the floor. I gave each child a brush and a pan of water, and a section that they were required to wash. They got more water and soap on themselves than on the floor, but it allowed me time for my own thoughts.

It had been over six months since Catherine died; five months since I had married Martin. Last night, our pretend marriage had finally been consummated. Did that mean that I could no longer receive an annulment? Perhaps I still could...after all, Martin had been drunk.

I did not think he despised me. Perhaps we could find a larger apartment, or even a house. We could then have separate bedrooms, and we could return to our previous life.

I should never have employed Constance's tactic to pressure Martin to share his bed. This was all my fault. I should have given him a year - or longer - to mourn. Then perhaps he might have grown to love me, at least a little.

And that was the heart of the issue. He married me only to care for his children. He did not love me.

But I loved him.

God help me, I loved him from the first moment he stepped into our house in Springfield. Twelve years old, to his twenty-five. He was so handsome, so witty. And so in love with my sister. I loved my sister. I did not want her to die. I did not want her husband. But now I had him. It was a sin. I had committed a mortal sin.

I had told Martin I would not wait forever. Why did I say that? I could not pressure him into loving me. When he comes home tonight - if he comes home - and if he comes home sober - I would tell him that I will raise his children, and take care of his home forever, and never ask for a thing.

So I went, around and around. The children and I washed that floor over and over. Any longer and we would have scrubbed down to the Giamettis' apartment.

I was finally brought out of my dismal reverie by the call down on the street from the fishmonger. "We got cod! We got flounder! We got blues!" I ran to the front window and leaned out. I hollered back, "I'll buy some flounder. Wait for me!"

I grabbed my coin purse and the children and we ran, wet and dirty, down the stairs.

"Fish! Fish!" I yelled. "Holler for the man!" I encouraged the children.

"Fish! Fish!" yelled Jonathan and Charlotte.

I felt a little better by the time Martin came home.

He came in on time and bearing chocolates. "From Helga's," he said, and the children claimed that was their favorite shop in the whole world, while also asking, "What is Helga's?"

"After dinner," I admonished.

We sat down to a mound of fish and potatoes, and Martin was buoyant and talkative. He described in detail his conversation with rotund Helga, who ate half of all her product and still made a profit. "And just like Jack Sprat, her husband is as skinny as a scarecrow. And they bicker all the time. They argue about the color of the sky," he said.

"The sky is blue," said Charlotte.

"You will not get an argument from me," said Martin.

He even offered to bathe the children and read them their stories and put them to bed. "So you can have a few moments to read your book," he explained.

Or to put off an unpleasant discussion, I thought. I hoped he would give me time to say goodbye to my few friends in New Haven before I was sent back to Springfield.

I did try to read, or at least sit with my book and not fidget.

When all was quiet in the parlor, Martin returned and I put the kettle on for tea.

"I promise not to drink like that again," said Martin, "but just for tonight, can I please have a little something in this tea?" And I took the bottle out and added a few tablespoons to his cup.

We sat. We drank our tea and looked at our hands.

"When I met your sister, you were just a little girl," he finally said. "A smart, outspoken, wise little girl. I was delighted to have a little sister like you."

"I adored you," I admitted, although I do not believe he took me as literally as I meant it.

"How could she leave me?" he asked.

"I don't know," I said.

"I can't think of you as anything but that smart little girl."

"I'm still her, that smart little girl … I can't be Catherine."

He covered his face.

"I'm so sorry I called you Catherine last night. I hurt you both. I don't know what to do."

"And I'm sorry I forced you to share your bed. You don't have to. I can put Jonathan in your bed and I'll sleep in the parlor with Charlotte."

"No," said Martin. "We are husband and wife. But I am not sure I can... do ... that... again."

I nearly didn't say it. God help me, I should not have said it. But I did.

"I know this is just horrid. Sinful. But... if you have the ... need... in the night in the dark ... it is all right with me... if you... pretend..."

Martin looked up. Looked at me in confusion. "Pretend?"

"Pretend I'm Catherine."

"Oh Lucinda! I'm so sorry."

"I know I'm appalling. I will go to hell."

"You're not appalling; our situation is appalling," Martin tried to smile, but it ended as a wry laugh. "We will go to hell together."

CHAPTER 31

IN JUNE, WE TOOK THE children to the Bronx Zoo, as we had promised. Every moment of it was exciting - and not just for the children. The day was glorious. The train ride to Fordham, then the trek to the zoo. And the animals! We saw every animal in Mother's big book, and even more we had never heard of: barbary lions, and crooked-horned kudus, and the most improbable thylacine, which looked like a large-headed striped dog, but had a pouch like a kangaroo. Charlotte could not contain herself when she saw peacocks spread their feathers, and I had to take her to the washroom for an emergency change of clothes. Jonathan skipped from one exhibit to another, greeting each animal with a formal, "Hello there, Giraffes," "Hello there, Elephants," and introducing himself, "I'm Jonathan Blaisdell and I am a human boy."

We ate frankfurters bought from a cart and lemonades and delicious ice cream cones that would have required another change of clothes had I brought any. Instead we washed sticky fingers and faces in a fountain, and overlooked the drips on the children's clothes. As a birthday present, we purchased a lovely cloth walrus for Jonathan. And for Charlotte, who did not understand the individuality of birthdays yet, a small wooden peacock. Mostly what was wonderful is that everyone we met in the crowded zoo took us for a real family. And indeed, we felt so.

We carried the sleepy children back to the train at the end of the day. Riding home in the waning light, Martin took my hand.

CHAPTER 32

Jonathan wasn't the only one celebrating a birthday in June. The following week was my birthday. I was eighteen.

Martin came home from work with a dozen white roses.

"For my child bride, who is no longer a child," he said, presenting the bouquet with a flourish.

"Why thank you, Sweetheart," I said with a dramatic curtsey.

Jonathan started to giggle. "Is Papa your sweetheart, really?"

"Yes, he is," I said, although in truth his father had not touched me since that wretched night.

"The roses are not all," said Martin, and, looking at Jonathan with a wink, "Sweetheart of mine." Jonathan giggled more and Charlotte attempted to curtsey as I had.

"I just stopped at the landlord's and Mrs. Battle has agreed to come up and watch the children, so we can go out to a restaurant. Just us two adults."

A restaurant. I had not been to a restaurant in more than two years. And New Haven had some fine dining establishments that I'd read about in the newspaper.

I found a vase in a cupboard to hold the roses, and quickly changed into the pink dress I was married in. I cut one rose and pinned it to my dress. I put my hair up and inspected myself by kneeling on the bed to get a glimpse of as much of me as possible in the small mirror that hung above the dresser. I thought I looked quite grown up. As Martin was washing up, I surreptitiously cut into a beet. I took a small hand towel and rubbed it against the cut beet. I applied a gentle dab to each cheek. Yes, I was certainly a grown woman.

"You look beautiful, Mama," said Charlotte. "I want to go."

"Not this time, dear," I said. "But you will have lots of fun with Mrs. Battle. She knows ever so many songs."

"She sings about angels and bathtubs," said Charlotte.

"Yes, isn't that wonderful?" I said, although I had not the slightest idea what the little girl meant.

Martin reappeared in a fresh shirt and a few minutes later Mrs. Battle arrived and clasped the children to her sizeable chest.

"I love these babies," she said, "so you two go out and have a wonderful evening."

And we did. Martin had chosen a small restaurant with candles and checkered tablecloths. The restaurant was called *Il Forno* - "The Oven" - said Martin, but how much nicer it sounded in Italian. Martin ordered fancy food - food I had never even heard of: Lasagna, Gnocchi, and oh my goodness, Cannoli and Sorbeto.

We drank wine. "Not too much for either of us," Martin warned, and we split a bottle, which I thought was quite a bit indeed, but the bottle was empty before our meal was finished. "We might as well drink now," he said, "Do you know what will happen in January?"

Well, I was proud that I read the newspaper each day. "The Prohibition Amendment has passed, and will go into effect in January. No more drinking for Americans."

Martin smiled. "You're probably happy about that."

"No, I like my beer. I used to drink beer with the O'Hara boys on Thursdays after work at the lumberyard. They always bought me a pint."

He laughed. "You are full of surprises, Lucinda! Can you drive an automobile too?"

"I think I probably could, if anyone would let me."

"I believe we'll have an automobile someday. And why not?"

"And perhaps a house of our own?"

"We were saving for that," Martin said, and just as suddenly the celebration turned solemn.

"We're trying," I said. "We're not doing so badly."

"It's awful," said Martin.

"But we are truly trying."

"Yes. We are."

"Martin, did you come here with Catherine?"

"No," he answered. "Never. This place is for you."

I decided to believe him.

The next day, I received a small package from my mother.

It was a bankbook for a savings account. The balance reflected all the money I had saved in the five years I had worked for my father. And more.

Mother had included a note.

Dear Lucinda,

Now you are 18. A grown woman. All your life you have done the right thing, and Father and I are proud of you – you are good, and strong, and beautiful. You dutifully saved your earnings as you promised, and unknown to me, your father matched each nickel with one of his own. Although he often argued with you about going on to college, he secretly wanted very much to see you earn a degree. Now you are dutiful again, taking selflessly the responsibilities of wife and mother. You have accepted a future not of your choosing. But I am convinced that one day you will have the opportunity to do the right thing just for yourself. Save this money for that time – to help you accomplish your goals.

Happy birthday, Lucinda. Be happy.

Love, Mother

I gave the children a nice lunch of hard-cooked eggs and ham, and settled them down for a nap. I let them sleep together in the big feather bed, and let them spread out all their toy animals at the foot of the bed, to guard them while they slept.

Then I sat down with a cup of tea in the kitchen, and the small blue bankbook, and had a long quiet cry.

CHAPTER 33

THE END OF JUNE TURNED very warm. Our third-floor apartment held the dry baking heat like my father's attic. We kept the curtains drawn in the hopes that the sun wouldn't find us and scorch us further. We all lay on top of our coverlets in the evening and opened the windows, hoping for one cool breeze - and no bats.

During the day, we stayed under the trees in the park as much as possible. Often, at the end of the day, when Martin returned from work, he would seek us out there, not even bothering to stop home first. We ate mostly sandwiches and fruit, as we could not bear to turn on the stove or oven.

One afternoon, the children and I were forced to flee the park as the clouds darkened and ran over us in threatening herds. Even Jonathan saw the comparison. "The clouds are like the buffalo in the zoo!" he said.

We didn't quite beat the storm, and we ran the last block in hard rain. I worried about lightning, but in truth, the soaking rain was such a relief, we started to skip and jump in puddles.

"Let's be ducks!" I cried.

And we quacked our way up the staircase, dripping wet and stomping on each step.

The door at the second-floor landing opened. There stood Mr. Giametti.

"Oh, I am so sorry," I apologized. "We are too loud and too raucous."

"It's all right," he said. "I am quite well today. I think the storm is clearing the air and lightening my burdensome head."

"The wind is pushing the rain sideways," I said. "If you open your kitchen window, you might be able to feel it on your face. It may be soothing," I suggested.

"Thank you. I do think I'll try it."

"And we will be extra quiet," I said. "I think we have gotten all the whooping out of us."

"Can I give one more quack?" asked Jonathan.

"You may," said Mr. Giametti.

"Quack!"

"Quack quack!" said Charlotte. "I had two!"

Mr. Giametti laughed.

"She has only just learned to count," I explained. "Of course, once she gets past three, I cannot guarantee the results."

"Mrs. Blaisdell," Giametti said, and it took me aback because, after six months of marriage, I still did not have much occasion to hear anyone call me that, "if you would like to get the children and yourself into dry clothes, and then come back downstairs, I could offer you all some cold lemonade. My wife has gone to visit a friend, and she has left me a large pitcher of her delicious concoction."

"Please, Mama!" said Jonathan. "I would like a *comtoction*."

"Yes, thank you, that would be wonderful!"

"We will be good!" said Charlotte.

"Why of course," said Mr. Giametti. "I will expect you soon. Would shortbread be in order?"

"Oh Mama!" said Jonathan. "Please!"

"We will be back in moments!" I said.

And we ran up the stairs (as quietly as the children could be, given their excitement) and I toweled their hair and put them in dry clothes. I quickly changed into a dry dress myself, and managed to find dry shoes for us all, which technically were just stockings for Charlotte, since she had only one pair of shoes that still fit - she had grown so much in the last few months.

Downstairs, I had Jonathan knock softly, just three raps, although it was all he could do not to bang repeatedly on the door. It was curious how excited they were. But I think they had been rather frightened of the forbidding mysterious neighbor, and were enormously relieved to find him pleasant and welcoming. Or perhaps that is how I felt myself.

Mr. Giametti had set the kitchen table for four. With pretty green napkins and the pitcher of lemonade set on a yellow cloth in the middle of the table. He had put out small plates with a generous slice of shortbread on each plate. As I had suggested, the kitchen window was open to the driving rain, and he had put down a towel on the windowsill and another on the floor to absorb the puddles.

The man himself was tall and very slender. He held himself straight with the stiff posture I had seen in people that were steeling themselves against pain. Like the assistant pastor in our church in Springfield, before he succumbed to a spreading cancer.

He had dark hair, worn a bit long over his forehead. He had not shaved that day, and the blue tint to his jaw was matched by heavy bluish shadows under his eyes. He was certainly not well. But his smile was warm.

The children were sweet and minded their manners. They sat at the table and held their lemonade glasses with both hands as if they were drinking something precious and delicate.

"Mrs. Giametti's *comtoction* is tasty!" said Jonathan.

"I will give her your compliments," said Mr. Giametti.

On a table in the far corner of the kitchen were four violins, one of which had no strings and another broken off at the neck.

"What do you do with the violins?" I asked.

"I repair them," said Mr. Giametti. "Since the war, I have not yet been well enough to return to work, but I have managed to make ends meet by repairing all sorts of musical instruments. I'm best at violins. And luckily, the college students at Yale are very hard on their instruments."

And he walked over to the table and picked up a violin. He played *After The Ball*, and oh, I thought my heart would break.

"Oh Mr. Giametti," I exclaimed. "You play like the angels! Why haven't I heard you from upstairs?"

"I don't like to disturb people, especially when I know they are trying so hard not to disturb me. I do my repairs when I have heard you go out... or when you are being noisy yourself," he added with a smile.

"Well, that would explain it," I laughed. "Although we do try, we are pretty much noisy most of the time."

He played several more songs for us, mostly slow and incredibly sad, but one lively tune from Italy that tempted the children to get up and dance. "Go ahead," he said. And they skipped to the beat of the music, holding hands, in sort of a comically fast ring-around-the-rosy.

"Thank you so much for the refreshments and the lovely music," I said. "It's time for the children to have their naps." The little ones groaned, but I could see they would be asleep within a minute of laying down their heads.

"I'm glad to have the company," said Mr. Giametti. "I am hopeful I will have more good days, and will be able to get about again. And have more visits."

I shook his hand and promised we would come again. Jonathan also gave Mr. Giametti a solemn handshake, and Charlotte kissed his cheek.

CHAPTER 34

B Y THE BEGINNING OF AUGUST, it was apparent to me that I was - to use the coarsest of terms - pregnant.

Martin had only been intimate with me that one night. Since that time, we slept in the same bed, but kissed goodnight only. My terrible offer to him that he had my permission to pretend I was Catherine was not acted upon. Although I had meant it at the time, I do believe that it would have been the end for us. We would wait, without explicitly telling each other so, until he could make love to me as Lucinda.

But here I was, in August, expecting a child conceived on the only night it had been possible.

I did not know how to tell Martin. But I knew it had to be done soon. My friend Constance had already guessed.

We had been seated at a bench in the park, watching our children play some silly game they had invented. I stood to call out to Jonathan to be a little more gentle, and a breeze blew my lightweight dress up against my body.

"You have that little roundness," Constance remarked. "The kind that for a slim woman such as yourself only means one thing."

"I'm afraid so," I confessed.

"Afraid? Not delighted?"

"Constance, I am eighteen and already the mother of two," I replied. I did not tell her that my husband did not love me and that only a drunken sopor had induced him to touch me. I did not tell her that he had touched me only one time. I did not tell her that he had married me at my father's insistence. I told her that I feared the amount of work involved.

"I only have Sadie," said Constance, "so who I am to give advice? But I am told that if you have enough children, the older ones tend to the younger ones, and allow you enough time to have a nervous breakdown."

I fell to my knees in laughter.

When I finally recovered, I asked, "Constance, did you go to college?"

"Yes," she said, "Smith College in Northampton."

"Smith! What did you study?"

"Music," she said. "I was a good musician at one time."

"Do you miss it? Are you sorry you are now a mother and not a musician?"

She shook her head at me, exactly like Catherine used to do when I said something that made no sense. "I am still a musician. And although I said that I was good at one time, I will make a confession to you." She leaned toward me and smiled. "I am still a very good musician." She called to Sadie to run faster, to try to beat Jonny in their race. "But I'm not sorry to be a mother. Women have to choose. And we don't get a lot of options to choose from."

"Are you bored sometimes?"

Constance laughed. "Are you?"

"Oh, my, yes! Am I a horrid mother to find it tiresome - all this housekeeping and cooking, and listening to small children's nonsense ?"

"No. You are not horrid. You are a smart woman who must spend most of her day in very trivial pursuits."

"Then how do I bear it - especially now, with another baby coming?"

She nodded towards the three children who were on their knees, heads together observing something in the grass, invisible to us. "Look how amazing they are - those curious little souls!" she said. "Keep that in mind, but keep in mind that you are a person too. Don't let the trivial fill you up. Why, most men work all day in the factory and much of that is boring too. Men might have more freedom than women, but we are not stupid or helpless. Learn. Study. Pay attention to the world. You can do that and love your children too. All three children."

I walked a step away. With my back turned to Constance, I watched the children still engrossed in some bug or flower. I said, "They are my sister Catherine's children. She died of the influenza."

Constance said quietly, "I wondered. Because you are not their mother, yet I see such a resemblance."

"I had intended to go to college. My father had recently consented."

Constance came to me and brought me back to the bench. "That is so much to give up."

"It was not so difficult a decision then. They needed me and Martin needed me. Catherine was happy with that life. I thought I could be as well."

"You are not Catherine."

"I am not enough like Catherine for Martin to love, and I am too much like Catherine for Martin to forget."

We sat for a while. She held both my hands in hers, as if trying to impart to me some of her strength through her fingertips.

Finally I said, "I have not yet told Martin about the baby. What if he is not happy?"

She shook my fingers. She said, "What if *you* are not happy? Take care of your own happiness. Let Martin take care of his."

I thought about this - and almost nothing else - for the next three days. Constance was right. I had to be genuinely happy about the baby myself before I could ever expect Martin to be. But what did I have to be happy about? That I was bearing the child of a man who did not love me? That I would now have a longer period as mother and the window of pursuing an education even more remote? That we were already in tight quarters in our little apartment? That I would have more diapers and dishes and fewer adult conversations? That my husband would not love my child like he loved Catherine's children?

And then my thoughts would go spinning in another direction. If Martin would love Catherine's children more, did it follow that it would be natural for me to love this child more than Catherine's children? The thought was preposterous. I had read too many fairy tales about evil stepmothers who did not love their stepchildren. Surely this was not me. Would having a baby make it be me? Those two little souls who called me Mama? I didn't resent them now. Why would I resent them after I had my own child?

My own child. That was the crux. My own baby might show me clearly that there was a difference between someone else's child and my own. But again, I loved Charlotte and Jonathan already.

How my head hurt.

Which brought me down to Mr. Giametti's apartment. Mrs. Giametti had since come home from her visit to New York City. She answered the door at my light knock.

"How is your husband doing today?" I asked.

"He is managing, thank you." She nodded her head towards the bedroom. "He is sleeping, and often that is a good sign. On his worst days, he cannot sleep. He cannot even bear to put his head down on even the softest of pillows."

"Could you tell me if there is medicine that helps?"

"Frank takes a powder of aspirin and caffeine. It helps a little. A cold poultice on the back of his neck sometimes helps too, although the truth is, sometimes it makes things worse... is someone in your family ill?"

"Just me. And not very ill. Just a very bad headache. I need to get on with my day before the children wake up from their naps. I was hoping there was something that would wash this away."

"I could give you some of the powders. It is quite strong, though. I would not want to make you sicker."

"Oh dear, that's true. Never mind. I will just go back to the children. I believe I hear them stirring."

Mrs. Giametti frowned. She was so pretty, even her frown was comforting. "Now that I have a good look at you, you truly do not seem well. You are so pale." She looked at me with concern. "Come and sit a moment. I will get you some cold tea."

She led me over to her kitchen table and poured me a glass of tea. It was quite refreshing. "There's mint in it," said Mrs. Giametti. "That also might help to clear your head."

I thought I heard noises up above. "Oh dear, I think the children may be awake - I must go." I rose quickly from the chair and felt suddenly faint. I swooned. I had not done that since I was ten and High Mass was interminable and I had not had breakfast.

"Sit!" ordered Mrs. Giametti. She led me, not back to the kitchen chair, but took me by the hand to the small bedroom off the kitchen. The extra room that our apartment did not have - the one they had been advertising unsuccessfully to let.

"You lie down right here for a few minutes, and let your head clear. I will run upstairs and check on the children.

I'll stay until they wake up, and then we'll all come back down together."

I did not have the energy to protest. I do not even remember if I thanked her. She was gone and I slept.

I woke hours later to much noise coming from the kitchen.

Mr. Giametti was playing a song from Italy on his violin. Mrs. Giametti was teaching the children the words to the song, singing in a sweet clear voice:

Tu scendi dalle stelle
O re del cielo
E vieni in una grotta
Al freddo al gelo

"Well, hello, you're back," said Mrs. Giametti. "We are just waiting for the children's Papa to come home. We are singing Christmas music in August. Just because it is so pretty and so easy for children to learn."

"Thank you so much," I said. "You are very kind. I am feeling ever so much better."

I saw from her beautiful small clock that it was after six. "Oh no!" I cried. "I'm so late. I have not made dinner... Martin will be home, and he will be tired and hungry..." I picked up Charlotte. "Come, Jonny, you can help me with dinner."

"Lucinda, you are obviously exhausted. Have dinner here," said Mrs. Giametti.

Mr. Giametti spoke up, "Yes, please stay. We don't have very much company. I've been enjoying the children. We'll wait for your husband, and we can all share a meal. Some nice sausage, perhaps. Nothing fancy."

"Oh, dear... I'm not sure.."

But the kind couple convinced me to sit and enjoy the music, while Mrs. Giametti cooked. It smelled quite good, and it was nice to feel hungry. I had not eaten all day. Within the hour, we heard Martin's footsteps on the stair. Mr. Giametti brought him in and explained that I had been ill earlier, and although I was feeling better, they insisted the whole family should eat with them.

"Are you all right?" he asked me, at the same time the children clambered up his shins to be lifted up and hugged.

"I'm fine," I said. "The heat was terrible earlier, and I did some ironing anyway. It was a bit much," I said.

"Come eat!" said Mrs. Giametti.

We sat around their table and ate and made light conversation. The children embarrassed me a bit - their appetites were so hearty I was sure the Giamettis would think that I was either neglectful or a terrible cook. I had not seen Mr. Giametti look so well. The conversation and companionship agreed with him. And with Martin too. They spoke of aviation in terms I had never heard, and with a passion that Martin had not shown since Catherine died.

The wine flowed, but I was careful to have a single glass. Martin showed discretion too. Since that night in June, he had kept his promise to me that he would be moderate in his drink. One bottle of home-pressed wine served all four of us easily.

As I watched the happy conversation, I realized that the couple was younger than I had thought. Not as young as I, but perhaps Martin's contemporaries. Martin would be thirty soon. Much older than I, but still a young man. He had only seemed old in his premature widowing and overwhelming grief. And I saw that worry and illness had done the same to the Giamettis. They were not old; they were worn with worry. But at least on this night, all three were young and without care for a time.

The evening passed so pleasantly that I hardly noticed that the children were nodding over their empty plates.

I announced that the children's bedtime was long passed and that I would be saying my goodbyes. I thanked Mr. and Mrs. Giametti *('Please, it is Frank and Sofia,' they said)* for taking care of the children when I wasn't feeling well, and now for providing us such a wonderful dinner and fine conversation.

Mrs. Giametti - Sofia - interrupted, "Why don't I come up and help you put the children to bed, and that way the men can continue to talk about airplanes and automobiles and we don't have to pretend we are not bored to tears?"

"That sounds very nice," I said.

And so Sofia picked up Charlotte and I carried Jonathan, and together we changed them into their night clothes and put them down. Sofia sang them a lullaby - a lovely song in a such a sweet voice it brought tears to my eyes, though I did not understand a word.

"I love you, Mrs. Giametti," said Jonathan. "And you too Mama," he added as an afterthought.

"I love you too, you fickle boy," I said.

"Let's have some tea before I go back downstairs," Sofia suggested.

So I put on the kettle and took out our nicest cups, as a way to repay her at least a bit for all her kindnesses of the day.

"Are you sure you are feeling better?" she asked. "You still look pale."

And I told her. I hardly knew her. And I had not told Martin. And yet I told her.

Her response was exactly what I needed to hear.

"A baby! Oh my God! A Miracle!"

It was. I had forgotten.

CHAPTER 35

THE FOLLOWING DAY WAS SUNDAY.
 I asked Martin if we could go to church services, as we had not been in several weeks, and I thought it would do us all good. He agreed, and we dressed the children in their finest clothes. We walked to St. Mary's, not far from our home. It was a lovely church, although, through lack of funding, its steeple had been waiting for decades to be completed. I thought of it as the Church of Patience. Which I sorely needed.

Jonathan fidgeted through the entire service. Charlotte wailed through the sermon. Martin whispered to me, suggesting we take them back to the vestibule, but I was determined to endure. I would soon enough have three children to contend with; I felt the need to prove I could handle two.

I prayed to St. Gerard Majella, the patron saint of expectant mothers. For the life of me, I could not understand why a man would be guardian of pregnancy. I think I would have been more comfortable with some jolly overweight woman who had birthed nine healthy babies. But I knew of no such saint. It appeared that most saints were emaciated tubercular souls who succumbed at a young age. And virgins too. I was nearly a virgin. Perhaps the Virgin Mary would be a better destination for my prayers. Once I shared my condition, I would ask my father to suggest the correct saint that would help me be a competent - and happy - mother.

Now that Sofia knew as well as Constance, it was imperative that I tell Martin right away. We had been honest with each other - even when it was painful. I wanted to do my best to make this news joyful. I prayed to Mary to find the right words.

I prepared a nice summer lunch of cold chicken in lemon sauce and a salad of garden tomatoes. I put the children down for a nap, but woke them after an hour. It was a beautiful day, and I wanted to do something special. We took the trolley a few stops to the large park that had a big pond with swans and ducks. I had two small sacks with stale bread and Jonathan and Charlotte ran down to the water's edge to feed the ducks. We found they needed close supervision - in the warm weather they thought nothing of walking right into the water. We also had to supervise the swans - they were so large and aggressive that when the bread gave out, we had to pick up the children and run for our lives. The children shrieked with delight, and we were breathless and howling ourselves.

A man at a cart was selling sorbetto. "Oh, let's have some," Martin suggested before the children even got to begging.

We sat on the lawn and ate our icy treats. A small dog wandered over and begged on his hind legs for a share. Jonathan was immediately smitten and fed the little scrounger right off his own spoon. I went to stop him, and Martin took my hand. "What's a few germs on such a fine day?"

The dog possessed an impressive collection of tricks, even though he appeared to be a stray. He sat, begged, shook hands, danced in a little circle, while Charlotte sang to him and Jonathan continued to give him small bits of sorbetto.

"I'm tempted to take him home," said Martin. "But Mrs. Battle would be mortified, and throw us out on the street."

"That's all right, Martin," I said. "You are already going to have another little mouth to feed."

He turned from the dog. "What did you say?"

"That I am expecting a child."

"My God! From the one time?"

"Apparently that was enough."

Martin watched Charlotte and Jonathan laughing at the dog's antics. "I love them both," he said.

"You will love a third as well."

"How I hope so."

That was my joyous news and reception. I hoped so too.

CHAPTER 36

WE DECIDED TO GO TO Springfield to tell my parents, as the news seemed too significant for a letter.

So Martin left work on Saturday at noon, and we took the afternoon train to Springfield. Martin worried that he should have hired a car - "the ride would be easier on you." Since my announcement, he had done nothing but worry. That the weather was too hot, that the evenings were too cool, that the stairs were too difficult, that I should not carry the children.

I did not remember him acting so solicitous when Catherine had been expecting. When I saw them during those periods, Martin had seemed relaxed and happy. With his current worry, I worried too - that he was compensating for his feelings of guilt because he did not want another baby. I responded with fake jubilance, and the insistence that I was the healthiest expectant mother on the planet, even when I was unable to stomach the smell of raw chicken, or was so exhausted at the end of the evening that I would fall asleep fully clothed.

Father picked us up at the train station - in his new automobile. Martin was overjoyed. Well, I decided that I could not fault him for caring more about the motorcar than our coming baby. He needed to feel some lighthearted excitement after a week burdened with responsibility. We climbed into the 1918 Oldsmobile Touring Car with Martin completely infatuated and Jonathan and Charlotte ready to jump up and down on the beautiful leather seats. Father proudly took the wheel and drove us in a rather indirect route back to the house. Just when we were about to step from the motorcar to the gravel path that Father had built for his new possession, Father said to Martin, "Would you like to drive it?"

"Oh my, yes!" Martin cried, and instead of climbing down from the car to run in and greet Mother, we took another spin around the block. Martin's face had not shown as much joy in the past year. I wanted nothing more than to throw my arms around my father and kiss him with my tears.

Finally back at home, Martin thanked my father for the wonderful driving lesson.

Father boasted, "Yes sir, this is a real man's car!"

Martin caught my eye, and I saw mischief there. "I do believe that Lucinda should take the wheel...just down the street and back."

My father looked horrified, but before he could protest, Martin had seated me behind the wheel, while he sat in the next seat giving me directions to get the automobile moving. I lurched forward and negotiated the vehicle down to the corner. Martin quickly helped me with the turn, and I drove back to the yard. To be honest, I sped back. The children were shouting all sorts of encouragement from the rear seat and I pressed the pedal harder and we flew back to the house. "Whoa!" I shouted, and managed to get the Oldsmobile stopped before I ran over the rose bushes. Martin and I held ourselves and laughed till we were giddy. I was so glad we had come.

By this time, Mother had come out with Amelia and Malcolm, and all three had been cheering on my accomplishment of not hitting the house. We all hugged our hellos and the little ones ran around us all with happy excitement.

Mother had outdone herself on dinner. A large, and I'm sure expensive, roast of beef, with potatoes that had browned around the roast, and what Mother liked to call haricots verts, but Catherine used to say, "Green beans, Mother. They're green beans." It was a family joke. But there was no one there to make it anymore.

Still, we remained buoyant. At the end of the meal, Martin turned to my Mother and said, "Thank you so much, Mother Benedict, for such a magnificent meal, and to you too, Father Benedict, for the pleasure of driving your admirable automobile. I am glad I can be so alliterative in my gratitude." We laughed, although I am sure Jonathan and Charlotte had no idea what they were laughing at, and I had my doubts about Malcolm and Amelia as well.

"Lucinda and I have some wonderful news," Martin continued. "Lucinda is expecting a baby."

Everyone turned to gape at me, including my own children.

My father stood. "No!" he bellowed, slamming his hand to the table and upsetting his coffee cup. He stormed out of the room.

I jumped up and ran after him. I heard the door to his office slam, but I threw it back open without the mandatory knock.

"How could you?" he asked. His whole body shook with rage.

"I don't understand..." I said quietly.

"You have fornicated with your sister's husband!"

"With my own husband! You are the one who wanted us - forced us - to marry."

"You will both be in hell. There is no greater sin."

"I am being a wife."

"You are NOT a wife. You are a sister! This is evil. This is incest!" Father began to cry. "Get out, get out!"

I fled the room. I ran up the stairs to the guest bedroom, to Catherine's bedroom.

Before dinner, I had taken out our Sunday clothing to release the wrinkling from the suitcase. Now I threw the clothing back into the suitcase. I was crying and trying to get the wretched case to close when Martin came in.

"We need to leave immediately," I said, choking on my tears. "If there is no train, we can hire a car."

"Lucinda, no. We cannot take the children out now. Your mother is reading them a story and then she will bring them up to bed. Your father is shocked, but he will calm himself. You'll see."

"No, he won't. I know him. You didn't hear what he said to me. My God, why did he want us to marry?"

I threw myself onto the bed, convulsed in tears. Martin stood watching, helpless.

Mother came in with the children, and I tried to stifle my sobs. The little ones were clearly upset and had never seen me so distraught. They cried "Mama, stop!" and clung to me.

"It's all right," said Mother to the children. "Mama is very tired from such a long day, but she will be all smiles again in the morning. You go to sleep now and you will see that everything will be happy in the morning."

I could not seem to move - nor could Martin. I heard Mother rummaging through the suitcase that I had turned into a disastrous jumble of clothes. By the time she had dressed the children for bed, I was able to regain enough composure to sit up and give the children my best imitation of a sincere smile.

"See, I am already feeling a bit better," I said.

"Is Grandfather angry?" asked Jonathan.

"Oh no," I answered. "He is just tired too."

"Maybe you should not drive the automobile anymore," suggested Jonny.

"I think perhaps you are right," I said.

My mother kissed both of the children goodnight and then came to me and kissed the top of my head. "The sun will shine again in the morning. You'll see," she said.

"Yes, of course," said Martin, and Mother touched his cheek briefly before leaving us.

When we came down to breakfast in the morning, Mother was alone in the kitchen with porridge and biscuits. And thankfully, coffee.

"Your father has gone to early Mass with Amelia and Malcolm," explained my mother.

We ate quietly. Even the little ones were subdued that morning.

Mother said, "Martin, why don't you take the children out to the garden? Perhaps you could pick some tomatoes and peppers that you could take home with you."

And Martin took both children by the hand and left Mother and me together.

Mother poured us each another cup of coffee and sat down at the table by my side. She took my hand.

"Your father," she said, "is a man full of contradictions. A man who does not always have the capacity to confront and acknowledge those contradictions. But last night he had to see the consequences of his actions. And he found it hard to accept.

He pushed you into marriage, but he told himself that it was just a union of propriety. To keep up appearances. He did it for himself, not you. And failed to recognize what was inevitable. That you and Martin would come to accept your artificial marriage as a real marriage. He finally had to see what he has not let himself see for many months: that Catherine is dead. And life has the audacity - the sheer bad manners - to go on. And it brings you new life."

I wiped away the beginning of a new round of tears. "Martin and I are not in a real marriage as yet. But we are getting there. He is still overwhelmed with grief. He has not really allowed himself to even try to be happy."

"He feels that being happy again is disloyal."

"Oh, yes!"

"Grief is a terrible thing. In some ways, you never want to get over it. You think it is not fair to go on with your life - to smile again without the one you love." She took a sip of coffee and I saw that her hand trembled.

"Nothing quite so horrid as bad manners," I repeated with a sorrowful smile.

Mother smiled too.

"Did you know," she continued, "that you had a brother two years older than you?"

"No! What are you saying?"

"Your brother Joseph. He died before his first birthday. He was taken by some fever he could not fight. I thought I would die with him. I thought I should have died with him. When I found I was expecting another child, I was so angry. I was angry with your father for ever wanting to have marital relations again. I was angry with you for thinking you could replace my darling Joe. I was angry with my body and with God, for making me continue to live."

I took her hand once more.

"When you were born," Mother continued, "it would be easy to tell you that suddenly all was right with the world and that I loved you and life was sweet again. It did not happen that easily. I refused to look at you, refused to nurse you. Your father had to hire someone to care for you. But gradually you made me curious. I heard your cries, I saw you be comforted by the nurse, by young Catherine, and yes, even by your father. Who was this strange demanding creature? One day I said, 'Everyone get out of the room and let me take care of my own baby!' And I held you and it wasn't so bad. I didn't forget Joseph. But I could love you too."

"If you did not forget Joseph, why didn't you ever talk about him? Why didn't you tell me I had another brother?"

"Just because I had joy back in my life doesn't mean the pain went away."

"And now?"

"The sorrow is always there. But so is the joy. I truly believe Martin will eventually see that too."

"Do you think Father will?"

"I don't know. He is a difficult man. But I know one thing - a baby is always a blessing. You were my salvation. Your child will save you too."

"I am not sure I can do it."

"If there is anything I know about you, Lucinda, it is that you can do anything."

CHAPTER 37

M Y FATHER DID NOT FORGIVE me. At least I do not think he did.

But I forgave him.

He also lost a son when baby Joseph died. He also lost a daughter when Catherine died.

And looking at my life with honesty, I saw that my father did not push me into marriage with Martin. That Christmas, when I learned of Father's plan, Martin had been willing to release me from that terrible agreement. But truth be told, I wanted to marry Martin.

I told Martin once that I had always adored him. But I let him think it was childish admiration. I knew the shameful truth. I had loved Martin with my whole soul. And I had thought in that immature soul - and still did in some ways - that I could replace Catherine. That I could have her life. That I could become her.

I replaced her with her children, because they were too young to keep her memory safe. It was up to Martin and to me to give her back to her children, with our memories and stories since they would have few of their own.

I resolved to do this.

I took down the portraits of my muckraking heroes that hung in the parlor. The room was now the children's bedroom and Ida Tarbell did not have to watch over them at night. I put those pictures into my trunk. Catherine's photo had its place of honor on the dresser in the bedroom, but Martin and I did not have to be reminded of her. She lived with us, and between us, night and day. So I moved that photo to the parlor and hung it in the spot that had been Tarbell's.

"This is your first Mama," I told the children as I straightened the portrait. Jonathan nodded as if he remembered, but I'm not sure he did. "Anyway," I said, "your first Mama loved you very much. She died in the great influenza epidemic. She didn't want to die because she wanted to stay with you, but she couldn't help it. So your Papa asked me if I would be your Mama, and I said yes. Because I love you and I loved your Mama. And that is how you came to have two mamas. And I will tell you stories about her, so you know her and love her too."

"Tell a story now, Mama," said Charlotte.

"You can't call her Mama anymore," Jonathan cried, and although it nearly broke my heart, I said with a smile,

"Oh yes. You both can call me Mama because I am your Mama too. I was not your first Mama, but you are my real children and I am your real Mama."

"Story!" insisted Charlotte.

So I told them about Catherine, and how she liked the ice from Grandfather's ice house, and how she would put honey on it, and let me have some, and share it with Aunt Amelia and Uncle Malcolm too. And we would go home with honey on our faces and Grandmother would say, "How did you get so sticky?" And Catherine would say, "The bees were kissing us!"

"She was fibbing!" said Jonathan.

"Yes, but she fibbed to make Grandmother laugh. And that is all right. Making someone laugh is sweet. As sweet as honey."

"Tell another!"

"One day, when you were very little, Charlotte, it was terribly warm. And we were out for a walk, but there was no place to escape the heat. And you fussed and cried. You couldn't talk yet, but we knew that you were saying, 'I need to get cool right now!' We came to a church and went in. It was cooler in the church because of the heavy stone walls, so I thought that was very smart of your first mama. But she had something else in mind. She picked you up from your pram and put you in the baptismal font. Clothes and all. And she said, 'A second baptism is always a good idea!'"

"Did she let me swim in the fountain too?" asked Jonathan.

"She certainly did."

"I like her," he said.

I felt a glimmer of hope that Catherine and I might be able to somehow share this home and this family.

CHAPTER 38

MY DELICATE CONDITION BECAME NOT SO delicate after all. I recovered my appetite - almost to a fault - and with September came cooler, more refreshing weather.

Sofia Giametti took a job as a seamstress in the corset factory. I was quite jealous watching her go off to work each morning with her lunch pail, arm in arm with two other young women. Not that I had any inclination towards sewing, or any type of factory work. I liked the idea, however, of earning my own money. As a result though, I did earn twenty-five cents per week, making sure that Frank had a nice lunch each day. I would have done that for free - I had quickly grown very fond of both Giamettis. We all had dinner together every Sunday. And they often came upstairs on weekday evenings after the children were in bed to play cards.

Lunch for Frank was served downstairs in his apartment, with his food. The children and I were delighted with this arrangement. Sofia purchased and prepared the most delicious pasta and sausages. Even her vegetables seemed more tasty than what I could buy and certainly more tasty that I what I could cook. There were times when Frank was quite unwell, and it was a difficult task to get him to come out from the bedroom and try to eat a bit. The children seemed to have a special sensibility for Frank's bad days. They spoke in whispers and Jonathan would even put his hand on Frank's forehead. And if by chance the children were also having a bad day, not in health but in temperament (which I will not pretend was rare), I would leave a meal set on the table and take the little ones home.

But luckily, Frank's bad days were becoming less frequent. Sofia worked five days a week, and on at least three of those days, Frank was well and in good spirits. We would go down at lunchtime to find him at work on an instrument, and we'd feast on Sofia's offerings. Jonny and Charlotte would dance to Frank's violin - or accordion or cello - even once a harp.

Frank was born in New York City. He was very proud that he was a true American. His parents had come through Ellis Island in 1885, and he was born five years later. When he was four his parents came to New Haven where The Sargent Metal Company was known for its good wages and willingness to hire Italian immigrants. Frank loved New Haven; his parents did not. They moved back to Italy when

Frank was fifteen, and he decided to stay. He went to work in the same factory, producing fine locks and was quite content. In 1912, when he was twenty-two, he desired a wife. He wrote to his parents and they found a suitable bride in Calabria. Frank paid for Sofia's passage.

"You didn't want to find a wife for yourself? To see her and speak to her and know that you were compatible?" I asked.

"Who would know better what was best for me than my own father and mother?" he replied. "If they said she would be a good wife, I knew they would be correct. And they sent me a photograph." He got up and went into the bedroom, and came back with a very worn photograph of a very pretty young woman. "Beautiful, no?" he said.

"Very beautiful," I agreed.

"She is a bit older than I," he said, which surprised me. "We wanted to have a house full of children, but it didn't happen. Then I went off to the war, and the gassing was a terrible thing. I returned with these headaches. It has been eighteen months now. But finally...finally... I am beginning to improve."

"I'm glad you are recovering. Maybe it is not too late for a family. Life is full of surprises. Look at me!" I said. Frank had met Catherine once or twice, and he knew that she had been my sister. I did not need to say more.

Knowing their history explained why Frank's English was perfect, while Sofia's, though excellent, was heavily accented. I felt a kinship with these good folk who were also united through an arranged marriage. They had been together nearly seven years and they had survived war, illness, and infertility.

This last tribulation was much harder on Sofia than Frank. In some ways, Frank was relieved there had been no children - his frequent incapacity caused him to struggle as a provider. And although he adored Jonathan and Charlotte, I believe that their noisy exuberance on a daily basis would have made his slow recovery all but impossible.

But poor Sofia. During one private conversation, she spoke of her heartbreaking barrenness. "I made so many novenas," she said, "that I wore down my rosary. But God must have known that Frank would suffer his injury and need so much quiet. My sister back in Calabria had two babies die in her womb. Terrible sadness but at least she knew that she could conceive. And so she was not discouraged, and now she has a lovely son. But for me, after all these years, nothing. I have lost hope."

"I'm so sorry," I said.

"We all have terrible disappointments. We say, 'What else?' and go a different way. I have a fine job and the pleasure of loving your little ones without bringing pain to Frank."

"Charlotte and Jonathan love you. And I have my own troubles with my family, so I am glad they have you to love."

After discussing the situation with Martin, we asked Sofia and Frank to be godparents to the baby I was carrying.

CHAPTER 39

OCTOBER BROUGHT CHARLOTTE'S THIRD BIRTHDAY. We received gifts from my mother, with a note sending Charlotte and all of us much love, but also mentioning that my father still needed some 'distance.' which I took as a kind way of saying that he was still filled with anger. Well, we could have a birthday celebration of our own.

Although the weather was cool, the amusement park at Lighthouse Point was still opened, and they offered a spectacular carousel. We took the trolley down to the point and the children (and we too, holding them) rode around and around until we were dizzy. And despite the children's wobbly legs, not to mention my proximity to a swoon considering my delicate condition, we took the ferry ride to Savin Rock and fed the seagulls. We bought a soft cuddly toy horse for Charlotte and a fine wooden carved one for Jonny. We ate spun sugar Fairy Floss and of course everyone's favorite, sorbetto.

We arrived home to dinner, which no one could eat, and birthday cake, which we ate although we shouldn't have, both prepared by Sofia.

She and I carried the exhausted children up to bed.

It took just one of Sofia's lullabies to send the little ones off to sleep. We sat and watched their sweet faces dissolve into their dreams. They amazed me at times like this. I now had a three-year-old and a four-year-old, and I was just eighteen.

Sofia whispered, "Do you think maybe God doesn't answer your prayers because He thinks you are selfish... always asking, asking, asking?"

I thought about it.

"Maybe," I said. "He might be tired of hearing people always wanting for themselves."

Sofia sighed.

I said, "What if we change places? What if I asked God to grant you what you want, and you ask God to give me what I want? Do you think we might sound more generous? Asking for good things for other people, not ourselves?"

"It might help," she said.

"Couldn't hurt to try. Of course, I think I would have the advantage in this arrangement - since you pray so much more than I do."

She laughed softly. "Well, then, you have some catching up to do. You better begin to pray for me immediately!"

I dropped to my knees. "Dear God, I am praying now not for myself but for Sofia here. Please make Sofia less bossy. Amen."

Sofia cuffed me on the back of the head with Charlotte's little horse. We both fell onto the floor overcome with giggles, and promptly woke the children and had to start all over.

I needed to hear from the non-religious side, so I sought out Constance at the park the next day.

"Do you think that prayer works?" I asked.

"No. I'm not even sure I believe in God, but even if He exists, why would He care about what you need any more than what some untouchable in India needs or even what that pigeon over there needs? Why would He be listening?"

"Why wouldn't He? Maybe He listens to us all, even the pigeon."

Constance stood. "Sadie! No throwing dirt!" She turned back to me. "I do believe there is a different benefit from prayer. Not God answering your prayer, but in prayer itself."

"Prayer alone without an answer?"

"Yes. Prayer for its own sake. Because when you pray and ask for something, you first have to decide what it is you want. What do you pray for? Once you decide you want something bad enough to pray for it, then you know what it is you desire. I think many people don't really know."

This made sense to me. It wasn't spiritual; it was practical.

She continued. "And once you know what you want, well, that is the most important step to getting it."

"Because then you are specific in your prayer?"

"Absolutely not. Leaving it to prayer is worse than just giving up. Don't let someone else decide what you get... not even God."

"So what do you do to get what you want?"

"When you know... exactly, specifically... then you go to war. You fight a war with anyone who tells you no."

Charlotte came running up with a handful of oak leaves she had picked up. "Very beautiful," I said. "Can you make a pretty yellow bouquet?" She ran happily back to the tree.

I wrapped my shawl around me. "I don't understand why these children never seem to be cold."

"You don't run around like they do," said Constance. "Plus, their little hearts beat faster."

"I didn't know that."

"Do you know what it is you want? Are you still burning to save the world?"

I watched Jonathan, Charlotte, and Sadie collecting autumn leaves while I thought about her question. I wasn't sure of the answer. I knew I loved the children. I loved the one still inside me. Being a world-changing muckraker seemed so naïve. How would one even go about that? I had wanted - it seemed like a lifetime ago - to fight for better wages for colored men. I recognized the injustice in my father's lumberyard, and I was proud of that extra nickel I had secured. But I recognized that I had a significant advantage in my very small victory. I could plead with a father who - at least at that time - seemed to love me.

What knowledge, what skills did I possess to achieve better wages from stubborn or hostile employers? But I certainly wanted to feel that satisfaction again. And where did Martin fit into all of this?

"I'm thinking about it," I said.

CHAPTER 40

THE FOLLOWING DAY I SAW the doctor. I didn't really intend to. Many women have a perfectly fine confinement without a doctor's help - or interference, as the case may be. But I had questions.

I had asked Constance that afternoon what it felt like to give birth and she said, "like Satan has taken possession of your body." She would give me no details. And I wasn't sure exactly how true that was, for if it were the truth, then I would expect all women to have only one child. After the one hellish experience, that would be the end of the sexual act forever, and human beings would have become extinct. And yes, I knew that men had power over women, but if the experience of childbirth was more than any could endure, women would have risen up. Of course, I did see the fallacy to this argument, since many women *were* trying to rise up.

I could not ask any of my other acquaintances because they were just that - acquaintances. The women in the park did not know that Jonathan and Charlotte were not my children. If some suspected, and perhaps gossiped, I was then even more determined not to give them the satisfaction of my admission. My closest friend, Sofia, offered kind support but had no first-hand knowledge.

My sister Catherine had seemed to manage her two births just fine, as did my mother. Mother was the person I truly wanted to speak to. But I could not ask these questions with a letter, or over the telephone in the landlord's apartment. And I could not visit. Not yet.

I went to the library.

I sought out the only woman librarian in all of the New Haven Public Library. I asked in the most discreet and polite voice for a book describing the process of childbirth. She replied, in her most indiscreet impolite voice, that her library did not have any books containing such vulgarity.

I took the children and left. But as I descended the marble steps, Constance's words stung me more than the librarian's rude ones. *Fight a war with anyone who tells you 'No.'* I spun around and the children lurched. I walked back into the library. I stood before the librarian. "I would like to point out to you that everyone that has ever lived, everyone you know, even saints such as yourself, was brought into this world by such vulgarity."

I turned and stomped out, head high and the children doing their best to keep pace with my steps.

On the next block was a doctor's office.

A woman doctor, unless of course a man had the unfortunate name of Dr. Sarah Howell, M.D., as declared on a small placard on the building.

"What is this place?" asked Jonathan, as I wandered through a dark hall, looking for the correct offices.

"A lady we are going to visit," I answered.

I found the room on the second floor. I knocked, and after a few moments, I heard footsteps, and the door opened. It was a young woman, as young as myself, with her hair cropped short.

"I am looking for Dr. Howell," I said, trying to seem less nervous than I felt.

"Come in," she said with a smile. "I am her niece and her assistant."

"I must be honest," I said. "I was passing by and saw your sign. I don't know of Dr. Howell - what type of medicine she practices. I have questions about childbirth and I have no one to ask."

The young woman smiled, and it was kind and genuine. "You have come to the right place. My aunt, Dr. Howell, is in general practice and has helped with many births. And she will be here any moment, with no conflict on her schedule. So take a seat."

I did and handed each child a book I had borrowed from the library before I alienated the librarian, and would most likely be banned forever. It was only two or three minutes before a well-dressed woman in hat and gloves arrived.

"You have a new patient, Doctor," explained the young woman.

"I can come back without the children," I offered.

"It's quite all right," the woman said. "Miss Howell will tend them while you and I have a chat in the next room."

"Plus I only have two dollars with me now, but I can pay you more next week," I said, thinking of my bank account, but also near to changing my mind about the wisdom of this impetuous visit.

"My charge today will be one dollar, because I think we will just talk and get to know each other."

I reluctantly followed her into the adjoining room, while the children seemed content to display their books to a new friendly adult.

I took a deep breath and started in. I did not have much to lose. She did not even know my name yet; so how badly could I embarrass myself?

"I am expecting a baby," I said, and she nodded. "The children with me are my stepchildren, and this is my first … um….time. I have no idea what to expect and I currently have no one to ask." I looked at my hands. "I am very afraid."

"I see," she said. "But that's quite normal. Are you afraid of the pain?"

"Yes!" I practically shouted with relief. "I am afraid I will not be able to bear it - or worse - that I might die."

"Very real fears," she consoled me. "You are not alone. And I will tell you that giving birth will hurt - there is much pain. But it is not unbearable pain. And when it is over, you feel quite well right away, because your own body wants you to heal quickly and be a good mother."

"Do many women die?" I asked.

"Many women used to die, but think about all the mothers you see now. Mothers do not die as they used to. Mainly because we are all much healthier than in days gone by. Centuries ago, women were malnourished and sick to begin with, so childbirth was very difficult."

"I am afraid to die because the children I have now have already lost their mother to influenza. They should not have me die as well."

"If you would like, I will help you when the time comes, and that may help prevent anything bad from happening."

"Yes, please!" I said, and I could not help it - I began to cry.

"Would you want me to examine you now, see how you are doing?" she asked.

"I do not want to interfere with your day. I am not on your schedule."

Dr. Howell laughed a bit and explained that she was still without many patients. She understood that it would take a while for people to accept a woman in the practice of medicine.

"That makes no sense!" I said. "How in the world would I expect a male doctor to tell me whether childbirth hurts?"

"Exactly right," she agreed.

She then guided me through a gentle examination. She found me to be in excellent health.

"I have strange feelings inside now and then. For the last two weeks. Like a bird is lightly flapping its wings around inside me. Is that a bad sign?"

"Not at all," Dr. Howell said. "It's a sign that your baby is healthy too. Babies move around inside you. They curl up and they stretch out. They kick their little feet."

"Oh my God! Really?" And I felt a bit foolish but there was no hiding the fact from this kind and experienced woman that I had no knowledge whatsoever of my pregnancy or anyone else's.

"And your little sensations also help me determine how far along in your pregnancy you are. I would estimate from the exam and the baby's movements that you might be having a baby in late Winter."

I knew that. But as honest as I had been with her, I could not bring myself to tell her that there was only one day so far in my life that I could have conceived. So I just thanked her.

"Why don't you come back to see me right after Christmas, and we'll see how you are doing? Jane can give you a day and time now, so you can plan on it. And perhaps find someone to watch your little ones? If you need to bring them, though, come anyway. It will be fine."

"My name is Lucinda Blaisdell," I said.

I was not going to tell Martin about my impromptu doctor's visit, but as soon as he came in from work that evening, the children began relating all about "Miss Jane and her magic necklace," and since I had no idea whatsoever what that meant, when he looked at me curiously, I told him I had felt a little weak on the way home from the library, and on impulse, stopped by at a nearby doctor's office.

He was immediately solicitous about my health, so I reassured him that the doctor said I was fine. That perhaps

I needed a bit more to eat that morning. When he asked me which doctor, I told him that her name was Sarah Howell, and he seemed taken aback that the doctor was a woman.

"I'm glad you sought help," he said, "but I'm not sure about that doctor. Catherine used a midwife, and you should have told me you were unwell. I would have brought you to see her right away."

"But if a woman could be a midwife, why couldn't she be a doctor?" I asked.

Martin ignored the question. "Just please tell me if you aren't well. I'll take care of you. I'm sorry that you felt the need to handle this yourself. I apologize."

Of course I had not even thought of a midwife, or asked Martin. It wasn't his fault at all, not that I could see. And somehow, I felt comforted. Not that Martin felt guilt, although I must admit there was a strange satisfaction in his remorse. It was Martin's reference to Catherine - the first time he had used her name without the depth of sorrow that had always made me feel like a trespasser.

"I'm healthy and the baby is healthy," I said. "Although I have no idea what the magic necklace could be."

CHAPTER 41

INEVITABLY, THE WEATHER GREW CHILLIER and we were upon the anniversary of Catherine's death.

Time had tempered Martin's grief, and he showed more affection towards me. At night, he occasionally wrapped his arms around me as we slept, my back up against his front. Beyond that, there was no attempt at intimacy. I had not thought to ask the doctor whether marital relations would be a danger during my confinement, but how would I have even thought of that, when the possibility had been so remote? I could always stop by Dr. Howell's office to understand any risk, although that would have required a bravery I did not think I could summon. But in any event, Martin never asked.

Catherine was buried in Springfield, and my parents had arranged for a mass to be offered in her memory. So

I put aside my hurt sensibilities and my father put aside his umbrage, and Martin and I took the children up to Massachusetts for the mass and graveside visit. We traveled on Friday and planned to stay through Sunday dinner, but Martin assured me that if I was disparaged for even a moment by my father, that he would pack us up and hire a car to take us immediately back to New Haven. His loyalty to me showed such decency as to instill in me some of the love I had felt for him as a child.

For in truth, over the long year, my love for Martin had not grown. Instead, my admiration for him had - and that was not the same thing.

The evening before we left for Springfield, I gave the children another little story of their mother after our bedtime prayers.

"Your first Mama, your Mama Catherine, could dance with the grace of the fairies," I said. "But oh, her singing voice! It was so dreadful. And she loved to sing so she didn't care a fig whether it sounded fine or not. She joined the church choir, and down in the pews, we could pick her voice out among the dozens of other children in the choir. Your grandmother would laugh - right during the service. Your grandfather would give her a stern look. One morning during Mass, your Mama Catherine was particularly terrible, and Grandmother could not suppress the giggles. And then we all started, me and Amelia, and even little Malcolm who was an infant. But not your grandfather! He frowned and scowled. 'Shush!' he said. And Grandmother said, 'That is our little frog croaking out her love for Baby Jesus.' And you know what Grandfather did? He let out one roar of a laugh and all the parish turned to look at him. And Grandmother said, 'Shush!'"

The children by the end of my story were rolling in Jonathan's bed, laughing and croaking like frogs themselves.

I turned to find Martin standing in the doorway. "I never heard that story," he said, "but I'm glad I heard it now. And I believe every word."

Later in our own bed, Martin asked me how often I talked to the children about their mother.

"Just once in a while. Perhaps once a week or so."

"What have you told them?" he asked.

"That Catherine was a champion marble player. That she could run very fast and often beat the boys. That she could read before she started school. How her hair curled in the warm weather. That she kept a kitten under the porch until the weather grew cold, and then informed my parents that she must keep it in her room until Spring - which she did. How her eyes were just like Jonathan's and her mouth like Charlotte's. That she liked to kiss their toes."

"Is it a good idea to keep reminding them? Maybe they should forget her and accept you as their only mother?"

"I'm not sure. I love them, Martin, and I want to be their mother. But I want them to know her too. I think their hearts are big enough to hold two mothers."

"Perhaps," he said.

"You seldom speak of her," I said.

His eyes grew dark. Angry even.

"Spare me," he said. "Spare yourself."

"Spare myself? From what? From what I see every day? From the hurt of knowing how much you loved her?"

"From the hurt of knowing how much I love her still!"

He rose from the bed and left the room. I heard him open the high cabinet that held the glasses. That held the whiskey.

And I fell asleep wondering if Martin's heart would ever be big enough to hold both wives.

We made it through the weekend in Springfield.

Mass and the visit to the gravesite were difficult but distant, like I was watching strangers through a November fog. Martin especially felt like a kind stranger, so polite and unfamiliar. I wondered if he was even aware of the people, the prayers, and the conversation around him. I thought perhaps it was Martin's strategy for surviving the next few days.

My father was stoic. He made no effort to reconcile, but neither did he criticize me further.

But it was all worth it, because I was able to spend time with my mother. Although the occasion was solemn, she was as overjoyed to see me as I was to see her. She was visibly relieved that I was healthy and the children were thriving.

Once all the commemorations were completed, Mother instructed Amelia that she should have charge of the children for the entire afternoon, so as to provide me with a respite. Amelia grumbled only just a little, to fill her required dose of complaining for the day, and led the children off to play. Mother told me that Amelia had dusted off her old dollhouse and that she had been secretly looking forward to playing with the children.

"She's near sixteen," Mother explained, "but that is an age when it is comforting to be a little child once in a while."

"She's more beautiful each time I see her," I commented.

"And more spoiled. Your father takes great pride in how Malcolm is doing at the yard; but Amelia is his darling. She will demand a husband who also treats her like a princess. A year ago I thought that would be impossible, but seeing how the young men swoon, it may be easier than I imagined to install Amelia in a castle."

"I am beginning to believe that women who demand more, get more. So perhaps Amelia is the smartest of us all."

"And how are your wishes, Lucinda? Are you seeing them fulfilled?" asked Mother as she brought me tea and honey.

And we talked. I told Mother all about our friendship with the Giamettis. I expressed concern over Frank's health, and she advised me to watch for signs that his recovery may be faltering, and worsening instead of improving. She had witnessed a similar condition with the neighbor's son on his return from the War. His improvement was so welcomed and applauded by all, that when his pain returned, he did not have the heart to inform anyone, and pretended for quite some time to be fine. He came to a tragic end, and Mother wondered if it could have been prevented had anyone discerned his suffering.

I found this information distressing, and Mother quickly added a reassurance that Frank's case sounded very different and his recovery was most likely on the horizon.

We discussed Sofia Giametti as well, that she was a sweet companion to me, and bestowed great love upon the children.

"In a way," said Mother, "You are both war brides. Making the best of your arranged marriages - and unlike Amelia, your expectations do not exceed your situation."

"Yes," I laughed, "Sofia and I are both doomed to reality."

And of course there was my coming baby. Mother reiterated her impression that I looked very well, and gave me some instruction as to how to let out my clothes temporarily. With Sofia being a seamstress, I thought that perhaps I might even be able to succeed, with her help. I confided to Mother that I had been consumed with worry, and had on impulse sought out a doctor. Mother was amazed but gratified that the doctor was a woman. I confessed that I had no knowledge of childbearing and had been embarrassed to ask. That when the baby moved inside me, I thought that something was terribly wrong, and that I might die. I described how kindly and efficiently Dr. Howell had reassured me.

"Oh my darling," cried my mother. "You will get through it all. I'm so sorry you had to have such worries all alone. But now you have a good friend and a good doctor. Don't keep your fears inside you. Let them out and then beat them with a stick!"

I checked in on the children who were still enthralled with Amelia's elaborate dollhouse.

"I'd like to go out for an hour or so," I told Amelia. "If you tire of the children, just put them down for a nap. They're overdue. Mother can help you."

"I can manage," said Amelia.

And the children did not even look up from their play to say goodbye, which was a good thing, I think.

I found Peter cleaning coal bins at the lumberyard. He was covered with soot, but whistling. He smiled when he saw me.

"I would hug you but you'd be dirty for a week," he said.

"That looks to be a very unpleasant job, Mister Dustbin."

"Oh, it's not so bad, because I have the place to myself. No one wants to help, and I like it that way."

I looked around. "Where are the horses?"

Peter wiped his brow, and surreptitiously his eyes, with the back of his dirty hand.

"Carthage died. Two weeks ago. I don't think I know of any horse living longer than that old fellow. But we haven't used the horses for months now. We've gone over entirely to trucks. Which leaves me cleaning coal bins, because I don't see well enough to drive on the streets. Your father would be a fool to let me loose in a motor vehicle."

"Which he is certainly not." I agreed. "So what happened to Zeke?" I was afraid of the answer, but Peter smiled.

179

"Ah, but that's the good news. Without Carthage as part of the team, Zeke hadn't much use. And he's practically as old as Carthage anyway. I found a farmer who took him to pasture."

"Really? What farmer would want one old retired wagon-puller?"

"Well, truth is... I'm paying for his board."

"Now that doesn't surprise me. You'd dress him up in a top hat if you could."

"Oh, but Zeke would look elegant in a topper! And there's more to this good deal. This farm - out in Longmeadow - it's splendid! And I'm going to work there. Your father really doesn't have work for me now that the horses are gone. So I'm going to get my farm after all!"

"You'll be owning it?" I asked, startled.

"Well, eventually. It's like this, Lucinda. There's this girl - Margaret. She's sweet and smart and has a bosom as big and soft as a goose feather pillow. I'm marrying her. Six months till the wedding - her father wants her to wait until she is twenty. And, well... it's her father's farm."

"That's wonderful, Peter. Do your brothers like her?"

"They do! And my father too. They're Polish, but Pop doesn't mind. They're Catholic and the Poles are very hard-working people."

"They are," I agreed.

"Just think. I am going to be farming with a good strong wife at my side. Why, she can pitch a bale of hay like a man!"

"I'm very happy for you Peter. And for Margaret too. You'll make a fine husband. She's lucky."

"Isn't it grand how sometimes Life works out?" said Peter.

"It is," I said.

CHAPTER 42

W E CELEBRATED CHRISTMAS AT HOME in New Haven.

My mother had invited us to Springfield, but now six months along, I had a good excuse to decline. In truth, I was feeling quite well during the day. I had no real complaints, but I was beginning to find it difficult to get a restful sleep. I was either uncomfortable with an aching back or uncomfortable because the baby inside me seemed to be most active at night. I would say to my expanding waist - *it is bedtime now,* so you must sleep - but this child had no concept of obedience. And on those rare occasions where my back and the child were quiet, my mind would pick that moment to consider all the tribulations of the world.

I took to napping when the children did, but even that was becoming more difficult, as Jonathan had seemed to outgrow his need for afternoon sleep.

"I just can't," he'd say. "My eyes keep opening up."

Some days when Jonathan's eyes kept opening up and mine kept closing, I would enlist Frank Giametti to help out. Jonathan was required to play quietly so as not to wake Charlotte, as she was disposed to whine and fuss without a good long nap. So Frank would sit with Jonathan in the kitchen and play with blocks or wooden animals, or read stories, while I slept a bit. As I was dozing, I could often hear Frank's descriptions of the ships that took him to and from the Great War or stories about his parent's hometown of Calabria, although he had never been there. His soft cadence in the background of my rest eased my mind.

Sofia - thank the Lord - gave me some cooking lessons, and I was able to take over more of the meal preparation. She was working long hours and often arrived home later than Martin did. So I had dinner waiting for all of us. We alternated between taking our meals in our apartment or the Giametti's. The benefit of going downstairs was the probability that Frank would pick up a violin or accordion or even a clarinet and bestow us with music as I cooked. The benefit to our dinners upstairs was the ease with which I could get the children into bed after dinner, and our adult conversation could continue. Either way, Sofia loved being able to read a bedtime story and make sure that prayers were said.

Jonathan and Charlotte took to calling them Zio Franco and Zia Sofia. I thought there was a very real possibility that the baby I was carrying would arrive with a clear understanding of Italian.

It was comfortable being one family.

The intimacy that seemed elusive to Martin and me when alone seemed within our grasp when we were all together. We smiled more. We laughed more. So we sought the company of our neighbors as a respite from being alone. It didn't matter what combination we made: Frank and Martin trying to fix a leaky faucet, Sofia and I baking bread, Frank and I talking about teaching and education - I learned that his ambition before the war had been to become a schoolteacher - or Sofia and Martin talking about life in Europe. I discovered only through Martin's conversation with Sofia that he had spent a year in Italy when he was studying engineering.

We spent Christmas Eve together. We included our landlords, Mr. and Mrs. Battle, when Sofia found out that their children and grandchildren were not coming for a visit, and that they had sat home without ceremony the previous Christmas.

We celebrated in the Italian tradition. The Battles were just happy to be included; they had no preference or disinclination for any type of holiday festivities. Their proclivity was only for wine, and they themselves supplied enough to last through New Year's Day.

Martin, having no brothers or sisters, admitted to being greatly indulged as a child, and mostly remembered the holiday as 'heaping stacks' of gifts, but no company or parties. And in my family, Christmas was spent mostly in prayer, which held no interest for me, to my father's dismay.

Although between the Benedict children and the scores of relatives, I still considered Christmas as a happy time with many festive visits and an abundance of hugging. But I couldn't think of any family tradition that I was heart-set on continuing, with the exception of decorating a fragrant tree - which, by the way, violated the terms of our lease, but considering that the landlords were grateful to be invited guests, they looked the other way at the small tree which stood in our kitchen.

So we went with the Italian tradition. Foremost, we had food! Our Christmas Eve table included more types of fish than I ever knew existed, and also eel and octopus, which I had no interest in trying. If there is any advantage whatsoever in being in the family way, it is the excuse to be as picky an eater as you would like. You say, 'Oh, I just cannot manage that' while you gently rub your belly. It also works for any physical labor or unpleasant conversation.

And there were fruits and pastas and delicious artichokes and eggplant - and panettone! I have resolved to never eat any other kind of bread.

After we had consumed as much as would perhaps set records not to be broken (until next Christmas), we carried our dishes to the sink, but re-set the table and left the remaining food, of which there was a startling amount. No cleaning up on Christmas Eve. The table was left for Joseph and Mary and the Baby Jesus, who were expected to come during the night. A lovely Italian tradition if you are not beset with mice.

We played Tombola, a numbers game on little cards. Sofia had provided prizes in the form of cookies made of fig and almond. Mr. Battle won nearly every game and was quite jolly from the winning and the wine.

Frank disappeared for several minutes, and returned with his violin. He played *Ave Maria* and *O Little Town of Bethlehem*, which we all sang. And then my favorite, *Hark The Herald Angels Sing,* which I love because it is rousing and you can go ahead and shout with joy at the end, which I did, even though I had abstained from the wine. Sofia chose *Silent Night,* which was perfect for her lovely voice, and surprised us by singing the verses, not only in Italian and English, but in the original German as well.

Then it was the children's turn. Sofia and Frank had taught them all the words to *Tu Scendi Dalle Stelle,* which Sofia had sung to them so many months before. They were well-practiced - which must have happened during my recent habit of afternoon napping. By this time, the children were dressed in their new white flannel nightdresses, and they looked and sounded like cherubs. Mrs. Battle let her tears run unchecked down her rosy cheeks.

"When the Missus starts the waterworks, it's our time to head home," Mr. Battle laughed. So they made their goodbyes, with kisses all around and Christmas wishes. Martin and Frank assisted the wine-afflicted couple down the stairs, while Sofia and I put the children to bed.

When the men returned, we played more Tombola and the gifts were kisses on the cheeks, with the losers kissing the winner each time, which caused us to become very silly no matter what the outcome. In any other circumstance this would have been shockingly inappropriate, and so it gave me great pleasure to imagine my father joining in.

Frank picked up the violin, but dispensed with the Christmas carols. He played songs we could all sing, like *Mary's A Grand Old Name* and *Bicycle Built for Two* and *My Wild Irish Rose*. Martin sang *Let Me Call You Sweetheart* both with the correct lyrics and a version that was so risqué that even Frank was blushing.

Frank struck up *And The Band Played On*. He pushed back the furniture and demanded that there should be dancing. I patted my stomach and demurred, and instead encouraged Martin to dance with Sofia. And they did. They were so lovely, my heart ached. I had never seen Martin dance. There was a lightness to his movement that I had never witnessed. Sofia closed her eyes and let herself be carried away. A Viennese waltz followed. It was more breathtaking than the first, if that were possible. As the waltz finished, Martin led Sofia back to her chair, bowed and kissed her hand.

The clock struck the hour. It was midnight, and it was Christmas. We hugged and kissed and wished each other Happy Christmas. Sofia said to Frank that they should run and catch at least a bit of midnight mass. And they hurried away.

Martin and I looked at the dirty dishes piled in the sink, and the plates of untouched food on the table. "Let's put what we can in the icebox," I suggested. "We can leave some of it out - the food that will keep. Everything else, out on the fire escape. If the animals eat it, well then God bless them."

"Absolutely," said Martin. "The animals need their feast on Christmas Day."

"I would ask the animals to wash the dishes, but those pigeons are so careless."

So we did the minimum cleaning and tumbled into bed. The children slept, including my little unborn, until the sun was well up and it was past eight.

Charlotte and Jonathan woke up shouting "Santa Claus, Santa Claus" - and sure enough, Santa had made a visit to the third floor of 30 Pearl Street. They had oranges and walnuts and chocolate candies in their stockings. And there was a doll for Charlotte with eyes that opened and closed. She hugged the doll to her breast and said, "My Amelia." And for Jonny, we found a tin car that looked very much like his grandfather's Oldsmobile.

We washed up and fed the children and hurried off to St. Mary's. The service was glorious, and the choir sang with exuberance. So many Alleluias! Jonathan got the giggles remembering the story of his mother singing in the choir and sang out, "Croak, croak, croak!" When the people in the pew before us turned around, I whispered, "Lord, Lord, Lord" and hoped for the best.

Back at home, Sofia had dinner ready. A marvelous ham with yams and apricots and snap peas. "An American Christmas dinner," she proclaimed. American or not, it was quite delicious, and even fussy Charlotte had a second plate. And then dessert! Sofia presented a very large, very fancy cake.

"American chocolate cake!" she declared. "Your favorite, Martin," she added.

"So it is," Martin agreed.

I was not sure whether Martin was being polite or if she had over the months of our friendship discovered a little fact from Martin that I did not know. Of course, I had never asked.

We had another round of gift-giving. The children were first, and Frank had made each child a most ingenious xylophone, with little tin discs fastened to a wooden frame and wooden sticks with rubber ends to tap the xylophone. The sound was pure - and thankfully soft. Frank quickly showed them *Twinkle Twinkle Little Star.* They repeated the first line over and over which was as far as their memory would go on this day. After two hundred repetitions or so, we declared it was time for their nap, and laid them down in the Giamettis' spare bedroom.

We poured coffee and exchanged our gifts to each other. Frank and Sofia gave us books. A lovely picture book of Italy for Martin, and for me, a book about Miss Helen Keller and Miss Annie Sullivan, her teacher. I could not have been more pleased. We gave Frank a fine pair of leather gloves - "to protect those talented fingers," said Martin. For Sofia, I had found a beautiful scarf in lavender trimmed with black fringe that I knew would flatter her delicate complexion. She threw it around her shoulders and the effect was startling - she was a glowing Madonna.

How fortunate we were to have such grand friends. That my parents and my siblings were not part of our celebration was sad, but I knew we would make amends eventually. They were family. That would keep.

"I love you both!" I cried as we said our goodbyes and carried the sleeping children back upstairs. It was all I could handle to carry three-year-old Charlotte, I had to stop halfway up the flight while Martin took Jonny to his bed, so he could return to take the little girl from me. There was no doubt she was getting bigger and I was getting clumsier.

"You must be exhausted," said Martin, as we finally got the children tucked in - in their holiday clothes, as I hadn't the heart to wake them.

"I am, but happy too. We've had a nice holiday."

"We still have gifts to exchange for each other," said Martin. "Are you too tired?"

"Too tired for presents? Is there any such thing?"

So we sat at the kitchen table and each opened another gift.

I had found for Martin a new shaving set. His was so worn the bristles fell out of the brush faster than leaves in the fall. The new set had a sleek razor crafted in Spain, a soft full brush with an ebony handle, and a sharpening strap of exotic leather.

"There could not be a finer set," he exclaimed. "And no better gift than one that is useful and beautiful as well." He kissed my cheek.

"And this is for you, Lucinda," he said, handing me a small package wrapped in delicate silver paper.

It was a music box. A square box of five inches, with an inlaid design of a sparrow in jade and mother-of-pearl.

I opened the box and heard the sweet melancholy notes of *Fur Elise*.

"Oh, this is lovely. A lovely box and a lovely song."

"I wish there was a song called *For Lucinda* but Elise is close. Elizabeth and Lucy are from the same root, I think."

"I believe you are right," I said, although I knew it was not true. The gift was truly intended for me. That made it the same.

"I'm so happy that you like it," said Martin. "I had no idea what to give you. I am so grateful to Frank. He found this and brought me to the shop to show me. He knew it would be perfect."

"It is," I said, although I knew it was no longer true.

CHAPTER 43

I N January the children broke a lamp. It was nothing much, except as an indication that things were getting a little crowded in the parlor. We still had the settee pushed into a corner, plus Jonathan's bed and Charlotte's crib, which she was outgrowing quickly. Climbing out was how the lamp was broken. And having our books in the kitchen was also a bad idea. I had already paid the library more than $1.00 for books that had "drowned" or "cooked."

The lamp upset Martin much more than I. He was feeling oppressed by the cramped quarters and began to speak of moving. We had not saved enough yet for a house, so it would mean moving to a larger apartment.

But I couldn't bear the thought of moving away from Frank and Sofia. Even the funny old Mr. and Mrs. Battle had become dear to me. And though I was not in close friendships with our other neighbors, I enjoyed exchanging pleasantries and hearing about their days. Pearl Street was home to me now, though I had lived here just a year.

I remembered what Constance had said about knowing what you want and standing firm.

I was about to give it a try.

We had dinner on a Thursday night with Frank and Sofia. We ate corned beef and boiled potatoes and carrots. The kitchen was aromatic and steamy from all the boiling I had done, but that just made it cozier. We had our coffee, and I made it particularly strong. I wanted to add whiskey but now that Prohibition was the order of the day, we kept what little we had, and saved our liquor for special occasions. In any event, I was now seven months along, and though I wished for a brace for my nerves, I had to make due with a large mug of black coffee. I stirred in a generous spoon of sugar, although I usually did not sweeten my coffee.

"I have a serious proposition to make," I announced.

"Oh really?" laughed Martin, believing I was joking.

"Yes, really. Please listen."

All stopped from their drinks and their conversation and turned to me.

"Our apartment is too small. Martin feels we should move," I said. Sofia and Frank shook their heads.

"Oh no!" cried Sofia. "You cannot leave us!"

"I agree," I said. "But there is a solution. You have had no luck in almost a year with renting your bedroom. It is still empty and your full rent is high. I know you work long hours, Sofia, in order to make ends meet. And Frank works on his instruments even when he is unwell. So here is the solution. We switch. Martin and I and the children will move into your apartment and you come up here and live in this one. Why we will hardly know the difference - we all spend our days in both places anyway."

Frank and Martin regarded each other. Sofia was already jumping up and crying.

"Oh let's do it! Please let's do it."

Martin frowned. "I'm not sure," he said.

"Why ever not?" I asked.

"Well, for one thing, it would be Mr. Battle's decision."

Sofia turned to him. "Mr. Battle knows we are both good tenants. He would not want to lose us. Besides, he likes me very much. I know he would miss my backside when he watches me climb the staircase."

"My God, Sofia!" said Frank, although he could not stay serious and started to laugh.

And we all began to roar.

"Two flights now!" I said to Sofia, although I do not know where I found the nerve to be so audacious. "He will be in heaven!"

And it was decided. A singular occasion. The women decided.

As Sofia predicted, Mr. Battle agreed. She was our emissary, explaining that they needed a less expensive rent, and that we needed larger living quarters. As soon as the new leases were signed - which happened within three days, we moved. By the following Sunday we had made multiple trips up and down the stairs.

Frank and I did not exactly pull our weight. He was in a bad way again with severe headaches, and I was too awkward to be of much use. So the majority of the work fell to Martin and Sofia, but they stayed in good spirits, laughing at their own awkwardness as they lugged bedding and chairs back and forth.

"You know," said Martin, "Maybe we should have just exchanged furniture as well as apartments and just carried along our clothing."

"Maybe we should have exchanged clothing too," said Sofia.

In the end, they left the extra bed in the Giamettis' spare room, as Charlotte could use it. And although they moved the chairs, they left the kitchen tables as they were. Neither of us had any particular attachment to the tables, and in any event, they didn't really match any of the chairs anyway, and we ate together most of the time. So it was settled.

I was responsible for clothing. The simplest way in my condition was to carry a small basket of clothes on each trip. The stairs grew much and I made a game of having Jonathan lower the basket down on a rope. He found this enormously entertaining, and filled the basket with our clothes to bring down, and on my end, I replaced those clothes with the Giamettis' and Jonathan hoisted it back up. Charlotte became jealous so we let her fill the baskets with her playthings and take a turn letting down the haul.

That night, in our old bed in our new bedroom, the baby inside me was restless from all the activity. The little soul kicked and kicked.

I took Martin's hand and placed it on my abdomen.

"Do you want to feel your baby dancing the jig?" I asked playfully.

He took his hand away. Silence.

I rose on my elbow and faced him.

"This baby, that is your baby and my baby, no matter how you feel... this baby had nothing to do with whether or not you believe we have sinned."

"I know. I'm sorry," he said.

He cautiously placed his hand on my round body. But the baby would not kick.

I sighed and rolled to my side, my back turned to my husband.

CHAPTER 44

M Y VISIT TO DR. SARAH Howell went well. She thought I was in fine form and the baby would arrive in late February. She remarked on how much more comfortable I seemed, how less anxious.

"I think I am just getting used to it," I said.

"That happens. And it's a good thing."

She warned me that from this point I should have absolutely no more alcohol. "Of course, with the new law, none of us drink anymore anyway," she said with a wink. Which is very much how everyone in the country was feeling, that I could see. She told me that I should not take any long trips, and I told her my parents lived in Massachusetts. She told me "Let them come to you," which was marvelous advice for a number of reasons.

She described what it feels like when the water breaks and I begin labor. It sounded awful, but she assured me it was not. She had her niece give me a card with two telephone numbers. "When all this happens, you have someone call up these numbers, and I will come. You will be just fine, but I'll come and make sure. Won't that feel good?" she asked. I nodded agreement, though with some skepticism.

"If anything - anything - does not feel right to you, then you go directly to the hospital and I will meet you there. If you must go, try to get to New Haven Hospital where the Yale medical students train. They recognize my practice there. Other hospitals ... well, it is more difficult for them to acknowledge a female physician. So New Haven, all right?"

"Yes, I understand. But how would I know if something is not right? I have no experience in this matter."

"Because you have a keen mind, Lucinda Blaisdell. Trust your judgment."

I had not brought Jonathan and Charlotte with me, and she asked after them. I said they were staying with a beloved friend for the afternoon, as Frank was feeling a little better and he was minding them for me.

"Sometime in February," said Dr. Howell. "Maybe six weeks. Perhaps just five. And there will another Blaisdell in the world. Get ready."

"How in the world do I do that?" I asked.

"Oh you cannot," she laughed. "So get ready to be surprised."

197

On Saturday, Sofia brought me some sweet infant clothing that she had made. She had knitted little caps and sweaters, and sewn beautiful gowns with embroidered hems.

I sat with my tea and the gifts in my lap, and I wept.

"Oh don't cry. You need at least a start."

"There are a few boxes in the cellar that Catherine stored away. I have been meaning to go down there and see what there is that may still be serviceable. But it's so difficult. I think of her folding all those little things in anticipation of her own next baby."

She patted my hand. "Let's bring the children up to Frank. Then I'll go with you. We will look together."

But when in the cold cellar and we opened the first box, it was Sofia who began to cry.

"So many pretty things. Like a little prince, your Jonathan was. And here I am, barren as an old woman. I'll never dress a child in such beautiful clothes."

"Oh Sofia," I cried. "I'm so sorry. We'll stop. We'll go back upstairs."

She made no move to leave. Instead, she sat on the hobby horse. Her frame was so small, she looked quite perfect on the little horse. She began to rock slowly. I sat by her on a trunk.

"It's not your fault, Lucinda. I'm just sad today," she said after a time.

"Maybe you will still have a child. It's not too late."

She shook her head. "I don't think so. There seems to be nothing inside me. I tried so hard - everything that all the women in Calabria used to do. And now Frank is so very sick."

"He looks to be getting better every day."

"No. I don't know. ... maybe."

We sat for a while, Sofia with her thoughts, and me, trying to imagine what her life has been.

"What was it like back in Italy?" I asked. "Do you miss it?"

"I miss some things," she said. "In my town in Calabria, it is very beautiful. And not so cold in the winter. It is very poor, however. Strange, though... even the poorest people in my village have chickens, have a garden. I am not so poor here as I was in Calabria, but where is my garden?"

"It's the hard part about living in the city." I took her hand. "Do you know?... I have a friend back in Springfield. He always wanted a garden. And now he has a whole farm! Sometimes you get your wishes."

"Oh, how fortunate. I would like to see that farm someday."

"I will go with you. We will pick beans and tomatoes and peppers and you can cook us something wonderful."

She smiled a bit at last.

"Why did you want to come to America and marry Frank?" I asked.

"Want? What is want? My father and his father decided."

"You had no say?"

"Did you?" she asked, giving me a hard look.

"In a way. I could have refused. But I chose to do it."

"Ah yes. To choose. I suppose I could also have refused. But back home... if I had refused, then no one would ever marry me. No husband. And no friends either. Not in Calabria. Not in all of Italy, I think. To disobey your father!"

She rocked a little more on the painted horse.

"But it is not so bad. Frank is a nice man. He is kind to me."

"That's true," I agreed. I thought to myself, Martin is as well. But is that enough?

"I had a sweetheart back in Calabria," she said, surprising me greatly.

"Oh Sofie dear! Did he wish to marry you? Did you wish to marry him?"

"Oh yes! We were very much in love. He was older than I - a widower. So it was like your Martin."

Not if being in love was the measurement, I thought.

Sofia continued. "Ernesto was a fine man. He was not handsome the way that Frank is, but he was handsome to me. But Ernesto and my father were enemies. They had argued many years before over some small thing, some silly game. Even when Ernesto's wife died - in childbirth - why do children mark our lives so? - my father would not go to the church to pay his respects. And then when I became a woman and Ernesto admired me, my father would not hear of it. Ernesto was willing to forgive - had forgiven, but not my Papa. And Ernesto would have been a fine match, even though he was near my father's age. He was strong and healthy. And not poor."

"Do you know what became of him?"

She laughed. It felt so good to hear her regain her natural good spirits.

"He married a stout widow with four lazy children! Poor Ernesto!"

And we went back upstairs to relieve poor Frank of his burden of minding two active children. Sofia insisted we take the box we had opened. "Such nice things," she said, "I'll wash them for you and they will be perfect."

CHAPTER 45

I WAS SO LARGE BY FEBRUARY I could hardly walk without swaying from side to side like the elephant we had seen in the zoo. The children thought it uproariously funny.

"Mama, you dance a big waltz when you make dinner!" said Jonathan.

We had a bit of a thaw at the beginning of the month, and the warm sun beckoned me. I got the children into their coats and we made our way - slowly - to the park.

I had hoped that Constance would be there, and was gratified to see her sitting on our bench while Sadie tried unsuccessfully to jump rope.

"I fear my Sadie will never run away and join the circus!" she called as she saw me approach.

"I've missed you so!" I said, giving Constance a kiss. "The hardest part of winter is the isolation."

It is a strange but true phenomenon that the first thing you do when reunited with a friend is to sit companionably in silence. Catching up on the news can be saved for later. First, you simply want to feel their presence and take in the comforting sight of a loved one at your side.

And so we sat for the better part of an hour, happily silent except for the occasional admonition or encouragement to our children.

"Well, I do have a small bit of news," she said at last. And she removed her knitted cloche to reveal that she had bobbed her hair.

"Oh Constance!" I said. "That is astounding! You look like a Hollywood screen star! And it is no surprise to me that you would be the first of my acquaintances to chop off her hair!"

"I feel ever so glamorous," she said, giving her head a shake. "And you would never believe how much more comfortable it is for sleeping."

"Does your husband fancy it?"

"Him? Oh dear, not at first. But now, he is finding it a bit of a novelty. He likes to show me off as his modern woman."

This struck me as a bit odd. I had the strong impression that Constance's spouse was a Bolshevik. Were not all Bolsheviks' spouses modern women? The number of incongruities in life seemed to only increase as one grew older. There never seemed to be any resolutions, just inconsistencies abiding side by side.

"I could cut yours for you too," Constance volunteered.

"Oh no, I couldn't do it! I am not so brave as you!"

"Well, you are beautiful just as you are," said Constance. "But if you change your mind, let me know. It will be such grand fun to turn you into a different woman."

I demurred, but a small piece of me thought it might not be such a terrible idea to change my appearance. Perhaps Martin would also like a modern woman. One who did not look so much like his dead wife.

CHAPTER 46

A S WAS BOUND TO HAPPEN, the baby arrived at the worst possible time.

I felt uneasy all day Sunday. Uncomfortable and restless. I felt the need to wash the floor and take down the bedroom curtains and rinse them out. They didn't dry, of course; the day was cold and threatening snow. But I ironed the curtains damp and re-hung them, standing on a chair that would be a precarious perch even had I not been nine months with child. I was oblivious to how foolhardy I was being, and Martin, who had been out with Frank - I believe looking to buy some bootleg gin - walked in on me just as I was trying to climb down from the chair. The children were holding my skirt in an effort to give me some balance, which I told them was helping, but was certainly doing no such thing.

Martin and Frank entered, startling me, and I almost fell.

"What in hell are you doing?" Martin yelled, and given that he almost never cursed, I felt both ashamed of myself and defiant.

"I'm working," I replied. "It's what I do. Wash things. Floors, curtains, beds, dishes, children. I would wash an airplane if we had one."

The children giggled.

"You are foolish," said Martin, but I could see Frank was trying not to laugh.

"Let me help you down," offered Frank. He reached up and picked me up and set me on the floor. I was surprised at how easily he lifted me. He sometimes seemed so frail, but there was a core of strength that reminded me that he had been a soldier, and was still a man. I cannot describe how nice it felt to have his hands on my hips, no matter how big and awkward those hips were now.

"I'm sorry," I said, "but I am overwhelmed with the need to do everything at once today. I feel thunderstruck by the idea that I will soon have three children and may never get anything done again."

"I am quite sure you will have everything under control. There seems to be nothing you can't do or a problem you can't solve," Martin remarked.

"Why thank you, but something tells me that it is perhaps not a compliment?"

Martin softened. "Please just try to rest for a bit. I'll even take the children, since I fear they will be up on chairs dusting the ceilings at any moment."

And I agreed, and laid down on the bed, while he took the children by the hand with promises of bread and butter.

I slept. And in my dreams I beat the carpets and polished the silver, although it was my mother's silver, and I was doing a very poor job. My father stood behind me and scolded me for all the tarnish I was leaving behind.

I learned later that it is quite common for a woman to tear about the house just before the baby comes. It is called nesting, although I do not believe that the kind of destruction I was engaged in could be considered building a nest.

I slept until dinner, when Martin sent the children in to wake me. It was already dark. I had prepared a stew the day before, and Martin had already set it on the stove to warm. The children and Martin had good appetites that evening, as did Sofia and Frank, who joined us after we sent Jonathan to knock on their door. After sleeping for hours, I found myself still tired but agitated at the same time. I took some tea, but could not eat. I began to wash dishes while everyone was still at the table.

"Please sit," begged Frank. "You are making us all very nervous. You don't need to do the washing up. Sofia can do it later." Sofia rolled her eyes at me. The men were always solicitous about our labor, but rarely offered to help.

"If you don't want this stew - which is excellent, by the way - I can get you something else to eat," offered Sofia. "What would you like?"

"Eggs. I would like some eggs," I said, only realizing when I said it that it was true.

So Sofia cooked me two eggs, and put some potatoes from the stew into the skillet, and got them browned and sweet from the tablespoon of lard with which she had oiled the pan.

"Why is it, Sofia, that your eggs taste better than my stew?" I let the children take a bite, and they demanded an egg for themselves too, and although Martin told them they had already had a full dinner, they protested that they were still hungry, and he relented and asked Sofia if she would mind terribly cooking an egg for each child. She readily agreed, and Martin added, "And one for me." Frank piped up, "And for me." Sofia in her good-natured manner, cooked eggs and fried potatoes for all.

We ended up with a good stack of dishes and bowls and pots and pans. Sofia insisted on finishing the washing that I had not completed, but I stood by her side to help wipe the dishes dry. After two minutes, Frank pulled up a chair and had me sit to dry. Sofia and I then began an exchanged of giggles that we could not suppress.

"Oh, our men are such a help - getting you a chair like that!" said Sofia. And we burst into laughter all over again.

The Giamettis didn't linger after the cleaning up was finished. They could see that I was tired, and both Sofia and my Martin needed to be up before dawn on Monday morning.

Sofia put the children to bed for me, and the couple said their goodbyes. "It is lucky we only have to travel upstairs," said Frank. "For it is snowing again."

Late at night, after Martin was asleep, I went into the bathroom and was sick. I didn't wake Martin, but quietly got back into bed. He mumbled something, and I responded that I had gone to check on the children.

About three in the morning, I woke with the realization that the baby was coming. As soon as I rose from bed, I felt my water break. Thanks to Dr. Howell, I understood what had happened. She had told me that the contractions might come first, but I did not think I had had any contractions during the day, unless I had misunderstood what my discomfort had been signaling.

I quietly cleaned the mess. I went to the kitchen and watched the clock, waiting for the pains. I felt all right, really. Dr. Howell told me that these things could take a long time. About forty minutes later I was sure.

I woke Martin.

"I don't think there is any need to hurry," I said. "But I think I will be having a baby before the day is out."

He dressed. It was near five in the morning. My pains were not yet quickening, so I put the kettle on for tea.

"Are you sure that you should have that?" Martin asked. I reassured him that it was fine, and he shook his head in the manner that had come to signal to me that he was trying to remember something. "I've been through this twice before," he said, "but I recall almost nothing. I must have been too young or too frightened."

I smiled. "Too young? I am younger now than you were then. Younger than Catherine was. And I am a little frightened, but not too much."

When the sun came up, I felt I had progressed enough to telephone Dr. Howell, as she had instructed. There was a heavy layer of snow, and although her office was not far from Pearl Street, I had no idea whether she would be there or where she lived if she was still at home. The card that her niece had given me had two numbers. I hope she would answer one of them.

We still did not have a telephone, so that meant waking Mr. and Mrs. Battle. First though, Martin ran upstairs and got Sofia. We were lucky to catch her, as she was just leaving for work. She had arranged with her boss to be excused from work on the day I delivered, so that she could tend to the children. We had been hoping against hope that it would be a Saturday or Sunday, since she did not work then. I felt bad that she would miss a day's pay for me. And Monday, of all days, was the busiest at the factory, because that is when the orders for the week were scheduled and delegated to the seamstresses. She assisted in that process and would be missed. But she came right downstairs and kissed me and told me that she would just run out and tell the women she walked to work with that today is the day, and she would not be in.

The children were up by this time, and I was still well enough to get them dressed and fed.

Martin then went down and pounded on the Battles' door. I could hear him from our kitchen crying, "The baby is coming! I need to ring the doctor!"

He was gone for quite a while, and so I filled that time with the certainty that Dr. Howell had died, or left town, or was seeing to another childbirth, or did not remember who I was, or her niece revealed that Dr. Howell was not really a doctor at all, but some escaped patient from a lunatic asylum, and so one could say that I waited quite patiently.

Upon Martin's return, he told me that Dr. Howell had not yet been in the office, but the clerk at the central exchange rang up the additional number that the doctor had given me, which turned out to be her home, just upstairs from her medical practice. Dr. Howell said that we should not worry, there was plenty of time and she was on her way. I was relieved that she lived right over her office since the walk would not be too long. Although Dr. Howell had said not to worry, and I had said to Martin that I was not afraid, in actuality, I was overwrought with fright and wanted her standing before me with her calm demeanor.

Certainly, I was not going to be reassured by Sofia. She was very nearly apoplectic herself, although with less fear and more joy. "The baby! The baby! Il bambino!" she repeated over and over, until the children were also shouting about the bambino.

Martin went back to the Battles, as he had forgotten to inform his own employer. I think perhaps he would have rather been at work than witness a childbirth, but he seemed determined to endure it. I am not sure what the situation had been with Catherine's children. Martin told me that she used a midwife, so I am sure she did not go to the hospital. But so many women did today. I hoped I had not made a terrible mistake. As Catherine had described it, hers were very easy births. I hoped we had that in common.

Although the snow had tapered off, and the sky even showed a weak sun, the streets were all but impassable. I hoped that Dr. Howell had decided to walk here. No automobile would make it through for hours. And it had been so long already.

I stayed in my kitchen, sipping tea and trying not to squirm in my chair when the pains built and then ebbed like the tide I had seen in New Haven harbor. Finally, Mrs. Battle knocked on our door. She had Dr. Howell with her.

"The midwife is here," said Mrs. Battle.

"The doctor," I corrected.

"Yes, so she says," replied the old woman, rolling her eyes at the doctor.

"So hello, Mrs. Blaisdell. I am told today is the big day! How are you right this minute?" said Dr. Howell, walking past Mrs. Battle and so dismissing her efficiently.

I sighed. "I think I am well. I have pains, not very close but not very far. And they are worse than they were a few hours ago, but not so bad, I don't believe."

"Time for you to take to your bed," she said, "so I can see for myself. Although I would say, you do look quite wonderful."

As she was settling me into the bed, she asked, "And where is your husband?"

"He is in the parlor with our friend Frank, I do believe he is afraid to come out."

"That is a wise decision, no doubt. And your children?"

"Frank's wife Sofia has taken them upstairs to her apartment."

"All good," she nodded.

I whispered to her, "Doctor, I am so frightened I think I may collapse with fear. I am just pretending to be fine."

She smiled. "Pretense is an admirable scheme when you are afraid. It tricks the mind - and the body - into calming down. I believe that all of bravery is rooted in pretense."

I thought about this and decided that later on I would ask Frank if this was true in war too.

My labor progressed slowly. The doctor was so much more patient than I. When I expressed that I needed to hurry this up, she explained - in terms that were probably not medically accurate, but that I could readily understand, even with my brain consumed by waiting for the next sharp pain to come:

"Your body right now is remaking a good piece of itself. It is what is called dilating. The exit of your womb and what the sensitive call your "delicate area," but which we of stouter heart shall call your vagina, those parts of your body are right now making themselves large enough for a baby to come through. Of course, your baby doesn't really want to wait any more than you do, and is determined to push its way out. And that hurts a great deal until you are ready. So the best thing you can do is be patient and bear it for as long as you can."

So we waited. I asked her why she had become a doctor.

"Oh my brother wanted to be a doctor, and I wanted to do everything he did, only better, which to tell you the truth was not that difficult. But it turns out that getting accepted into a medical school was very difficult. That made me want it even more badly. I truly believed that I was going just to prove to my father that I was as smart as Matthew. But a funny thing happened. I loved it. Women are supposed to be too delicate to handle the coarseness of the human body. But we aren't delicate, are we?"

She uttered that last sentence just as I was screaming out some extremely coarse words. She laughed with her head thrown back. Like Catherine used to. I think that is when I saw this doctor as a real woman. An educated woman who would be my friend in a different circumstance.

The pains were coming quite close together now.

I said, "Before I lose all my ability for rational thought - which perhaps is just seconds away - I need to ask you something else. Our dear friend Frank is very ill. He was gassed in the war, and although it was considered a mild case at the time, the effects now are very bad. He needs to see a doctor who is educated in the illness brought on by the mustard gas."

She said that she would see what she could do.

"I think you are an accomplished doctor," I said. I waited for the next stab to pass. "And I would never want to offend you, but as much as I love Frank, I am not sure he would be quite ready for an examination by a female."

"Understood," she said. "I know of a doctor - a man for your manly friend Frank - who is in Bridgeport, and he has studied extensively the aftereffects and complications that many soldiers are experiencing due to their exposure to the poison gasses. I will put you in touch with him. But later, because right now you have a baby about to be born."

And ten minutes later, at 3:06 in the afternoon of the twenty-third of February in 1920, my daughter came into the world.

She was so tiny, but Dr. Howell assured me she was the perfect size for a newborn. She had dark matted hair and a purple face all scrunched up. Her fingers and toes were the most delicate things I had ever seen. I was so unprepared that I was surprised when she came out attached to me by her little belly button.

"Oh, Lucinda, how do you think your baby got nourishment from you?" laughed Dr. Howell. "But now we separate you two, and for the very first time, she is her own little person." And with that, Dr. Howell laid the baby on my chest. It was beyond belief. Five pounds and a new and complete human being. She was no longer me. She was herself.

Dr. Howell instructed me in bringing the infant to my breast. I could nurse her as soon as I felt up to it. She assured me that although I wouldn't have real milk for a few days, my body was producing a type of nourishment that was exactly what a newborn would need.

"And she will need it often. Be prepared to be very tired. You have three children now - sleep whenever you can. But not right this minute, because you need to introduce this baby to her father."

Dr. Howell left the room, and returned with Martin.

"A girl," I said simply. "She is not so pretty, but I have hopes for her."

"She's lovely," said Martin. "You have done well. I hardly believe your strength." He touched the baby with two fingers only. His hand was so big compared to her tiny frame. He stroked her dark hair.

"I thought...perhaps... we could name her Catherine," he said.

I nearly agreed. I nearly said it was a fine idea. I nearly gave my consent to giving my child the name of a ghost - however beloved a ghost - who had haunted me for more than a year and who would haunt me all of my life. I nearly allowed the ghost to inhabit my daughter who was minutes old, my daughter who trusted me after only those few minutes to always protect her.

"No!" I cried. "I can't be Catherine no matter how hard I try. And I don't want this child to have to try. She is her own person! She is not Catherine!"

He took his hand from the baby. There were tears in his eyes.

"Oh, Lucinda. I'm so sorry. I don't want to hurt you. I'd never want to hurt you."

"I know you don't want to," I replied, and then added very softly, as Dr. Howell had returned and was standing in the doorway with Sofia and Frank, who had our children by the hand, "But you always do."

"Please, Lucinda, name this child whatever you wish, and I will love her as her own being."

"Come in, everyone!" I said. "Charlotte, Jonny... come here and meet your new little sister."

Sofia nudged them forward. They seemed a little frightened, the way they were in the park this fall when a small barking dog approached them. I tried very hard not to look the same way. Pretense. Thank God for it. "She won't bite you," I said. "Look, she's sleeping, I think."

"She's very pink," said Charlotte.

"She looks sticky," said Jonathan.

"Yes, she's both of those, but Dr. Howell says that this is how all new babies look. And that she will get prettier and prettier every minute."

"Pretty? Oh my, she takes my breath away!" cried Sofia.

"Come and sit on the bed and hold her," I said.

"For a minute only," said Dr. Howell to me, "because within that minute you will realize that you are past exhaustion."

Sofia sat beside me and I put the baby in her arms. She wept, but not the tears of grief and loss she shed down in the cellar a few weeks before. Her tears were those of pure joy.

"Her name is Annie Sullivan Blaisdell," I said.

Martin looked at me in surprise, but there was acceptance there.

"What a marvelous name," said Frank. "I love you, Lucinda, and I love you, Annie Sullivan Blaisdell."

"I love you, Annie Sullivan Blaisdell," said Sofia.

"I love you, Annie Suvvan," said Charlotte.

And around the room, each person in turn expressed their love for this small child, named for a woman who changed the world because she taught a child who changed the world.

CHAPTER 47

ANNIE WAS HUNGRY EVERY MOMENT of the day. The older children were jealous every moment of the day. I was bone-weary every moment of the day. How preposterous it now seemed that a year ago I had thought that minding two children had been difficult. Two children were so easy. Two children, who, when I was at the end of my fragile patience, I could occasionally hand to their father. Two children who slept at night and let me sleep.

If I had been unprepared for motherhood a year ago, I was completely unskilled and unsuitable for a newborn infant. It took an hour to nurse Annie, as she plodded along, half asleep, and half-heartedly suckling at my breast. When she finally gave up, exhausted, she slept poorly, and it seems like it was only minutes until she was hungry again. She wailed for hours on end. Normal, everyone agreed. Normal.

How do new mothers not throw themselves in front of a train?

I had two salvations. The first was Annie herself. I marveled at the very miracle of her existence. Fussy, yes. But she would stop in her ineffective attempts to nurse and regard me. *You are everything*, she would say with those round blue eyes. *You are my whole world.*

My second savior was Frank. Martin was working longer hours than ever. He told me with suppressed excitement that his project might change aviation. It was gratifying to see him optimistic about the future after grieving for so long - although I knew objectively that it had not really been so long. A year for the love of your life is a short span of mourning, after all. But nonetheless, it cheered me to see him show the possibility of happiness, and as a result, I was hesitant to demand more of him at home. He loved all his children, without a doubt, but he was a man whose identity was attached to his labor. I understood this. I had lived in my father's house for seventeen years, and worked by his side for five.

And Sofia. How she loved the children! And they responded to her. She allayed the fears that filled Charlotte in her new role as middle child. "*I want to be the baby*," Charlotte would cry, and it was Sofia who would tell her all about the marvelous privileges she had as big sister - though for the life of me, I could not see an advantage for poor Charlotte. But Sofia would give her special responsibilities, like setting the table, and it was a very good thing indeed our dishes were not priceless. Sofia also made several beautiful dresses for Charlotte, explaining to the little girl that the infant Annie could not be trusted to wear something so nice, as she was sure to spit up on the fine lace. And Sofia had ribbons for Charlotte's hair, and best of all, she made a sweet baby doll for Charlotte that resembled Annie, and when I fed Annie, Charlotte would put the doll to her breast and say *"Try harder, darling."*

But Sofia was also advancing at her work. At the undergarment factory, it didn't take them long to see what a talented seamstress Sofia was. And well-organized, and not afraid to take responsibility, which was very unusual in the immigrant women that they were inclined to hire, who were almost always reluctant to stand out. Sofia had received a significant promotion and increase in her wages, so financially the Giamettis were benefiting, but she worked hard, and returned home late and weary.

So it fell to Frank to save me. And he did.

He had no experience with children, other than the last few months with Charlotte and Jonathan. But he was so natural, so calm. He spoke quietly at all times. I never heard him raise his voice, and yet the children listened to him.

He came down to our apartment every morning about nine for just a half hour, so I could get myself washed and dressed. If Annie was fussy, which was often, he held her on his shoulder, performing some soft little dance to quiet her. At the same time, he supervised the older children's breakfast, serving them whatever I had left for him on the stove, oatmeal or eggs with potatoes. I usually made enough for him to eat as well, and he would stand at the stove, eating right out of the pan, with the baby on his shoulder.

I think I would have been in my nightdress until noon if he did not provide me with that half-hour.

Frank would go back to work repairing his instruments until mid-afternoon. Then he would reappear and give me another hour, and sometimes longer. I'd nurse Annie just before he arrived, and with luck, she would be asleep in her crib by my bed. Frank would put Charlotte down for her own nap, and then read or play some quiet game with Jonathan, who most days refused to nap. I had no such qualms. I slept.

I was usually awakened by the baby, or by the still-sleepy Charlotte crawling into my bed for a cuddle. And Jonathan of course, determined not to be left out.

Frank would lean in from the doorway, and smile at me and my brood. "See you later," he'd say, and take his leave.

He saved me. And the cost to him was significant, because he had not recovered from his injuries. His headaches had not diminished. Many days he was so ill, he could not eat or sleep. He would not return to his apartment to work on his violins. I found on one occasion when I went to hang laundry, that he had only made it up a few stairs, where he sat with his head in his hands, hoping for the pain to pass.

But he came. He never complained and never showed the children anything but his sweet genial demeanor. I never told Martin how ill Frank seemed. I knew that Martin would not trust Frank with the children. But I had no such worry. No matter how Frank may have suffered, I knew in my soul that he would never fail the children. So I slept.

Fortunately for myself and for poor Frank, and indeed, for everyone in the building not hard of hearing, Annie eventually left behind her colicky stage and grew more contented. By May, I was the mother of three happy children, and a woman who once in a while stayed awake through dinner.

Dr. Howell stopped by once to confirm that the baby was progressing well, and I suspect to determine whether or not I had collapsed from nervous exhaustion. Annie was already settling in when the doctor stopped by, and remarkably my dress was clean and my hair brushed, and so I believed I passed the inspection properly. She seemed to ignore the fact that Jonathan was barefoot and that I had dishes in the sink.

"It will be easier before you know it," said Dr. Howell. "Your little boy will perhaps be starting school in the fall?"

"Yes!" Jonathan shouted. "I am going to be five, and I will go to school. Mama is going with me."

This surprised me.

"No, sweetheart," I gently corrected, "you will go to school with the other children who are five. Mama will stay home with Charlotte and Annie."

"But you say all the time you want to go to school. You say so to Zio Frank. You can go to school with me."

Dr. Howell smiled at him and regarded me with a questioning look. "Children hear everything," she said. "And mostly they get it right."

"Not this time. School may have been in my future before I became a mother to three."

"You're very young. You will still be young when they are on their own."

"No mother of three is young."

She laughed. "Well, I do believe you have a point."

Dr. Howell's other mission was to bring me the name and address of a doctor who might be able to help Frank. Given the throes of childbirth, I hardly even remembered asking her, but she had not forgotten. The doctor's name was Leonard Crane, and he practiced in Bridgeport. He had spent the years since 1918 gathering information and studying the late effects of poison gas on the soldiers coming back from the Great War. He was especially interested, according to Dr. Howell, in the cases of soldiers whose original exposure was not considered severe, but were now suffering badly.

"Frank still has good days," I told her, "but he is not at all well lately. He has tried to hide it, but I see how difficult it is for him to disguise his pain."

"Get him to Dr. Crane as soon as you can," she advised.

I didn't wait. As soon as Dr. Howell had taken leave, I grabbed the baby and ran up the stairs, with the two other children following behind.

I knocked on the door, but entered before he could answer.

Frank was not in his usual chair in the kitchen. He was in bed, and although it was inappropriate for me to enter, I did so regardless. I sat gently on the bed. Charlotte and Jonathan stood near.

"Frank, dear," I said, "are you asleep?"

Frank opened his eyes and saw the children and winked at them.

"Now isn't that a silly question?" he asked. "If I were asleep, how would I ever answer?"

They giggled. "Very silly," said Charlotte.

I could see the strain on his face, and I loved him all the more for keeping it from the children.

"I have good news!" I said.

"Another baby?" asked Frank, and I laughed so hard the baby spit up a bit on my shoulder.

"No Frank, you will not have another child to tend anytime soon. Dr. Howell was just here and she knows of a good doctor who is treating soldiers like you."

"Italians?" he asked.

"Now who is being silly? Soldiers who were gassed and are still suffering. The doctor is in Bridgeport and I will use Mr. Battle's telephone to arrange a visit."

"I can't go to Bridgeport. It is too far."

"It is a short train ride."

"I cannot go. I can't do it alone and Sofia must go to her job."

"Sofia will make the time, and if she cannot, I will go with you myself. I'll take all the children if necessary. They love the train." I added, "But I'm sure Sofia will go."

He sat up and sat next to me. He was wearing his trousers but only an undershirt. I pretended not to notice. I pretended that it was fine that we should be sitting together on his bed. That we were so close I could detect the fine lines around his eyes, the warmth of his hand placed so near to mine.

"I don't want Sofia to know," he said. "Come with me, and we will not burden Sofia until we have some understanding of my health and what the doctor may be able to accomplish."

I didn't know how we could do this. Because, as Dr. Howell had just recounted, the children hear everything. And tell everything. How could I ever keep this a secret?

And yet I said, "Of course. I promise."

CHAPTER 48

I THOUGHT ABOUT THIS DILEMMA FOR three days. I wanted to call Dr. Crane immediately but I had to make sure I had a plan, so I needed to find a solution to the problem of accompanying Frank to Bridgeport without the children. It was bad enough that they had heard the discussion - a train ride and doctor's visit would be more secrets than their little heads could bear.

Mrs. Battle was too old, and perhaps not sober enough, to handle three children for more than an hour or so. Furthermore, she was more likely to reveal our visit than the children, as she discussed everyone with everyone else, usually to my delight.

I considered my mother. Annie was nearly two months old, and my mother had not seen her as yet. She was planning to come and visit in June, when I had planned a birthday celebration for Jonathan as well as a christening. I could ask her to come sooner. Jonathan would be jubilant that he could have his fifth birthday party a bit early.

But I could not. As much as my mother would love to see all the children, and would want to support me in my efforts to help Frank, she would not be able to condone keeping a secret from Martin. I gave serious consideration to confiding in Martin despite Frank's wishes. If I could tell Martin, we still may be able to keep Sofia uninvolved until we had some definite answers. I could stay home with the children and Martin could take Frank to Bridgeport.

I indirectly proposed the idea to Frank, asking him whether he would be more comfortable seeing the doctor with a man rather than with me. He was adamant that I should go with him.

"You have put this plan before me, and the only way for it to stay confidential is if goes no further than the two of us," he stated. "Besides," he added quietly, "I need you with me."

As a last resort, I turned to Constance. She believed that women were better decision-makers than men, and strong enough to handle any situation on our own. So three days after my visit from Dr. Howell, on a warm sunny day, I dressed the children for a romp in the park and put little Annie in the pram. Charlotte was distraught over giving up her coveted ride in the carriage. I coerced her with the promise of gelato, and she stifled her tears and walked alongside the carriage with Jonathan.

I was disappointed that Constance wasn't there. I bought Jonathan and Charlotte their ice cream and set them on the grass to eat it as neatly as was possible, which caused them to be extremely slow, and so their treats melted and both children were sticky, deplorable messes before long. I told myself that it was no tragedy; I could clean them up by dampening one of Annie's extra diapers in the fountain. But no use for that now. I would wait until they were thoroughly unrecognizable - and finished.

Annie was content - asleep in the shade in her pram. She had decided to be an angel lately, and for that, I was thankful.

"I guess I should buy Sadie a gelato too, but perhaps she could just lick Charlotte's dress," said Constance, coming up behind me.

"Oh, please, let her have a go," I said. "It will be ever so much more effective than my scrubbing."

Constance gave Sadie a nickel, "Go get your ice cream from the man right over there," she said to the little girl.

"I will go with you!" said Jonathan. "I know that man. And he will give you a fine treat for three cents!" And they ran off together, with Charlotte trailing behind, as usual. We watched Jonathan tell the vendor what Sadie wanted, as she shook her head vehemently "No!"

"He must have chosen the wrong flavor," said Constance. "Sadie knows exactly what she wants, and is never afraid to say so."

"Jonathan is used to ordering Charlotte around. She never defends herself, and she lets Jonathan decide everything."

"Charlotte will get along better in life than Sadie. But I'm still gratified that she is so headstrong. We need more fighting women." She peeked into the carriage. "And speaking of modern fighting women, let me see that baby!"

Constance reached in and picked up Annie. "You knew it was a girl!" I remarked.

"I saw you from the trees, when you picked her up earlier. I didn't think your Martin would let you dress a boy in so much lace."

"My friend Sofia made this dress. And she didn't know at the time whether it would be a girl. She believes all babies should be decked out in as much lace as possible."

"Well, your little one is perfect then." Constance gave her a kiss and the infant rewarded her with her new talent of a genuine smile. "Oh, she is definitely perfect."

"Her name is Annie Sullivan Blaisdell, and I'm so happy that you like her, since I came looking for you specifically to ask a very big favor."

"Ask away."

I told Constance about Frank and his illness, and about the doctor in Bridgeport. I told her honestly of Frank's wish to hide his appointment from his wife, not wishing to alarm her, and how Frank had been so good to me and the children despite his condition.

"I could go with him to Bridgeport, but I need someone to watch the children," I explained.

"Done," she said immediately.

"Three is difficult. I cannot even explain how difficult. But I can pay for a nurse or a servant who can help you that day."

Constance continued to play with Annie, turning her this way and that, making the lacy dress spin, while Annie minded not in the least. "Next week is Sadie's birthday. A five-year-old, can you imagine? She and Jonathan will go to school together and it will be so much fun bringing them to school in the morning, and much more fun for us once they are gone for hours at a stretch! Heavenly freedom! But anyway, if you can schedule Frank's visit someday next week, I will have a birthday party the same day. I will invite some of the other mothers and children I know, plus we can hire a girl if we need to, so there will be plenty of adults to watch the children. And Charlotte and Jonny will be so busy they will not even know you are gone!"

It was a wonderful plan, and I thanked Constance for her brilliance and generosity. She also offered to take the baby as well, as long as Annie could take cow or sheep milk and not my own. I hadn't even thought of that. I decided that Annie would come with Frank and me and that way if we were delayed, she would not go hungry. She would hardly divulge our secret.

"I must go home and telephone Dr. Crane," I said.

"Come to my house," Constance volunteered. "It is very near here, and that way you will know where to come on the day of your friend's appointment."

We rounded up the children, who were now all three sticky with gelato, and walked around the corner to Constance's home. She lived on the second floor of a glorious old mansion. We tried to get the pram up the stairs, but after several ineffective attempts and much laughter, we picked up Annie and left the pram in the foyer.

Opening Constance's door was like entering Timbuktu or the Taj Mahal. Gold walls and red draperies. Oriental carpets and black lacquer furniture with designs of peacocks. "Are we in heaven?" asked Charlotte.

"I think so," I said to her, taking it all in. "Oh Constance, it is so exotic!"

"My sensibilities are not for everyone. The landlord threatens me with eviction every once in a while. But come, you need to make that telephone connection."

She led me into a small room in silver and deep purple, with a glass door and a horsehair settee near a small table holding the telephone. Imagine having a room just for speaking on the telephone! I still had Annie in my arms and Constance took her from me and left me in this lovely cabinet to make my telephone call. I had been carrying Dr. Howell's note in my shirtwaist for days, and I now took it out. Martin had made most of our rare telephone calls over the year, and I was nervous that I would sound foolish or give such incorrect information as to end up speaking to the Pope. But the exchange assistant was kind, and in no time at all I had reached the offices of Dr. Leonard Crane.

I identified myself and my connection to Dr. Howell, and explained Frank's medical issues. Before long, Dr. Crane himself came to the telephone and asked me several particular questions - the frequency and descriptions of the headaches, and whether he had also been burned in the poisoned gas attack. I did not believe he had been burned - I had only seen the upper part of his chest and his arms recently, but they looked fine - more than fine if truth be told. The doctor explained that the burns would most likely be on his head and neck, but not always, as sometimes the chemical had been absorbed by the soldier's uniform. I expressed my belief that Frank had been spared the burns, and described the headaches as completely as I could. He also asked me the exact date of the injury, but I did not know. I told him I could find out easily enough and telephone back, but he said that would not be necessary. He would ask Frank when he saw him. I was overjoyed at this - Dr. Crane had agreed to see Frank. We set up an appointment for eleven in the morning on the following Thursday, exactly one week away.

I rejoined Constance and the children who were waiting for me in the parlor, and Constance quickly led us to the kitchen where we finally were able to clean little hands and faces. The kitchen was modern and clever, with a large ice box and the latest in washing machines.

"This is like a dream," I said. "Your husband must be very successful. And obviously very tolerant of your eclectic taste."

"You have been honest with me, Lucinda," she said, "so I will be honest with you. I have no husband."

"Oh my!" I exclaimed. "But you have spoken of him! Have you recently divorced?"

Constance offered me a seat and a cup of tea. She sat opposite me.

"Lucinda, I have never been married. I call Sadie's father my husband just for propriety's sake."

I was stunned. An unmarried woman with a child. But she looked content and well cared for and most of all, unashamed.

"Sadie's father... where does he live?"

"With his wife."

"Constance!"

She patted my hand. "I know this is all terribly shocking. It was for me too...at first. I met Thomas in Boston. He was so handsome and successful. I didn't know for the longest time that he already had a wife. But then there was all this," she waved her arms signaling the apartment and all the fine things, "and he is very nice. And I find that seeing Thomas twice a month is really quite sufficient. Sadie and I are happy living this life."

I didn't know what to think. This was just scandalous. Constance sat before me - a kept woman - telling me that she was happy. Happy! I had given up my own happiness to do the right thing. But here was a sinful woman, immoral and not in the least interested in morality. Happy!

I looked at Sadie, the product of this immorality. She had brought out a wooden model of the London Bridge and was showing Jonny and Charlotte how her little china dolls could all be set up walking across the bridge. Sadie looked like my children. She did not look disgraceful.

Constance still sat with Annie on her lap. Annie had fallen asleep with her head on Constance's breast and her hand clutched to a button.

Constance sighed. "If you don't now hate me, I am still willing to watch the children while you seek medical assistance for your friend." She kissed the top of Annie's head. "I may be a disreputable woman, but I am a very good mother."

Charlotte jumped up and ran to Constance with one of the dolls. "Look, Mrs. Constance, this baby has hair like you. So pretty."

"Why, sweetheart you are right. Now why would this painted doll have bobbed her hair? She must be very modern indeed."

I decided.

"Yes," I said. "Yes, I would be grateful if you could take the children next week. Thank you."

"Thank you for trusting me," she said.

"Does that other offer still stand?" I asked. "For you to cut my hair?"

She laughed. "Truly? I would love to. Right now!"

We did it. Constance threw a towel around my shoulders and bobbed my hair. Not too short. A bit longer than my chin but not near touching my shoulders. A bit shorter in the back –"That's so stylish right now," said Constance. My hair curled quite a bit without the additional length, and indeed, we had eliminated a full twelve inches. Charlotte handed me back my hairpins, although I certainly had no use for them now. I rubbed the back of my neck and shook my head. I felt weightless.

"Whatever will you tell Martin?" Constance asked.

"That I am a modern woman," I said.

CHAPTER 49

MARTIN WAS NOT HAPPY ABOUT my bobbed hair, but he was restrained in his reaction.

"Why ever did you do that?" he asked, but kept his voice genial and soft.

"I was with my friend Constance today," I explained, "and she bobbed her hair a while back, and she looks so nice, and she also said she sleeps ever so much better without being pinned down by lying on her own hair. So I thought, Why not?"

"Well, I suppose 'Why not?' might have been answered with the realization that a woman's hair is her expression of femininity," Martin said. "And yours was so lovely."

This surprised me. Martin had never expressed his views about femininity before. Or complimented my looks. And I had gotten the distinct impression that he supported the suffragettes, and many of those strong women had shorn their locks.

"But you let me drive my father's car!" I said.

"What in the world does that have to do with you cutting your hair?" he asked.

Well, I knew, but it was difficult to express. I shrugged.

"Ah, so be it, it will grow I suppose." And he turned back to his book.

When Frank and Sofia came down for dinner, their reaction delighted me.

"You look so sophisticated!" said Sofia. And she spent a few minutes finger-styling it, and changing the part, and trying different looks, each time stepping back from me a bit and saying, "Nice, nice, so pretty."

Frank's reaction was best of all.

"You are stunning! You are uniquely you and perfect!"

I blushed.

"Come now, it's just hair," I said, attempting some modesty that I was not at all feeling. "Let's eat."

And Martin again said, "It will grow."

After dinner, I had the opportunity to speak with Frank for a few seconds, as Martin was showing Sofia an article he had found in the newspaper about the Italian economy.

"I have secured an appointment for you with Dr. Crane on Thursday," I whispered. "And my friend Constance will take Jonny and Charlotte for the day."

"I am not sure I can do this," he whispered back.

"Yes you will. You need to. Please."

"For you," he said. "I will for you."

Later, in bed, lying in the dark beside my sleeping husband, I found myself quite irritated with Martin. I almost wished he had become angry over my shorn hair. But then again, if he had been angry I would have worried that he was upset that I no longer looked so much like Catherine. And that would also have stung.

But his lack of strong opinion had me just as vexed, as that could mean that he just did not care one way or another what I looked like. It was just not important enough to get angry over.

And looking back, I realized that he had never really lost his temper or seemed angry with me in over a year of marriage. I ought to be grateful that he was kind and considerate. There were occasions when he seemed to take pleasure in our life together. But extremes of emotion?

Of course, I was much the same. No elation, no fury.

We were both so careful in our emotions. We could live the rest of our lives just as carefully. It would be an honorable and polite existence. It would be decent. Would it be sufficient?

My anger softened. This was my fault as well. I needed to be a real wife to Martin, not just a mother to his children. I moved closer to him in the dark, and I tentatively touched Martin on the place on his body I had never touched - in truth, had never looked at. I felt him respond, and I rose to my knees and turned my body to straddle his. I loosened the strings on the bodice of my nightdress. Martin reached up and grasped me by the shoulders. In one movement, he turned us both over and our positions were reversed - with me lying on my back and Martin on his knees over me. He leaned forward and kissed me. I felt a passion in his kiss that was absent from his goodnight kiss an hour earlier, from all his previous kisses. I returned his fervor.

Our eyes met and he smiled at me. I reached up and gently brushed back his hair from his brow.

He flinched.

Catherine had done this. I remembered it. I had seen it. In my mother's kitchen, I had seen Catherine tenderly smooth the hair from Martin's brow.

Martin rolled off me. He spoke into the dark, not looking at me. "I'm sorry, Lucinda. You are sweet and loving and beautiful. But I can't."

We lie side by side in the dark. Silent, eyes open, unmoving. We could have been in our coffins; two more victims of the cursed influenza.

After a long while, Martin took my hand, and we continued to watch the darkness, waiting for morning.

CHAPTER 50

ON THE DAY OF FRANK'S appointment, I woke
with anxiety and guilt. The guilt was simple
to identify - I had kept our intentions a secret
from Martin. He did not know I was leaving his children
with what most of mankind would consider an immoral
woman, and traveling by train with a man not my husband
to complete a mission that included neither of our spouses.

The anxiety stemmed from the audacity of my plan.
I had never been to Bridgeport in my life, and now I had
decided to travel with a seriously ill man and a two-month-
old infant. I needed to locate the doctor's office, and secure
transport to and from the office. I had no idea how long we
would be gone, whether we would find any answers, what
the treatment would be, whether further trips would be

required, and what we would tell Martin and Sofia when we returned.

And yet I was determined.

As soon as Martin was off to work, I dressed Charlotte and Jonathan in party clothes, and explained that they would be spending the day with Mrs. Constance and Sadie, and wondrously, they would attend a birthday party. Their excitement helped keep me from my own imminent panic.

As the children were finishing breakfast, Frank appeared. He was also nervous, but ready. He volunteered to stay with Annie while I walked the older children to Constance. She had offered to come and fetch them, but she had been generous enough.

The sun was shining. I hoped that was a good omen. And Constance responded to my knock with effusive enthusiasm. She promised that the children would be kept busy and happy, and not to worry about what time I should return. As if not worrying were an option open to me.

It was over a mile from Pearl Street to the train station, and Frank's determination flagged as we neared the train. I so wished I had had the foresight to arrange for a car to drive us to Bridgeport. It would have been so much simpler - and less strain on Frank's precarious health. I was truly not cut out for the role of advocate.

It was not a long train ride, though Frank's headache had become significant, and the strain was apparent. I tried my best to distract him.

"Tell me," I asked, "how you became such a magnificent musician."

"Magnificent?" he smiled as well as he could manage. "Do you mind....?" he asked quietly, and then he rested his head on my shoulder. I stroked his brow lightly.

"Does that help, or does that make it worse?" I asked.

"Helps," he said. "Greatly." He closed his eyes. "Well, my father was the one who was a magnificent musician. And his father as well, from what I understand, although I never met my grandfather. And when I was very small, my father gave me a little violin - they make small ones, you know, for a child's small hands and fingers - and he said, 'Now just play.' And I squeaked out some notes just by copying what I had seen him doing from the time I was an infant. Oh, I was so bad! And Papa said, 'The secret to music is to never stop. When you make a mistake, you must just go on. If you never lose the rhythm, then you never lose the music, and in the end, it becomes very good music.' And so that is what I did. I never stopped for a wrong note. I just continued. And that's all there is to it. You continue."

I thought about my own years of piano lessons, championed steadfastly by my mother, but ultimately unsuccessful. And I could see the truth of Frank's philosophy. I had always stopped for every mistake, repeating passages again and again, trying to fix my music. But in the end, I lost the music, because I lost the rhythm.

We arrived in Bridgeport within the hour, and we had a bit more than an additional hour to make our way to Dr. Crane. I had at least practiced the minimum prudence in that I had gone to the public library the prior day, and checked a map of Bridgeport. The doctor's office was adjacent to Bridgeport Hospital, and the hospital was two miles from the train. I did not think Frank was up to the walk. So when we disembarked from the train, we made our way directly to the station director's office, where I asked how and where I might be able to hire a motorcar to bring us to our destination, and then wait for us to return us to the train. The stationmaster was very kind, and within ten minutes, the hired car had pulled up to the station and the accommodating driver brought us directly to the office of Dr. Leonard Crane.

The doctor was an elderly man, ascetic and pale, with a mustache that had been the style around the year I was born. He greeted us warmly. He remembered my telephone conversation, and if he was surprised that I was carrying an infant to my friend's medical examination, he did not show it.

"Mr. Giametti, I am so honored to meet you," Dr. Crane said. "You have suffered your injury fighting a war in place of old frail gentlemen like myself. I think perhaps my kind is more expendable than yours."

"Well, I thank you for seeing me," said Frank. "I'm hoping your expertise can save me from these terrible headaches. Perhaps then neither of us will be expendable."

Dr. Crane showed Frank to the examination room. Frank turned to look at me, entreating me with his eyes to come with him. But I sat with the baby in the anteroom, and said, "It's fine... see the doctor and I will wait here."

They were gone for near to thirty minutes. Then the door opened and Dr. Crane called me in.

"I would like to take Frank over to the hospital for an x-ray," the doctor said. "Often we don't see much when we radiograph the skull, but it will eliminate any skull fracture or calcification."

Frank looked very frightened.

"I'll go with you," I said.

"I have called and they are waiting."

Annie started to cry. It was nearly noon, and she was hungry. But Frank - I could not let him do this alone.

"Let's go," I said.

And I put the wailing baby on my shoulder, took Frank's hand, and we followed the doctor across the street and into the hospital and down white corridors to rooms that seemed to be made of steel.

I kissed Frank's cheek as the doctor and the technician took him into the radiography room.

Then I did the most appalling thing. Right there sitting on a hard chair in the corridor, I unbuttoned my blouse and let the baby nurse. It was disgraceful, I know, but I was desperate. I resolved that should anyone approach me to castigate my reprehensible behavior, I was going to pretend to speak no English.

I think I was so audacious because I was so afraid for Frank. I knew nothing about x-ray science. A machine that can take a photograph of the inside of your body - how could it not burn through your skin? Perhaps it was worse than the mustard gas itself. All I could hope was that Dr. Crane would not cause Frank any further pain.

It was not a long wait. I had no sooner covered myself and changed Annie's diaper - not knowing what to do with the soiled one, I walked down the hall to where I found a trash container and I threw it away - when Frank reemerged on Dr. Crane's arm. I was so relieved I jumped up, startling Annie back into a momentary wail.

"Oh, Frank!" I cried, "Did it hurt?"

"No, not at all," he answered and took Annie from me. She immediately quieted.

We followed Dr. Crane back to his offices. He showed us into a room that was dominated by a large cluttered desk. He did not sit behind the desk, but instead joined us in three very old leather chairs in a corner of the office. Frank still held Annie, and when he took his seat, he arranged her on his lap so that her feet were against his stomach and her head was by his knees. She was fast asleep.

"Doctor," I began, "if you need to speak to Frank privately, I will step outside..."

"No, please, Lucinda," said Frank. "The doctor has already given me some of his thoughts, and I'd like you to understand."

Dr. Crane leaned towards us. He spoke quietly, whether not to awaken the baby or not to alarm us, I was not certain.

"Here is what I see, although there is no way to be sure. But I have had four other patients in very similar circumstances. And I have a colleague in New York who has seen perhaps twenty-five more cases. We are working together to try to discover what has happened and what might be done."

It was not good news. Dr. Crane and his associate had identified dozens of cases where what had originally been considered minor exposure to poison gas had within one to two years had become serious secondary trauma.

"Do you see," the Doctor asked, "anything extraordinary about Mr. Giametti's eyes?"

I had not noticed before, but searching now, I saw that Frank's right pupil was much larger than his left, as if his right eye was looking into the darkness, while his left eye was adjusting for bright sunlight.

"The separate reactions to light may occur due to several conditions, but one condition with this effect is a tumor in the brain."

I stared into Frank's eyes, willing his pupils to be normal, willing myself not to see the abnormality, just as I had not seen it before.

"Given also his severe and progressive double vision" - I shook my head in denial; Frank had never confided this to me - "and the frequent headaches, as well as the lack of any skull fracture in the x-ray analysis...well, when I take all this into account with what we have discovered in the long-term effects of mustard gas poisoning, I do believe there is a tumor, perhaps more than one."

Frank did not look at me. He stroked Annie's tiny fingers and said nothing.

"There must be something you can do," I said. "If you know what this is, there must be some action that you can take..."

"With the patients I have seen, and the others I have studied... as of yet, we see nothing that can be done. We keep looking."

I felt my tears begin and I willed them not to fall from my lashes. "Those other patients? How have they fared?"

I asked, though I was frightened to hear the answer. I was frightened to have Frank hear the answer.

"Of the four I have seen, three have died. One is doing quite well. My New York colleague has also witnessed the passing of most of his patients. I am sorry to say that I believe Mr. Giametti, like his fellow soldiers we have seen, has a cancer of the brain. Most likely, an effect somehow associated with the mustard gas."

Frank spoke then. "What happens next? Or rather, what do you think will happen for me?"

Dr. Crane answered, "I think you have a bit of time. Your condition does not seem as poor as others. But I think it will progress, perhaps rapidly. With the other patients, the headaches can either intensify or - in a few cases - they have blessedly subsided. I think you will probably lose your vision quite soon." The doctor leaned further toward us and touched Frank's arm. "Then...I'm sorry," he said.

"What if we had more money?" I asked, thinking about my secret bank account.

"Oh, Mrs. Blaisdell," said the doctor. "It's not money. I would cure this fine man for free if I could."

I saw Frank use his thumb to gently brush a tear from where it had fallen onto Annie's leg. Dr. Crane, I think saw this too, for he turned to me.

"This is a very sensitive thing I must ask. Very coarse. And I must apologize. But we are trying to learn all we can about the long-term effects of the gas, including those that may pass to other generations. So I will ask, although it is offensive: Is Mr. Giametti the father of this baby?"

I was stunned. Frank immediately straightened. He answered for me, "No this baby's father is Mr. Blaisdell. Mrs. Blaisdell and her husband are loving friends. The only thing you are correct about is that the question is offensive."

"Frank, it's all right," I said. "I understand. Dr. Crane wants to ensure that the children of those soldiers that have been poisoned are well. If this was your child…" I could not finish. *If only,* I thought. And then I was stunned again, because I had thought it.

The doctor stood. "I'm going to give you a stronger medicine for the headaches," he said. "It should help quite a bit. It's very potent, so you need to take care. Take it as you need it, but try if you can to be judicious."

"That's all?" I asked, unwilling to even get up from my chair. "Frank will die and you give him some drug for a headache?" I could hardly believe I could be so rude. I had come for a cure. I wanted the doctor to give us a cure.

"Lucinda!" said Frank. "Easing the pain will be a great benefit. More than I hoped for."

I stood and took the baby from his lap. "You hope for too little!"

He touched my shoulder, "You are probably right, Lucie. But then I will not have to bear such horrible disappointment."

The doctor walked with us to the door. He followed us out to the street, where our car was still thankfully waiting. "You can call me or come back anytime, Mr. Giametti," he said. "And I will send you more medicine any time you need it." He hesitated, and whispered to Frank - it was surely not meant for my ears, but I heard, "I will send you more than you need, if the time arises."

It was a silent ride back to the train station. Neither of us knew what to say. Finally, Frank took my hand.

"The baby was very good today," he said.

"Yes, she was an angel. Thank God she is over the fussy stage. Can you imagine if she had screamed throughout the examination?"

"Maybe that would have been better... to not have heard."

"Where is a wailing infant when you need one?"

We laughed then. What else could we do?

We arrived at the train station about forty minutes before the next train was due. This was good timing, for although we were anxious to be home, it was also nearly two and we had not eaten. Frank insisted he had no appetite, but I purchased two sandwich biscuits with ham from a street vendor and Frank ate a bit. I found a shop that sold me lukewarm tea in a paper cup, and Frank drank a full cup. I didn't have time or any additional money to go back and buy one for myself, but it was just as well, since I did not see any ladies' facilities, or at least none that I was willing to enter.

The train at that hour was half empty. We took two facing benches, with Frank offering to sit in the backwards-moving seat. Not that the seat moved backwards of course, but that he was sitting looking out at where we were leaving. I could never have managed that without vertigo, and I didn't know how he could, given his painful headache and what I knew now was double vision. Perhaps it did not matter. I knew with a healthy head that I would be ill if I could not see where I was going.

Frank was quiet. He put a hand to his forehead occasionally, but said nothing. Annie enjoyed the sway of the train, and cooed and smiled, and soon was asleep.

Frank took from his pocket the bottle of pills that Dr. Crane had given him. He read the label, opened the bottle, and took one. He shrugged his shoulders.

"Maybe I should take them all now," he said.

"Oh Frank, stop that talk," I cried.

"It would save everyone so much trouble."

"Except for the conductor who finds you in New York."

"Not New York," he laughed. "You're going the wrong way."

I sighed. "All my life."

"Oh, now you're the one who should stop that talk. You are not even twenty yet."

"Not even nineteen," I corrected.

"Worse," he said. "The words 'all my life' do not even apply to you." He closed his eyes. "But I, on the other hand…'all my life' is right here before me."

I could not restrain my tears. In the deserted train car, I cried unashamedly. "Oh, Frank, whatever will we do?"

He leaned towards me and took my hands in his. "Lucinda, there is nothing we can do. Life will go on for you, and it will not go on for me. You will be okay, but you must promise to look after Sofia. You are the nearest thing to a sister for her. She has no family here. Just me... and just Martin and you."

"How can you say this as if it was acceptable? As if you don't mind?"

"Lucinda. I mind. I am so fearful of dying at this very moment that I feel the train is hurtling down the track, not towards New Haven, but towards death itself. I can't stop the train. My destination is terrible but I cannot stop it."

"You cannot die," I cried. "I'll find another doctor. Dr. Crane doesn't know."

"He does. And we knew. You knew yourself. You found Dr. Crane because you knew something was terribly wrong."

"I want someone to fix it. I want you well."

"I won't get well. So stop. Please."

Frank rose and sat beside me. He held my hand in silence for the rest of the trip.

We were both composed when we arrived in New Haven. It was well after three; we'd been gone for less than six hours, but it seemed that the world had changed. It felt unrecognizable. I felt unrecognizable - I would not have been surprised if the children did not know me.

We made our way to Constance's home. Frank asked me to keep our day in confidence for a short while, to give him some time to reflect and decide the kindest way to share his condition with Sofia.

"Perhaps," said Frank, "I am more resigned to my fate because I was a soldier. When you go off to war, you have no choice but to recognize your own mortality."

I shifted Annie more comfortably in my arms. "That's a significant difference between men and women. For when you give birth, you recognize your own immortality."

"Knowing that part of you goes on - I think that it very comforting. Poor Sofia. She came here for a husband and a family. Soon she will have neither."

"Do you think people can be happy alone?" I asked.

"I don't know. Maybe. Some people seem to be right with themselves."

And at that, we were at Constance's door. Constance, a woman who seemed quite right with herself. She was a woman alone but not withdrawn from the world.

She answered the door with a smile and a gesture to indicate that quietness was in order. We tiptoed in. There amongst tissue and boxes and toys scattered about, Charlotte and Jonathan and Sadie were asleep on the floor.

"The other children have left," Constance whispered. "And these three little elves played until their last bit of energy flowed out onto the floor, and I have just let them lie here. With any luck, your two will be awake enough to walk home, and then go directly back to sleep."

I introduced her to Frank, and I was glad that either the medicine or his sheer determination had taken hold, since his color was good and his stance was strong. I knew his pride had already been assaulted by his incapacity and Constance's knowledge of it.

We gently woke the children. Although sleepy, they seemed delighted by the surprise of seeing Frank standing before them.

"Zio Frank!" said Jonathan. "We have been to a big birthday celebration. I never saw so many children in one spot. It must be just like school!"

"Oh yes," said Frank, "You will have so many playmates at school that it will be a celebration every day."

Looking around the room strewn with toys, I was suddenly shamefully aware of my terrible bad manners. I had been so preoccupied with Frank that I had not brought a gift for my own children to give to Sadie. I apologized, and Constance said, "Oh shush now... Sadie has more possessions than any little girl should have. What she needs are good friends. When you are comfortable enough to fall asleep together, that's where love starts."

"I can't thank you enough for minding the children. Someday I will repay you with more than a doll for your child," I said.

Frank said, "Well, I owe you too, Mrs. Hadley. It was an enormous support for Lucinda to accompany me today. And she is a stylish companion too, thanks to your skill with the scissors."

Well now, that was just embarrassing, so I quickly got the children to say thank you and goodbye, and we headed out the door.

"Where did you go, Mama?" asked Charlotte.

"Oh, I had a nice time. It was such a fine day, and Zio Frank was feeling so much better, so we went for a long walk. And we had ham sandwiches and tea."

"We had cake and apricots," said Jonathan.

"How wonderful!" I said.

CHAPTER 51

TWO DAYS LATER, ON SATURDAY afternoon, Sofia ran into my kitchen without knocking.

"I have such good news!" she said.

"Good news? Oh my! What good news?" I asked, so startled I almost dropped the dish I was drying.

"Frank saw a new doctor a few days ago, and this wonderful doctor has given him new medicine, and he is already ever so much better!"

At that, I did drop the plate. It clattered to the floor, and broke in half.

"Oh dear," I said. "My hands were wet and the plate was so slippery!"

How could he? How could Frank tell Sofia he was getting better when the doctor told him he would die? I did not know whether to find this lie a form of cruelty or kindness. Or perhaps cowardice. Wouldn't Sofia be even more heartbroken to believe he would be cured only to discover that his medicine existed to save him from pain, and not from death itself?

I picked up the two halves of the plate.

"It's a straight crack, perhaps you can glue it," Sofia said.

"Frank…" I started. But of course I could not tell her. I had no right to tell her the truth. I saw that I had already been disloyal to Sofia and to Martin as well, keeping such a secret. But if I betrayed that secret now, I would be disloyal to Frank as well. "Tell me all about Frank." I finished. "I will get us some tea."

We sat at the table. Jonathan was playing with the toy animals and blocks, trying to make a bridge with the blocks like Sadie's bridge. I would have to ask Constance where she found such a nice toy, as Jonathan's birthday was coming up. Charlotte and the baby were both asleep.

"So Frank…" I said.

Sofia smiled. "Well, yesterday, Frank told me he had seen a doctor last week. That the doctor had contacted him, because he is doing a study of soldiers who were gassed. So he went. All the way to Bridgeport. I don't know how he had the strength to do such a thing all alone. And the doctor gave him some new medicine that has been found to stop the headaches. Frank told me that he is already feeling much relief. And I see it! I saw today! He was ever so much better. He finished a violin today and started on another. And he was singing while he worked. Singing!"

I tried to sound lighthearted. "How marvelous!" I said. "I am so glad his pain has diminished. What else did Frank say... I mean did the doctor tell him about what causes the headaches? Will he need to take the medicine for a long time?"

"I don't know. Frank didn't say. I think Frank will have to see the doctor again, after his examination results are finished. He says for now, all we should care about is that he is feeling better."

From this I gleaned that perhaps Frank had only sought to explain his new pills to Sofia. The news of his brain cancer was still to come.

I took a sip of tea and set the cup down so hard it rattled. I really could not be breaking china every time I felt disconcerted.

"I would have to agree that it is best to be grateful for each good moment as it comes," I said.

"Yes. But...." Sofia looked away from me. She kept her eyes on the curtains, as they shimmered a bit in the light breeze. "I need him to be better."

Sofia began to cry. "It is so hard, Lucinda. Frank is a hero. A soldier hurt in the war. I'm very proud of him. But it is so hard to have him sick every day. I know it is selfish. I am older than you by many years, but still, I'm young. I don't want my life to be so sad."

Poor Sofia. All my heart had been with Frank all this time. But Sofia! She came to America for a husband and a family. I could imagine her excitement to start a new happy life. And found herself barren, and with a husband going off to war and returning injured. And soon - though she still did not know this - soon he would be blind. Then dead. Sofia, now thirty and beautiful with no children and no husband. And me, Lucinda, eighteen, with three children and a husband who still mourns his true wife. We were sisters after all.

"Will you pray for us?" she asked.

"Yes, of course," I said, although I had stopped praying a year ago.

I did not get the opportunity to speak with Frank until Monday when both Sofia and Martin had gone to work.

Sofia and Frank came to dinner on Sunday, and they were in good spirits. The pain pills appeared to have worked wonders for Frank. His spirits were high and we laughed throughout dinner, about silly unimportant things, which was blessedly normal. Frank insisted on holding Annie throughout dinner, and the two older children were envious. So Sofia taught them a new song in Italian - I believe the words praised summer and all the fun of the warm weather. We all sang together. We could hear them still singing as Sofia put them to bed, as she loved to do.

"Did you see?" Frank said on Monday when he came down to help with the children. "Did you see how happy she was?"

I sent the children to their bedroom to retrieve their xylophones.

"But it is a lie!" I whispered. "How could you tell her you are well?"

"I didn't," he said. "I started to tell her the truth, but I only got as far as seeing the doctor and receiving the medicine, and she was so eager to clasp at this hope. She was overjoyed that I seemed better. I need to give her some happy times to remember. At least for a little while. For as long as I can."

"For how long?" I asked. "You certainly do seem very well right now."

And Frank then confessed to me that although the pills were helping to control his pain, some of his good spirits was just pretense. The headaches had not completely abated, nor had his double vision cleared.

"So it will not be long, I fear," Frank said. "I will tell her next week that the doctor has telephoned with bad news as he has received the results of my medical tests. But first, let's plan an outing to the seashore. Let's have the most wonderful time we can."

And so we did. On Sunday, we went to the new state park in Madison, a short train ride from New Haven. It was a bit difficult - not to say hilarious - on the train with the children and picnic baskets and extra clothing. I fear we looked like something out of a Keystone Kops moving picture, with someone always precariously off balance and sundry items falling loose and children jumping up and down.

But we made the trek. The beach was quite crowded, considering it was still May. But it was very warm and sunny, and the new park had been the topic of much praise in all the newspapers in Connecticut. We found a spot not too far from the water and spread out our many accoutrements. Blankets, towels, a parasol to keep the baby from the sun. And food. "I do believe we have enough to live here for several weeks," said Martin.

The water was still frigid at that time of the year, but that didn't stop Martin and Sofia from venturing in, at least a little. Frank and I watched the two splash gently, while the little ones laughed from the shoreline. They withdrew in short order, and took to building sandcastles with Charlotte and Jonny.

Sofia wore a very modest swim dress, but still looked radiant and appealing. Martin was dashing in his swim costume as well, like a hero in a book. Frank had not changed from his summer shirt and trousers, and I wore a lightweight dress - and even a shawl for modesty for nursing the baby. It was as if Frank and I were the chaperones to the outgoing young couple. I am not sure how much Frank with his failing vision could see. He seemed content to just take in the sun.

I suppose I should have been jealous. And I was - a bit. Moreover, though, I enjoyed watching Martin play with the children and with Sofia. I realized that I had not seen him so carelessly happy for nearly a year, since our trip to the zoo. I had felt us come together as a family that day. And I was seeing a family again. But the mother - the wife - was Sofia.

Frank lay down on the blanket, shielding his eyes with his arm. I desired nothing more than to lie next to him, but that would have been sinful. So I remained sitting by his side. Annie reached up to me and put her hand to my face. I in turn put my hand on Frank's. He took it without looking and held quite tightly. We became a comfortable tableau, and after a while I felt both Frank's and Annie's hands slip away as both fell asleep.

The four people I watched making sandcastles, and the two sleeping here secure that I would protect them - this was my family. My heart ached with love for all of them. Martin, my husband, the engineer, carving a moat for his castle with precision. Sofia, sister of my heart, placing a crown of shells for the tower. Jonathan, mud-covered and laughing as his drawbridge tumbled down. Charlotte, self-contained and serious, patting little mud-pies and setting them in a row. Annie, a tiny human just beginning to be curious about the world around her, a mystery waiting to unfold. And Frank. Who was Frank to me? The artist I loved who I was about to lose.

Several months ago, Sofia asked me to pray for her. I had confessed at that time that I was not successful at prayer. And just this week, she had asked me again. Sitting in the sun on this beach with the love around me so complete, I tried. Perhaps I would be more successful by praying, not for a miracle, but for some small blessing. So I prayed that this day would linger in all our memories and give us comfort in the future.

CHAPTER 52

M Y FAMILY CAME DOWN FOR Annie's christening, and we added a little birthday celebration for Jonathan as well. I did not especially want to do both on the same day, but my father believed that hotels were the nesting grounds for disease, and he certainly may have been correct, and our apartment was too small for the four Benedicts to spend the night. So we squeezed both occasions into one Sunday.

Father had originally pressed for us to travel to Springfield instead, but Frank and Sofia were to be Annie's godparents, and I did not feel that Frank was well enough to make such a long trip. I had rarely ever defied my father, but since the results of my obedience had not gained me any of his favor, nor God's as far as I could see, I was steadfast in my insistence that the christening should be here in New Haven.

The family arrived early in the morning in my father's motorcar, which delighted Jonathan. We stood at the side of the road, and everyone disembarked in a different direction. Mother ran straight to the new baby, and cried tears of joy, which Annie rewarded with one of her new genuine smiles. Amelia went straight to the porch, announcing that she was unbearably overheated - but to her credit took Charlotte on her lap anyway. Malcolm shook hands in a very adult manner with Martin, and then scooped up Jonathan and sat him in the car. Father, who had gone straight to the boot for their gifts, was encouraged to climb back into the automobile and give Jonathan a ride around the block.

"Let's go to the park!" Jonny cried. "We can see if Sadie is there... she doesn't believe that Grandfather has an automobile."

So the men took off, with Martin giving directions, all happy to have the opportunity to impress a five-year-old girl with their fabulous motorcar.

"Good!" said Mother. "We women can visit and have some lemonade and recover from the fumes and the dust! I hope they are gone for an hour!"

We went in, and Mother and Amelia were surprised that we now lived in the second-floor apartment. I had forgotten in my letters to mention that we had exchanged apartments with the Giamettis.

We sat with our lemonade and tea cake that Sofia had left for us. Frank and Sofia would join us at noon for the walk to the church for the christening. Amelia took a turn to fuss over the baby, so Charlotte could sit with my mother and stem her rising jealousy.

Mother looked around the table and declared, "Was there ever a more attractive group of women in the world than we Benedict girls?"

"Wait until you see Annie in her christening dress," I said. "She will be the prettiest of us all. Sofia made the dress almost entirely of fine lace that she carried with her from Italy." I saw Charlotte's face fall. "Oh, there is a surprise for you too, Charlotte. Zia Sofia has made you a lace dress too, as befitting the princess sister of the princess baby."

"Father would not allow us to bring a change of clothes," complained Amelia. "So we had to ride in our nice dresses. I fear mine is just ruined - dirty and wrinkled."

So I immediately had Amelia change into my summer robe, while I brushed the road dust from her dress, and ironed her wrinkles. She looked lovely, even sitting in my dressing gown, and when she donned her now-immaculate outfit and emerged from the lavatory with her hair brushed and cheeks gleaming, I had to admit that Father was right all those years ago, and she was the loveliest Benedict of us all. I felt as jealous as Charlotte over the unfairness of younger sisters. I hoped that Martin and Frank would not fawn over Amelia, or I should be likely to have my own little tantrum.

The male contingent of Benedicts arrived at last, with Jonathan gloating over his triumph with Sadie. "She was there! We gave her a ride around the park!"

"I'm sure Sadie was quite impressed," I said.

"Her mother is a Bohemian!" said Father. "And why, I must ask, have you cut your hair?"

"It is wonderful to see you too, Father," I said. I was not going to let him spoil our celebration. He was here, after all. I had had my doubts whether he would even come. I was determined to remain happy for that. I picked up Annie from Amelia's lap and handed her to my father.

"There!" I said. "Your newest granddaughter. Annie Sullivan Blaisdell. She has your brow, don't you think? But fortunately not your temper." And I kissed him.

I suppose that unexpected display of affection shocked my Father into submission. He bent over the infant and scrutinized her tiny face.

"Yes, she definitely has my brow. But she has your fine beautiful mouth. Let us hope she has not inherited your tendency to use that mouth for salty language." He scowled, but then immediately softened as my mother gave him her most admonishing countenance. He bent and kissed Annie on the top of her head.

"You had better take her back," he said to me. "I am out of practice with the fragility of infants." He placed her quite gently in my arms, and said, "She is lovely, Lucinda." With that surfeit of sentimentality, he quickly added, "I trust you are not intending to have her christened in that poor rag of a dress."

"Oh, Father, you won't be disappointed," I said over my shoulder as I took Annie into the bedroom. Charlotte and Annie were not the only ones with a new dress for the occasion. Sofia had made one for me too. It was pale summery yellow, and instead of an abundance of lace, it bore just a small lace collar of a warm pink - to soften the yellow against my face. It was loose and breezy - a dress the flappers would like - if the flappers were going to church, that is.

I quickly changed and added pale stockings and shoes to suit the dress. I ran a brush through my hair. I looked every bit of a modern woman. And then Annie. I dressed her in the delicate lace gown, so long a gown that its hem hung nearly to my own. She had a sweet bonnet and lace shoes to match.

"Here we are!" I announced, as we stepped back into the kitchen. All ready for our big day.

"Oh my!" exclaimed Mother. "Two angels have come from heaven."

I smiled, gratified. "But wait a moment - more angels will join us." I admonished Martin to change into his church suit, and I hustled the two older children into their bedroom. There I changed Jonathan into a smart little outfit of pale gray shorts and vest, and affixed a white bow tie. Then Charlotte. I dressed my solemn little child in a dress made of the peachy-pink lace of my collar, with a yellow ribbon for her sash.

"You are as beautiful as your Mama Catherine," I told her.

"She liked to sing very loud in church," Charlotte said.

"Oh she was a happy loud singer," I said, "and the most beautiful loud singer in the congregation."

"I will sing just as loud," she announced.

"You go right ahead if you are feeling it!" I laughed. That should do it for revenge on my father for his comment on my bobbed hair.

I ushered them back to join the rest of the family.

"More cherubs!" gushed my mother. "How will I ever come back to earth?"

"I'm not a cherub at all!" protested Jonathan. "I am five years old and I will go to school and read and play baseball."

"I will teach you this summer," offered Malcolm, and Jonathan said, "I will not call you Uncle Malcolm when we play baseball because that would not be right."

"How about Mal, the greatest pitcher in Massachusetts?" offered Malcolm.

"That sounds good. Are you really the greatest pitcher in Massachusetts?"

"A little humility might be in order," warned my father.

"Well, as I'm on my way to church, I have to say there might be one or two better," said Malcolm.

"That is not quite the humility I expect," said Father, although I did see him smile for a second.

Martin, looking successful and handsome, ran upstairs and returned in just moments with Frank and Sofia. Sofia looked lovely in sky blue. Frank was pale and I recognized the look of pain veiled over with the effort to disguise it. But he shook Father's hand and complimented my mother on all her fine children and grandchildren. Sofia held back tears as she said that she and her husband were honored to join this family by standing as godparents for the baby.

And with that, Sofia took Annie in her arms, and I took the other two little ones by the hand, and we walked a few blocks to St. Mary's, my Church of Patience, as I had dubbed it, where Annie was baptized and Charlotte sang her Italian song of summer in her loudest expression of joy.

After the christening, it was Jonny's turn. My parents gave him a set of blocks more intricate than the baby toys he had been playing with. From Malcolm, a baseball, and Amelia had found him some wooden frogs to join his zoo. From Sofia and Frank, he received a small flute, and I expressed my wish that it would be at least a year before he learned to make a sound with it. Constance and Sadie came over as well, and presented Jonathan with a sailboat for the small pond at the park. And from Martin and me, there was a duplicate of the London Bridge toy that had so captivated Jonny when we were visiting Constance. She had arranged for her 'husband' to send one down from Boston.

Poor Charlotte was feeling quite left out, and I was glad I thought to have Sofia make her doll in a christening gown similar to Annie's. And Sofia had also fashioned a change of clothing for the small doll, of a dress made from the scraps from Charlotte's own.

Martin fetched Mr. And Mrs. Battle to join us for cake, and some mild libation that Martin had been saving for a nice occasion. It was a successful day from start to finish.

As the family was preparing to leave for Massachusetts, my mother followed me into the bedroom where I was changing the baby and thanked me for putting aside my father's disapproval. I had given this much consideration over the past week. My father had been wrong and cruel to condemn me for acting as a wife to the husband he had pressured me to marry. But I had decided that if he came to Annie's baptism it would mean that he was recognizing her as a child of God. And so it would be acceptance - of her and of me. He was still wrong, and it still hurt. But we were all in this situation that none of us understood.

"He is still my father," I said. "How could he not love another grandchild?"

"I was fearful that perhaps he might not," Mother said. "But I think Annie's sweet nature may have won him over."

She also asked after Frank. "Your friend does not look well," she said.

It had been over two weeks and yet Frank had not yet been truthful with Sofia, so I could only say that Frank is under the care of a physician, and is trying a new medicine, and we were all hoping for the best.

"I will pray for him," she said.

And I found myself angry. All this prayer. To what effect?

CHAPTER 53

I T WAS ALMOST MIDNIGHT ON Wednesday when we heard the knocking on our door.

Martin ran to the door grabbing a skillet on the way, in case he should need a weapon. This probably would have been comical had it been any other time.

It was Frank.

"I'm sorry," he said. "I need to tell you."

"Tell me what?" asked Martin, still holding the skillet.

"I have a cancer. Cancer of the brain."

"My God!" said Martin. "Are you sure?"

Frank sank into a chair. He laid his arms on the kitchen table and rested his head. I stood watching from the door of the bedroom, standing barefoot in my light summer nightgown.

"I've known for weeks," said Frank, not raising his head. "I hadn't been able to find a way to tell Sofia. But she was going on and on tonight, so happy that I was better, and making plans for the future, and I couldn't bear it. I told her."

Sofia! I ran from the bedroom and out the door and up the stairs. I did not have to go far. She was sitting halfway up the steps. Just staring into the darkness.

I sat by her side and put my arms around her. She did not cry. She just continued to stare at nothing. At the empty world she was facing. We sat for a long time, perhaps an hour.

Finally, she said, "I am cold. Do you have a shawl?"

I took her hand and led her down the stairs. Frank and Martin were still seated at the table, a bottle of homemade wine between them, nearly empty. There were no glasses.

I found a nice goblet in the cabinet, and poured the remainder of the wine and handed it to Sofia. She held it with both hands but did not put it to her lips. I'm not sure she was even aware she was holding it. I fetched a blanket and put it around her shoulders.

Frank watched her. "I'm sorry," he said. "I wish I could be well. I don't want to die and I don't want to hurt you and leave you."

Sofia turned to him. "It was the war. The war has killed you. I knew it from the moment you went away. I knew you had already died. War ruins everything. I told you that, but you went anyway." She sobbed and made an angry animal sound. "You would have been better off dying in France. I wouldn't have to watch you die."

It was a terrible thing to say, but it was grief that had taken hold, not hatred. Frank rose and knelt by her chair and she stroked his hair, and finally let herself cry.

Martin turned to me. "Frank has told me that his new medicine is to control the pain only. It was never a cure. And now he is going blind, which the doctor tells him is inevitable."

I nodded. I was complicit in this horrible knowledge, but Frank, even in his agony, had kept my role a secret. So I feigned ignorance and hated myself for doing so.

"We will do everything we can for both of you," I said. "Anything."

And we sat in silence until the sun rose.

Sofia rose, saying, "I must go to work. Things will be all right if I go to work."

I took her hand. "No," she said. "Let me go. I need to go."

Frank nodded and I released her. Martin had fallen asleep at the table just a short while before. I woke him gently.

"Martin, dear, it's morning. You should get to work."

"Morning?" he muttered. And when he realized he was still at the kitchen table and remembered all that transpired, he asked, "Should I stay?"

"No," I said. "Go. I will stay with Frank. We will be fine."

The children were waking, the baby was crying, and my breasts were aching and heavy. Frank offered to go back upstairs, but I told him he should stay. He tried to lie down on the settee in the parlor but the smallish piece of furniture had been uncomfortable even for my much smaller frame, and I ended up encouraging him to lie down on my own bed. At first he demurred, but his exhaustion finally got the better of him, and he acquiesced. I told the children, still in their nightclothes, to sit on the bed with Frank and play a game where they had to be statues and not move. Then I gathered wailing Annie to my breast, raced up the stairs with the baby latched hard onto me, and found Frank's pain pills. I rushed back down, rather amazed that the baby seemed oblivious, as famished as she was. I reentered the bedroom to find the children safely in giggles as they struck their statue poses, one on either side of Frank, who lay very still with the strain showing on his face.

I handed him a pill. He took it from me, and grinned, which confused me at first and then I realized that I still had the baby at my bare breast.

"I thought you were supposed to be blind!" I said.

"Not yet, Lucinda," he laughed. That laugh was as sweet a sound as I had heard in years.

Frank slept for hours. The children begged to go out to play, but I was fearful of leaving Frank. About two, Frank finally came out of the bedroom, a little sheepish.

"I had so much wine last night," he said. "And then the pill on top of that. I'm sorry to have ruined your day. I will go home now, and leave you alone."

"Stop that," I said. "All the pretense is over now. You are sick and you are allowed to be sick."

"I was capable of caring for myself yesterday, and I can still," he said. "I will tell you when I cannot."

I realized that he was angry. Well, he had a right if anyone did. And he did not need me to turn him into an invalid before his time. Or take away his pride.

"You're right," I said. "And you smell of old wine and slept-in clothes. Go clean up. I'm going to take the children to the park. Perhaps you can find something to eat - I didn't wait on luncheon for a man who sleeps during the day."

"That's better," he said. "Have fun, kids!" And he smiled when putting the emphasis on the word 'kids,' which he knew my parents had never allowed me to utter. He straightened and I heard him stride purposefully and rather loudly up the stairs. It may have been pretense, but it was a pretense that we needed to hold to for a while.

"Get your new sailboat, Jonny," I said. I went to the park with a much lighter heart, although I left the door to our apartment unlocked, and Frank's pills on the table where he could find them easily.

And so we went on for the next few weeks. We measured the days by hours, the hours by minutes - and the minutes alert to the slightest change or deterioration. If we broke it down into the smallest increments, then there was less change to see. Frank looked the same as he did five minutes before; it was only when you compared him to the week before that his condition worsened. So we tried desperately not to look at the larger picture. We all became inured to the fact of Frank's impending death in some way or another. Frank and I had a head start on Martin and

Sofia - that was the only difference. We sometimes even made light of it.

"I just could not bear to see women get the vote," he declared one day.

"Oh, I think it may have been prohibition that has done you in," I said.

"No reason to go on," Frank agreed.

Frank and I made another trip to Dr. Crane. Ostensibly - for Sofia's sake - Frank explained that since I was his daytime companion, it made sense that I should meet the doctor and receive some guidance as to the best method of care. But for Frank and I, our real purpose was to understand better the timetable of his demise. How bad would it be? What could we expect?

For this trip, we did not go by train, but rather hired a car. As before, Constance took the older children, but no secrecy was needed. Dr. Crane greeted us with affection, commenting politely on how Annie had grown and looked the picture of health. Frank's health, however, was not a sunny picture.

"A few months, I'm afraid," said Dr. Crane. "Perhaps four. Maybe only one before your sight is completely gone. You may find yourself hard of hearing, but often it is just the opposite, with small sounds being magnified. You may hear voices. Hallucinations are not uncommon. There will be days when walking is difficult, or your hands may tremble uncontrollably. I know it sounds frightful, because it is. But on the positive side, you may have some wonderfully clear days - where your mind is sharp and your body steady. Enjoy them. Take all the pleasure you can whenever those moments appear. And for the bad times, I will give you more medication."

"Tell me honestly," said Frank. "Am I better off taking all the medication now, and ending it immediately?"

For a moment, I thought the doctor would be appalled, perhaps refuse to give Frank the drugs, maybe even refuse to see him. But then I recalled overhearing the doctor on that first visit, when he appeared to offer to give Frank enough pills to end his life.

"Mr. Giametti, the time may come when the pain is too much to bear. But I have found - and this is the truth - that the other soldiers with your condition have found it not so bad at all. With the pain under control, they chose to live as long as they could manage. For you never know when there may be a sunrise that you glimpse through you failing vision, or a song that you had never heard before. Or maybe a child's laughter or embrace. You may not want to miss the possibility for one good day." He paused. ... "But I do not judge," he added.

Dr. Crane instructed Frank to sit in the anteroom for a moment while he spoke with me privately. But I refused. "Whatever you tell me, you will need to say in front of Frank," I said. "I can't live with any more secrets."

And so Frank listened while the doctor instructed me as to Frank's care when blind, and how to handle hallucinations, and when he might soil himself. We listened stone-faced. As if hearing about how to light a new stove or tune a violin. It was just techniques. It was not us.

"You may want to buy some tin cups and plates," he said, as he walked us back to our hired car. "It will save the expense of broken china."

CHAPTER 54

THREE DAYS AFTER WAS MY birthday. I was nineteen. I felt the responsibility, not only for the three children, but for the other three adults with me as well. Neither Sofia nor Martin had asked any details of Frank's medical appointment. They concentrated on their working day, and at night attempted to keep the atmosphere cheerful. I do not think they were trying to avoid the burden. I believe they knew that the burden would grow larger with sharing.

The night before my birthday, I was awakened by a soft knocking on my door.

It was Sofia.

"Please, Lucinda, I need some help. Frank is in such pain, and he will not take a pill from me. I do not think he knows who I am."

And I flew up the stairs to find Frank standing at the foot of the bed, looking as if he was standing on a rock in the middle of the ocean, afraid to take a step for being crushed by the waves.

"Can you see?" I asked.

"Oh, Lucie!" he cried. "For a few moments I could not. And there seemed to be so much noise. I fear I have frightened Sofia near to death!"

"I'm here," she said.

"I see you now. I became so confused. But my head is clearing now. Please don't be angry."

"I'm not angry," said Sofia. "But you knocked the pill out of my hand, and I don't know where it is."

We all searched the floor on our hands and knees, and it was Frank who came up with the missing pill.

"Isn't that something?" he said. "My vision may have gone to hell, but my fingertips are working."

"Well, feel your way back to bed, and stay there," I said. "I can hear the baby crying right through the floorboards." Sofia and I helped him back to bed. It was no harder than assisting a man who had gotten a little tipsy and a little giddy.

And now we sat over dinner celebrating my birthday with a bit more of the Giametti's homemade wine.

"Prohibition hasn't made much of an impact on 30 Pearl Street," remarked Martin. "We certainly found the right neighbors."

I was comfortable enough with our makeshift family that I was nursing the baby at the table. Charlotte and Jonathan were singing, some type of Italian birthday song that Sofia had taught them.

"One of these days," said Martin, "it will be surprising to us that these children know any English at all." He hugged them to him and said, "Ti amo, figli!"

"Oh my God!" I said laughing. "Will I be the only one left whose only Italian is 'gelato!'"

"Speaking of which, it is time for cake!" said Sofia.

And we all gathered around and feasted on Sofia's delicious cake - with gelato on the top, of course. It felt as if we had turned the clock back a year, and everything was right again. I could taste the hope baked into the cake, and I knew I had made the right decision.

Before I could announce what I had been considering since seeing Dr. Crane, Martin announced, "It is time for the children to go to bed. We are in need of some adult conversation."

So Sofia and I took the children to their room, and prayers were said and kisses were plentiful. They were asleep before Sofia finished her third lullaby. I took Annie to the bedroom and laid her in the crib. She had been asleep through most of the festivities. She had become so sweet-natured in the past two months. As if being included in the most horrible of medical issues had induced her to support us with her calm and loving demeanor. Holding her helped me from collapsing.

Back at the kitchen table, the second bottle of wine had been opened. Reminded that I still had birthday gifts to open, I picked up the small box from Martin. In the box was an elegant bottle of perfume.

"Tabac Blond," explained Martin. "It is what all the emancipated women are wearing."

"Well, that is perfect for me then," I said.

"You can wear it when you vote in November!" said Sofia.

"Not all the states have passed that amendment yet," Martin warned with a laugh.

"They will," I said. "And I will be voting - except of course, I will have to wait until I am twenty-one."

"Ah, yes, we forget you are yet a child," said Frank softly. He took from his shirt pocket a small piece of fabric that had been sewn into a little bag with a drawstring. Sofia's work, I was sure, and I was already thinking about how Charlotte would love that to hold the little pebbles she was always picking up.

"From Sofia and I," he said. "With more love than we can ever say."

It was a bracelet made from tiny beach shells.

"It's lovely! Thank you so much."

Martin looked around the table, and his eyes were wet. "I have some important news," he said. "Connecticut Aviation is closing. I have known for some time that things were not well within the company. The owners were too focused on military uses for aircraft, and especially with military dirigibles. I could see that demand for that product was diminishing. Commercial aircraft is the future, but they would not listen."

"That's terrible," said Frank. "You will have to find other work right away."

"Yes," Martin agreed. "But it is only terrible in part. Because I knew this was coming, I had written to Wright's Company quite some time ago. They are operating a large plant in Ohio. They have reviewed some of my ideas and designs and they want me to come and work for them immediately."

"Ohio?" Frank gasped. "You will move to Ohio?"

Martin avoided looking at Frank. He spoke directly to me.

"I should have told you first. At any other time, this would be the best news in the world. This is the job I have always wanted, and the pay is very good. We can have a house and a motorcar. I am told that the area around Dayton is beautiful." He paused. "But I know with what is happening now...I know how difficult it will be to leave. I'm sorry for that. I don't know what else to do. How to make it work..."

I did. I knew. This was what I had been planning for the last several days. The idea had been in my head for at least a month prior. The only difference was the location. Ohio. Why not?

"Listen to me," I said. "I have been tormented with the awfulness of our circumstances. But I have a solution. It is completely untoward, as irrational and shocking and terrible as the situation is itself. But I believe it would be best. That of all the horrid things that could happen now, taking this step might be the least horrid. We may even be happy."

I looked at the three people at this table - the people I loved as much as a person could love. I took a deep breath.

"Martin, I love you very much and I believe you love me. But we do not love each other as husband and wife. I have come to the conclusion that we never will. You were meant to be my brother. Not my husband. You cannot love me as a man should love his wife." He started to protest. He picked up his hand as if to brush my words away, but he let it fall again, and he looked away.

I continued, "But I think you deserve a loving wife. Sofia could be that wife. I have seen that you love her. You could love her as more than a friend. And Sofia deserves a healthy husband and a family. She deserves sweet and beautiful children. She loves Charlotte and Jonathan already. She would be a wonderful mother to them. I truly think that Martin and Sofia should go to Ohio as husband and wife."

"My God, Lucinda," said Martin. "What in hell are you saying?"

"It is hell," I agreed. "But I am trying to find a way back to salvation. And here is the rest of it. Although I cannot love Martin as my husband, not as a woman should love a man - I have that love for Frank. I love Frank with all my heart." At this I began to cry, but I kept going. I looked at Frank, and I hoped that he could see me clearly. "I can't bear the thought of losing you. I know you don't have much time, and so I want to spend every second with you.

Is it sinful? Maybe it is. But I don't think so. I think we were all of us thrown together in this house so that we could find each other. So that we could set the world right. So that we could set ourselves right."

There was a silence through the room that felt like the air before a strong thunderstorm. But sometimes thunderstorms are exactly what the air, the ground, the animals of the earth, need.

After several minutes where I sat motionless - waiting - the first to speak was Sofia.

"I would say yes," she said. "If Frank would release me from my vows."

Frank cried out. "God help me," he said. "I would release you now with all the love in my heart. You will be free of me soon enough, but I would rather you go with love now. I would be content knowing that a man as fine as Martin was your husband. That you could be a mother as you always wished." He stopped and found my face. I am sure he saw me. "But as much - as much as I want the best for Sofia - I want to spend the rest of my life, how much or how little of it there is, with Lucinda. If she can bear to see me die, it is in her arms that I would choose at the end."

We were all weeping. We were together in our agony, and perhaps in our hope.

Martin looked at me in confusion. "You would abandon the children?" he asked.

"Oh Martin," I answered. "This has been the hardest part of my decision. But I am not abandoning them. I am ensuring that they have the best mother they could have. I would keep Annie with me, because she is still at my breast, not because I love her any more than I love Catherine's children. And when... when Frank... leaves me... I will join you and Sofia. I will join you as your sister, as I was meant to be. The children would be together again."

"I am not a religious man," he said. "But I am not sure I can reconcile this with God."

"God?" I cried. "God? You are afraid that God will condemn us?" I raised my voice. "God does not care. If God cared, Catherine would be alive - she would be here with her children enjoying a beautiful summer evening. If God cared, you would still have your wife; your children would still have a mother. If God cared, Sofia would not be barren. If God cared, I would be at Mount Holyoke happily studying literature and believing that I would change the world. And if God cared, there would have been no war. And Frank - my darling Frank - would not be dying.

I have come to believe that God doesn't decide. He gives us the wonder of a free will and a superior intelligence. He sees if we use it. If we lead good lives and find our own happiness."

"How could we do this?" Martin asked. Then he asked again, although with a slight difference that was all the difference in the world.

"Could we do this?"

"Could you love Sofia?"

Martin looked at Frank, who had posed the question. He looked to me, and I nodded slightly, in an effort to let him see that he was not hurting me. Then Martin looked at Sofia. He smiled for the first time in this astonishing conversation.

"Yes," he said.

CHAPTER 55

O NCE WE HAD DECIDED TO do this terrible and wonderful thing, the logistics all fell into place. Within days, Martin accepted the position in Ohio, and the company found him a home that they would make permanent if he found he liked it. He filled out his paperwork with his wife listed as Sofia Blaisdell. They arranged to leave in a week. Martin's and Sofia's excitement and optimism began to grow, although there was often a certain undercurrent of melancholy.

We worried about the children. I was fearful of their reaction. They had already lost one mother - how could I hurt them again?

Martin and I sat with them on Sunday morning. I took Charlotte on my lap and Martin held Jonathan. I explained that their Papa had a wonderful new job in a beautiful place called Dayton, Ohio. So they would take a long train ride and go there to live. And Sofia wanted to go to Ohio very much, so she would go too.

"Do you remember all the stories I told you about your first Mama?" I asked. And they nodded and told me how she danced and ate honey and let them swim in the baptismal font and made everyone laugh. And I reminded them that before I came to live with them and take care of them, I was Aunt Lucinda, and not Mama.

"I came here to love you and take care of you and be your new Mama until Papa found just the perfect Mama for you. And Zia Sofia loves you and Papa so much, that we know that she is the perfect Mama for you."

"Zia Sofia is our Mama?" asked Jonathan.

"She would like to be," said Martin. "She loves you so much."

"But what about Mama?" said Jonathan looking at me sadly. Charlotte snuggled in tighter into my lap.

"I need to stay a while and take care of Zio Frank," I said. "And then I will come and we will all be one family with Papa and Mama Sofia and Aunt Lucinda and little Annie."

"And Zio Frank!" said Charlotte.

"Oh, yes," said Martin. "Zio Frank will come too."

And I left the children with Martin and went into the bedroom. I closed the door and cried for a very long time.

We told Mr. and Mrs. Battle that all of us were moving to Ohio - that Martin had found a new job and that the

Giamettis had decided to move as well. I knew I could not stay on Pearl Street with Frank. The Battles may have been kind people at heart, but this concept of us exchanging families was too shocking to share.

Besides, I knew when I was formulating this plan where I wanted to go.

Constance helped me. She was so adept at finding just the right person who would have the knowledge and the resources. Within four days, she had put me in touch with a businessman who had a small beach cottage to let in Madison, Connecticut. Madison, where I first realized that I was in love with Frank, and first saw the slight possibility that we could change our fates.

I took a six-month lease on the house - from July first through Christmas. As a woman, and only nineteen at that, I could not sign the lease. I returned with Martin and he signed as my brother. I paid the rent in advance with my college nest egg.

Five days later, Martin, Sofia, Jonathan, and Charlotte boarded a train for Ohio. Frank and I saw them off at the station. We kept it cheerful on the surface for the sake of the children. But it was difficult. Sofia clung to Frank, hiding her heartbreak by crying into his shoulder. I wrapped my arms around both children and told them one more story about their mother - how Catherine on her first train ride told everyone that six invisible horses were pulling the train. Invisible to everyone but her.

"There are three black horses and three white horses, and they have the most delicious - her word - tails.

And Grandfather told her she was being frivolous, but Grandmother said, 'I believe you.'"

Martin kissed me and held Annie like the precious gift she was. "You have the most generous soul, Lucinda," he said to me, and put the baby gently back into my arms.

And they were gone. Frank and Annie and I got into the hired car that held a few suitcases and Frank's violin, and our newly acquired tin dinnerware, and went to the beach.

CHAPTER 56

THE HOUSE HELD TWO SMALL bedrooms, and a kitchen so tiny you had to step to one side to open the oven, and a big parlor with a sofa as well as a kitchen table and three mismatched chairs. All the furniture was ancient - with sagging springs on the beds and sofa, and pieces of paper under the table legs in an ineffective attempt to stop the wobbles. But it was also a modern home as cottages go, I was told, because it boasted indoor plumbing and a telephone - both of which were requirements for me, given Frank's condition and a baby three months old.

There was no crib for Annie, but considering we had not brought (nor owned, to be truthful) very many clothes, we took a drawer from the dresser, lined it with a blanket, and put it on the floor. "Do not step on the baby," I warned.

And there was a bookcase, with old books - history, poetry, the complete works of Alexandre Dumas, Charles Dickens, and Jane Austen.

And a porch. There was a glorious screened porch with a view of the water, with the beach down a short path through some reeds and saltspray roses. As I looked towards the water, a rabbit hopped across the path.

And so, yes, the house was perfect.

The gentleman who owned the house, once he understood Frank's failing health, had contacted a local market, who agreed to deliver to our cottage. Frank was tired and wanted to sleep for a while, so he lay down on the creaky bed, and I set off with Annie to find the market. It was less than half a mile from our cottage, so an easy walk during the nice summer weather, but I foresaw days when I would not want to leave Frank.

The shopkeeper, Mr. Vincent Longo, was a genial man, and had been expecting me. He addressed me as Mrs. Giametti (which was sweet to my ears) and expressed his appreciation for Frank's military service, pointing out that he was also Italian-American, and was glad to help out during what he called "my husband's convalescence." I gave him a list of my most urgent necessities - coffee, tea, flour, eggs, and some chicken and various fruit and vegetables. It seemed odd that I needed such small quantities and did not need to prepare food for the children.

Mr. Longo would not let me take the groceries, especially since I was carrying the baby, whom he called the prettiest little Italian face he had ever seen, and I agreed. He assured me that he would send a boy around in an hour or so with all my packages.

"That is very kind," I replied. "I hope you will understand if I need to take the coffee right away."

When I returned to the cottage, Frank was still asleep. I put the baby in her drawer, smiling at the comical but practical simplicity of her new bed, and set to work rearranging the furniture.

I dragged the small bed out from the tiniest bedroom, and put it on the porch. I did the same with the kitchen table and chairs. We would live outside as much as possible during the day. There was some phlox in bloom on the side of the house, and I snipped a few blooms and put them in an old jar on the table.

I was sitting on the porch with coffee, reading an old book on the history of Connecticut when I heard Frank stir. He came out to the porch and sat with me.

"How did you do this?" he asked.

"It was magic," I said.

"From start to finish," he said. "Is there coffee left?"

We watched the sun go down, and I prepared a simple dinner of chicken and lima beans.

"You put a bed out here," Frank noticed.

"I thought if you needed to sleep during the day, and the weather was hot, this would be comfortable."

"I may sleep here tonight," he said. "It would almost feel like I was under the stars."

"That sounds very nice," I said, "but it is a very small bed. The bed in the bedroom is big enough for two."

"Well, that sounds very nice too."

And that was all there was to it. When we turned out the lights, we lay down together in the bedroom, with Annie at our feet in her makeshift bed. I fell asleep holding Frank in my arms, and I felt that I had set myself right with the world. "Goodnight, my husband," I said.

I had an onerous task to complete the next day. I wrote to my mother. I attempted to explain to her that I had not been a wife to Martin, and that I had gone away - I did not say where - to care for Frank, whom I loved. To write, 'Frank is dying' caused me to stop and walk down to the beach. I had left Frank with Annie, and so I did not stay long - just enough to cry a bit and regain my composure. I wrote:

You and Father may never forgive me, but I hope someday you will understand. I should never have married Martin - he and I can never love each other in any way but as brother and sister - as it should always have been. He has had a wonderful offer to work in Ohio, and I have persuaded him to go there without me. I have gone away with Frank. Frank is dying, and my love for him is so deep that I could not bear it if I could not spend these final months by his side. Sofia and Martin understand, and have given us their blessing. Sofia has gone with Martin to Ohio. She will take care of Charlotte and Jonathan, and I believe she will be a blessing to them as a mother. I also believe that Martin and Sofia will be able to love each other the way a husband and wife should - the way Frank and I do. I have Annie with me. It is my intention that after Frank no longer needs me - a few months at best - I will rejoin Martin and Sofia and the children - as aunt, not mother, and we will all be together again. This arrangement is sinful in the eyes of the world, I know, but I am hoping that someday you may see that it is honorable and that it is right for us. But whether or not you can accept my decision to abandon my marriage, please know that the children will not be lost to you - Martin has pledged that the children will visit you with loving affection whenever possible. Do you remember what you wrote when you sent me my college nest-egg? You wrote "You have accepted a future not of your choosing. But I am convinced that one day you will have the opportunity to do the right thing just for yourself." Mother, this is my time. It is right for me to love Frank while I still may. I may never find such love again.

I gathered Annie in my arms and walked down to the market to post my letter before I could change my mind.

The next few weeks were blessed by glorious summer weather and a respite in Frank's condition.

We would breakfast on our porch - I moved the table again once I realized what spot was bathed in morning sun - with coffee and a loaf of bread that Mr. Longo would send over the previous afternoon. Then Frank would take my arm and we would walk the short distance down to the beach. I would spread a blanket and pillows. I had even learned, with Frank's instruction, to set up a small tent with sticks and towels, so the baby would have a shady place to sleep. Frank and I would lie in the sun, often silent, but sometimes we would share our favorite childhood memories. I would read the newspaper that Mr. Longo provided - one day late, but what would that matter to us? The world could be years ahead of us, and we were happy to let it race ahead while we remained in the sun, listening only to surf and seagulls.

If Frank was content and relatively pain-free, we would stay most of the day. I would run back to the cottage at noon and return with a basket of fruit and cheese, and a jar of iced tea. Sometimes we would see other folks as they walked along the beach, and we'd exchange pleasantries, "We hope you are having a wonderful holiday," they would say, and often Frank would shout back, "It couldn't be more wonderful," and then under his breath to me, "except for the dying."

I would look at him sternly and say, "Well, husband of mine, you can't have everything." And we would toast ourselves with iced tea in our tin cups.

Occasionally, on very warm days, if no one else were to be seen, I would strip down to my petticoat and venture into the water, returning to sprinkle the cold droplets on Frank while he cried out in mock protest.

It was clear during those first two weeks that the sea air and the warmth of summer had a beneficial, though superficial, impact on Frank's health. He seemed stronger.

He often would carry the picnic basket back to the house at the end of the evening. He even offered to carry Annie - "She would fit in this basket easily now that we have eaten everything" - but I knew how precarious was his strength. I could not risk his falling. If he fell, I was not sure if I was strong enough to get him upright, and if he fell with the baby...well, neither of us would soon forgive ourselves. Besides, by the end of the two weeks, although in his bravado he made a good pretense, I knew that he was completely blind.

It rained only three days in all of July. On the first rainy day, I took out Frank's violin and strummed lightly on the strings, so he would know what I was holding.

"Do you think you can still play?" I asked.

"My hands are not steady - I am afraid I will damage it," he responded. "I would love to hear it though."

"Maybe you could teach me. I want to learn in the way your father taught you. To play through no matter what. To ignore my mistakes and stay with the music."

"How bad a pianist were you?" he asked with a smile.

"I struggled. But I know the notes and measures. With your help, I might be able to translate them from piano to violin. How hard could it be? It is so much smaller than a piano - therefore it must be much easier!"

"Oh, Lucie, you are so vain!" he laughed.

"Are you afraid you are a terrible teacher?" I asked.

"I am the best teacher," he responded.

"Oh, now who is vain?"

So he named for me the strings, and how I would place my fingers to achieve different notes. At the end of the lesson - almost two hours, I could play a scratchy octave.

"Enough for today," Frank said. "I need to rest. Preferably someplace very, very quiet."

That evening, I fell asleep listening to the rain tapering off. I was awakened after midnight by Frank reaching for me. I thought perhaps he needed his pain medication. As I searched to find his pills on the nearby table, he pulled me to him instead. He kissed me with more than the sweetness of his usual morning and evening kiss, more than the kiss he gave me at dinner as I put a peach into his hand. I felt a passion that had been unknown to me. I have no words to describe sexual intimacy; I have no experience except for that one momentary grief-filled act from Martin more than a year before.

Frank found me through his fingertips, not his eyes. He found my breasts and my hips. He caressed my shoulders and my waist. He outlined my ears and traced the length of my legs. He took the hem of my nightdress and coaxed it over my head and tossed it to the floor. Then his hands and mouth explored once again.

"You are as soft as the peach I touched today - and as delicious," he whispered. We made love with an exquisite and gentle urgency.

"I love you, Frank," I said. "I love you, my husband."

"Te amo, Lucia, my wife."

We made love often after that night, each time with the fervor - and perhaps desperation - brought by the knowledge that it could be the last time we could touch each other and hold each other. How the world might change, I thought, if all marriages recognized the possibility of loss with every touch. How much more tender we would be to each other. This was the gift given us in recompense for the coming sadness - that in acknowledging our certain parting, we gave to each other our complete souls.

CHAPTER 57

J ULY ENDED AND AUGUST BROUGHT scorching days and evening thunderstorms. We adjusted our days accordingly, going down to the beach earlier so that we could return before the heavens opened up on us. We were caught a few times, and it was both thrilling and frightening to find our way back to the cottage through black clouds and lightning. We could not run - not with Annie and not with Frank's blindness. So we walked. Drenched and terrified, and fell into each others' arms in relief when we were finally safe. I thought perhaps it might be a good way to die, but for precious Annie, who did not cry out in terror but laughed through each burst of thunder. She was too brave to surrender. I needed to go on for her sake.

One day, instead of the young boy who brought our groceries, Mr. Longo came himself.

Frank was not having a good day - he was weak and feverish, but he roused himself and was cordial and courteous to the man who over the past month had taken to choosing our food purchases himself, so that I seldom needed to walk to the market or leave Frank alone. He also, I believed, consistently undercharged us for our food. The boy would say, "Oh, but Mr. Longo said the grapes were a gift" or "Mr. Longo said that he could not charge for the bread, as it is yesterday's," as the youngster would hand me a loaf so fresh it could float from my hand.

Mr. Longo arrived with a bottle of his own wine. He could see that Frank was ill, but his good manners required him to overlook this and treat Frank as a respected soldier and not an invalid. I poured three glasses of wine into our tin cups, handing one to Mr. Longo and putting one into Frank's hand.

"Saluti!" said Mr. Longo and we all drank. It was very good wine. The pain that showed on Frank's brow lessened a bit with the familiar pungent flavor.

"Alla tua salute!" responded Frank.

And there was an animated conversation in Italian. I wondered if Frank missed Sofia, if hearing Italian made his heart yearn for her and her sweet song and sweeter heart. But I was also comforted to see him rally a bit.

At some point, I understood that the conversation had turned to me. We all have a sense of being spoken about, even when we can't understand the words.

Mr. Longo left after a while, saying to me in English that he would stop by again, and that it was an honor to meet a soldier who had sacrificed so much in the war.

That evening I asked Frank what he had said of me. He explained that Mr. Longo thought I was quite beautiful and wondered how we had met.

"I told him you were the sister of a very dear friend, and that we loved each other from the first moment we met."

I liked the idea of that. But it also made me curious. "I don't think it was exactly at the first moment," I said, "so tell me... when did you know? When did you first think you might love me?"

He leaned back in his chair and closed his eyes. He could not see, but his memory needed him to look inside. He smiled.

"It was when you cut your hair. It was not that it made you more beautiful... you were already beautiful. It was in the way you were happy and defiant at the same time. This, I thought, is a woman of spirit!"

"Did you really think I was already beautiful?"

"Oh yes... and I wanted nothing more that instant than to touch your short, rebellious hair! So come here and let me do that now."

We had another visitor in August. Constance came with Sadie.

Sadie was disappointed that Jonathan and Charlotte were not here, but we distracted her with sandcastles at the edge of the water. Constance and I had a lovely visit. She was gratified to see that our cottage was to our liking, and that we had plenty of food in our cupboard.

We had gone to the beach without Frank. He was not up to the walk that day and instead lay on the bed on the porch, with his head propped on pillows. He had the newspaper on his lap, though he could not read it. It gave him comfort to feel its familiar rustle and smell the inky print.

"I'm fine," he said. "I will probably doze off in a minute or two... so you girls - all four of you - go down to the water, and I will listen to the breeze carry your sweet voices back to me."

I put a pill into his hand if the need should arise, and Constance and I took Sadie and Annie down to the beach. Sadie ran back and forth between the water's edge and our blanket, where Constance held the baby and caught me up on the gossip of the other women from the park. She told me that the women's voting amendment was about to be ratified. "I don't think it will make a real difference in the world," she said. "At least not at first. I think it will be fifty years at least - perhaps a hundred - before women will have to power to vote for each other, and not for men. Then the world will change."

"Well, when I am twenty-one, I shall vote. I will shake things up!" I laughed. "I will do it alone if the ladies won't help."

"What would you change?" she asked.

"Wars. Cancer. The way we judge one another."

"I have something else to tell you," she said. "Your father came to me. He drove from Springfield, and he waited in the park, where he remembered he had taken Sadie for a ride. He confronted me and wanted to know where to find you. He knew you were in Madison, or at least had been there at the time you posted your letter. He wanted me to tell him exactly where you were."

"Did you say?" I asked, trembling.

"I told him I didn't know. I believe he intended to take you back to Massachusetts. That could be for the best. But I fear that it would not."

"No, I will not leave. My father may want to give me another chance to change my life - to make it right with God. But I am right with myself. And I owe that more to you than to anyone."

"You owe me?" she said.

"You live how you want. You don't measure yourself by any of the standards that our good and righteous society has imposed upon us. Once I saw the freedom and the happiness it brought to you, I knew that I could do the same."

"I am not always happy, Lucinda," she said.

"But you *choose*," I said. "You have satisfaction and sustenance that the choice was yours."

"I do," said Constance. She wiped sand from her hands. "Tell me, Lucinda," she asked, "do you still want to save the world?"

I thought about it.

"Sometimes I do. In a smaller way. I think I could be a good teacher. I remember what you told me - that changing the world could start with the children."

"I think you would make a fine teacher. You should go to school."

"I've always wanted that. Maybe one day I will."

Constance laid back and shielded her eyes. Then she rose on her elbows and squinted at me, in that way that told me her sharp intellect had been at work.

"Martin may be on his way to becoming a rich man. He could send you to college."

"Martin has three children to support!"

"And two wives!"

"Oh Constance, you always make me laugh!" I stood and scooped up Annie. "Let's go back and see Frank."

When we returned, Frank was awake and a bit improved. I put the kettle on for tea, and picked up the violin.

"Look, Constance, what Frank has taught me in a mere four weeks." And I played a shaky but recognizable rendition of *Fur Elise*.

"That's quite good for just a short period of time," she encouraged.

"Ah, but that is her whole repertoire," said Frank. "I should like her to play three songs well before I am gone."

"Then you had better live a long time," I said.

"May I?" asked Constance, putting her hand out to take the violin.

I handed it over and she played. How she played! Constance played *Fur Elise* as if the music had been written for her, and then followed with an adagio so lovely that my heart filled with tears.

"My God," cried Frank. "You play like a goddess! Like an artist and goddess!"

She smiled. "My father and my uncle are both with the Boston Symphony Orchestra. I think I would be too, if I were not a woman. No place in the orchestra for a skirt. According to them, anyway."

"But you have played professionally? You must have shared this gift! What a loss if you could not!" I cried.

"I play in small circles. The men find me a novelty." There was a trace of bitterness in her words, but she shook them off. "That is how I met Sadie's father, by the way. I was playing for a small party of people well connected in the music world of Boston. A patron of the arts, is Thomas. And he was quite taken with me. I seduced him with my bow, you could say."

It was a rather shocking thing to say, but Frank and I were no longer appalled by illicit love. We reveled in it. How quickly our lives had turned.

"Oh, there is seduction in the violin, no doubt," said Frank.

"This is a fine instrument," remarked Constance, turning the violin in her hand. She handed it to me. "I must go. The car I hired will be here in a few minutes. Let me get Sadie out of her muddy clothes and into something she can sleep in. She will be fast asleep as soon as we drive away."

And we kissed and hugged. I was loathed to let her go. I had seen so few people in the last six weeks, and her visit had cheered me enormously. To have so loyal a friend that she would defy my father, and yet come to tell me, in case I should change my mind. I knew that she would have taken us all back with her, had I asked.

Later that evening, Frank said, "I wish we had a Victrola. Then it would be perfect here. I would like to hear music that beautiful every day."

"Done," I said. "I will find one. I swear there will be music - and not my poor excuse - in this house before the week is ended." I did not know how that would happen, but I knew I would do it. I could do anything. I was in a cottage with Frank and my baby. A year ago it had not even been an idea. And then I dreamed it. And then I realized it.

"I need to tell you something," said Frank in bed that night. "About the violin. Constance recognized that it was a fine instrument. Well, it is more than that. It is very rare. Very valuable."

"I'll treasure it always," I promised, and kissed him.

"No," he said. "I do not want you to treasure it. I want you to sell it. The money from that violin would take care of you and Annie for a very long time. If you do not wish to go to Ohio, or you go but you aren't happy - well, you will have recourse to do whatever you wish. It would give me comfort to think I could provide for you, that I could give you a gift of the freedom to go and do and be whatever you wish."

"Frank, you have already given me that freedom," I said.

"Still," he said. "Remember you have it. And Constance's lover - Sadie's father - he is probably the person to contact. A successful man and a patron of the arts. He would buy this violin or put you into contact with someone who would. And he would not cheat you, because he loves Constance - and Constance loves you."

"I'll remember," I said.

The next morning, I gave Frank a light breakfast, got him comfortable on his bed on the porch, kissed him, took Annie in my arms, and set off to Mr. Longo's market.

"I have a great need," I said. "And you are the only person I know here in Madison."

I explained that I needed to buy a phonograph and as many records as I could, and I needed to have it delivered to the cottage as quickly as possible. Frank is a musician, I explained, and he needs music.

"I should have thought of it weeks ago," I cried.

"Do you not know, Mrs. Giametti, that I can procure anything you need in one day? Why, I am famous for it!"

"I have nearly one hundred dollars left," I said. "It must last for a few more months. That doesn't count Frank's burial money. We have that set aside already. So we will only need food and perhaps firewood when it gets cold, if we are still here."

"Oh, my dear!" he exclaimed, "You mustn't speak like that. Frank will recover!"

And so I told him the truth. That Frank was not convalescing. That he had cancer of the brain, and he had come here to die. Mr. Longo wept.

"You will have a Victrola today!" he said. "And it won't cost you a penny. I will loan you my own. The best phonograph in Madison. And I have recordings! Classico, Italian, Opera... your Frank will be delighted. I promise, I promise!"

And that afternoon, Mr. Longo drove up in a truck with his Victor phonograph tied on the back. He set it up in our parlor. Then he went back to the truck and came back with stacks of recordings. It took him three trips to bring them all in.

"I have even brought my grandson's recordings of children's songs. Just in case your baby might like them. Keep it as long as you need."

"But you obviously love music yourself," I said. "Whatever will you do?"

"Play the accordion!" he said with a laugh.

And oh, we had the most glorious music. My favorite was Enrico Caruso singing *"Che gelida manina"* from *La Boheme*. Frank translated it for me, and the words were as wonderful as the sound, as Rodolfo falls in love with Mimi while they search for a light in the darkness.

Frank loved everything. He loved the traditional Italian songs, as well as Beethoven and Schubert, and the patriotic songs of the Great War. We listened every evening for weeks.

As the weather got cooler in September, Frank's health started to fail. He could no longer hold a cup steady, and had to lean on me to walk. His pain was intense, so I doubled his medication. Then his hearing became erratic, often overly sensitive, and we often had to stop the phonograph in the middle of a song, as he could not bear the sound. He slept fitfully unless he took even more pain pills. I would hold him for hours and stroke his brow. In the morning, he would be filled with remorse, apologizing for making my life so difficult.

This was the path I had chosen. I had known the outcome going in. But still, I was not prepared.

The day that Annie sat up by herself for the first time, Frank could not sit up at all.

He spoke to me sometimes in Italian. Whether he thought I was Sofia, or perhaps had just forgotten his English for a time, I didn't know.

Frank, in quiet moments, liked me to read to him. He liked Dumas much better than Dickens, but soon he was unable to follow the story. Instead of allowing the words alone to soothe him, he would become distressed at his failing comprehension. So I took to poetry, reading Whitman and Wordsworth.

The weather grew too cool for sitting on the porch, so I moved the table back inside. I left the bed, in the hopes that we would have a respite as often happens at the end of September, with a few days of fine mild weather. I hoped to perhaps give Frank some additional moments in the sunshine - as if feeling the sun on his face would bring him back to the good health and strength I had seen in July.

I received a letter from Martin. He was well satisfied with his new work, and the house was large and comfortable.

He had purchased a motorcar and the family drove out to the countryside every Sunday afternoon. Jonathan had started school in Dayton; he was learning to read. Charlotte was losing a bit of her shyness - and she had a good ear for Italian, she easily skipped back and forth between the languages. *'They are happy,'* Martin wrote.

At the bottom of the letter was a postscript from Sofia.

My English writing is not well, but I would let you no that I have made sure that Martin tells the children a story of there mother Caterine evary week. They will not forget her. For me, I tell them a story of when you were there mama. They like best when you spend the dinner money on wodden animals for there ark. I am happy. I love Martin. I am happy also that you love Frank. We miss you both. I have a gardin.

I sat for a long time, holding the letter. I gave it to Annie, and she happily tore it apart.

I telephoned to Mr. Longo's market.

"I'm very sorry to bother you," I said, "But I am wondering if you might be able to stop by some time today to visit with Frank? It is selfish of me, I know, but I feel a strong need for some fresh air. I would just like to take a short walk, but I am afraid to leave him."

I think Mr. Longo knew by the tremor in my voice that I was in despair.

"I will come as soon as my wife comes to help out at noon. I will be there, Mrs. Giametti. Do not worry. I'm coming right away."

An hour later, the old truck pulled up to the cottage. Mr. Longo was not alone. There was a gray-haired woman with him, in a floral dress and big black shoes.

"This is my wife, Millie," he explained. "When I told her I was coming to see Frank, she insisted that we close the store and she come too. So she can watch your little one and you can clear your mind and take a nice walk."

It was impossible not to cry. These people that I barely knew would give up an afternoon's revenue so that I could take a walk?

"Go, go now!" said Mrs. Longo as she took Annie from me. "I was born to tend to babies. I had nine of my own and now I have fourteen grandchildren. And take a shawl. And don't wear those shoes - it is too cool. And take as much time as you damn well please."

I walked nearly two miles along the beach. I stopped when I reached the state park. The seagulls were the only creatures I encountered, and they paid me no mind. Despite Millie's warning, it was quite warm, and on the way back, I took off my shoes and walked in the water. The coldness of the water and the roughness of the pebbles beneath my feet reconnected me to the world. I'm still here, I thought. I am nineteen. I have a dying husband who is not my husband and a living child who is mine alone. The trick in music is to go on, to keep the rhythm, to not stop, to not worry over mistakes. I will go on.

I returned with my composure - and my determination - restored.

Mrs. Longo was seated on the sofa in the parlor with Annie on her lap. The baby was sucking on a large wooden spoon.

"She's getting a tooth," said Mrs. Longo.

I looked at my daughter, whose very existence had been peripheral to my life for several weeks now. She held the spoon out to show me her great toy.

"I need to do better," I said.

"Nonsense. Your baby is fat and healthy and very happy. You are doing a damn fine job!"

I sat next to the woman, and she put Annie on my lap. The baby immediately turned her head towards my breast.

"Can I ask you something embarrassing?" I said.

"Nothing is embarrassing to a lady who's had this many kids."

"Will it hurt? When I nurse her, I mean... *with teeth?*"

Millie Longo laughed. "Hell, yes! But Annie will try to be gentle with you. And you can start weaning her off your tit. Don't feel bad about it. Kids grow up. It's a good thing. You'll sleep better and you'll need it. She'll be crawling in just a few weeks. Then you are in for a hell of a time."

From the bedroom, I heard Mr. Longo weaving some kind of tale in Italian. Frank gave a short reply, and I heard him laugh. Frank laughed! And Mr. Longo burst forth with a booming laugh and continued his story.

"What are they talking about?" I asked.

Millie listened for a few moments.

"They are discussing the technique of a certain very limber prostitute!" And she threw back her head and roared.

CHAPTER 58

THE NEXT MORNING WAS THE warm, fine day I had been hoping for. With difficulty, I got Frank on the bed on the porch. It was the first of October, and the angle of the sun did not fall onto the bed as I wished, but it was light and the air was fresh.

Frank was in much pain, so I gave him three pills. He calmed after a short while.

"Where is your hand?" he asked.

I sat on the bed and nursed Annie, holding Frank's hand. When the baby was satisfied, I took his hand and showed him the little bump of her tooth.

"She's getting big," I said.

"What is her name?" he asked.

"Annie Sullivan Giametti," I answered.

Annie fell asleep, and I set her on a blanket on the floor. I took off my clothes and laid down with Frank. He instinctively put his arms around me and it felt good.

"Do you hear the seagulls?" he asked. "How I love that sound. There must be dozens of them."

I listened to the continued quiet.

"I scattered bread for them, so they would visit," I lied.

"The church bells too. Did you order them up?"

"Yes. I did."

"I'm glad the wolves are gone," he said.

Later, I rose and dressed. I hugged my baby and she pulled my hair and laughed. Then I set her on the floor with the wooden spoon, and picked up the violin.

I played. I played the three songs that Frank had taught me. *Fur Elise* and *Ave Maria* and *After The Ball*. I played them over and over. I did not stop for wrong notes. There was no need to fix mistakes. There was only music if you stayed with the rhythm.

I laid the violin next to Frank. With Annie in a shawl on my hip, I walked along the beach and then made my way to the market.

"Frank has died," I said.

CHAPTER 59

A RRANGEMENTS WERE MADE. I SENT a telegram
to Ohio.

*Frank passed October 1. All is well. No need
to come.*

I spent the next few days cleaning the cottage. I scrubbed
the floors, the walls. I shined the pots. I washed windows.

The weather was cool, but I bundled Annie and we
walked on the beach. We walked for miles. I had never seen
so many seagulls.

Constance came and we had a small funeral. Just Annie
and I, Constance and Sadie, and Vincent and Millie Longo.
And the young boy who had brought our groceries.

Constance had her car take us back to New Haven. She
wanted us to stay with her, at least for a few days - "Or
as long as you wish" - but I was anxious to go on. So we

spent one day only. Constance watched Annie for a few hours so that I could make a trip to the bank. I withdrew the remainder of my nest egg. Constance forged Martin's signature. That evening, Constance cut my hair, which had grown quite long, but I would keep it short now forever. Sadie played on the floor with Annie, encouraging her to roll over, and Annie obliged.

"Can we have a puppy, Mama?" asked Sadie, and I couldn't help but laugh - the similarities were certainly obvious.

In the morning, we took Sadie off to school.

"I love school," Sadie said. "I learn like a boy!"

"You learn like a girl!" said Constance, "which is ever so much better, because you can do everything boys do, and have babies too."

The little girl hugged us both and ran into the school.

"That was kind, but perhaps not completely true," I said to Constance. "Women can't do everything men do. We can have our babies, and we can love them, but we can't support them. I can't go to college now. It's hard enough for a woman to be accepted. And now I am a widow with a baby."

"Martin and Sofia will help you," she said.

I nodded. "I know. But... well, I know it's selfish and foolish... but how I wish I could do it by myself."

Constance took me by the shoulders and spun me around to face her. On my hip, Annie laughed at the sudden dance.

"You are not selfish!" Constance exclaimed. "And we could all use more foolishness! You wish you could do something 'by yourself'? Mother of God, Lucinda, you are nineteen years old and you have done more things *by yourself* than most men and women could ever dream of!"

We went back to the house for my belongings and walked slowly and silently to the train station. We passed a different school, not Sadie's, a school with dark-skinned children in the yard. Skipping rope. Running. Shouting. Laughing. Being children.

"Do you know," said Constance as she stopped to throw back a wayward ball to a small boy, "that there are schools so poor and so in need that they often hire teachers who have not even been to college?"

We walked on to the station. She handed me the suitcase she had carried for me.

"You are my best friend, Lucinda," said Constance. "Never let anyone judge you. Do what you believe is right. If you want something, try. If you're not happy, stop. That's all there is." She embraced me and kissed me. "And if you need to breathe a little slower, come back anytime."

I watched her walk out of the station, with her head high. Men all turned. Women looked too. They looked because she had the life that they all wanted and were afraid to pursue. She had freedom.

She turned back and yelled to me in the most unladylike way, "Vote for women!"

I approached the ticket counter. I had one small valise, a violin, and a seven-month-old baby.

The ticketmaster said, "Where to, Miss?"

I hesitated.

Martin and Sofia and the children were waiting for me in Ohio. My sister Catherine had told me years ago to follow my heart. 'Be light,' she had said. Constance believed with her own heart that you should discover what you want and never allow anyone to stop you.

"Come on, miss, there are folks waiting. Where to?"

"Boston," I said.

I took my seat on the train, with Annie on my lap, facing me. She smiled.

"We are going to see a man who wants to buy a very good violin," I said.

The violin was precious, but it could provide for something more precious. For me. For Annie. And for the infant Francis who nestled safely inside me.

Thank you, Frank, for everything precious.

ABOUT THE AUTHOR:

Nancy Roman is the author of JUST WHAT I ALWAYS WANTED, available on Amazon. She writes weekly about aging, kindness, and living a happy life on her popular blog, notquiteold.com.

Nancy lives in Connecticut with her loving husband, four mysterious cats, and one disobedient but adorable dog.

Blog: *notquiteold.com*
Twitter: *@notquiteold*
Facebook: *facebook.com/nancyromanauthor*
Instagram: *nancyromanwriter*

28187477R00199

Made in the USA
Lexington, KY
11 January 2019